Over the Wall
—Tales from Ancient Chinese Plays

Adapted by   Chen Meilin
Translated by   Sun Haichen

Foreign Languages Press Beijing

First Edition   1997

ISBN 7-119-00342-9

© Foreign Languages Press, Beijing, 1997

Published by Foreign Languages Press
24 Baiwanzhuang Road, Beijing 100037, China

Printed by Foreign Languages Printing House
19 Chegongzhuang Xilu, Beijing 100044, China
P.O. Box 399, Beijing, China

Distributed by China International Book Trading Corporation
35 Chegongzhuang Xilu, Beijing 100044, China
P.O. Box 399, Beijing, China

Printed in the People's Republic of China

Contents

Introduction

Traditional Chinese plays, like Greek tragedies and comedies and the Sanskrit dramas of ancient India, represent the earliest achievements of world drama. Their origins can be traced to early antiquity, and their formative period encompasses hundreds of years in which elements from ancient poetry, story telling, dance, music, painting, sculpture and architecture were incorporated. By the Song and Yuan dynasties, drama had become a full-fledged art form portraying the full range of social life and capable of developing plot and presenting conflicts by means of the words and gestures incorporated into the dramatic roles.

The Yuan Dynasty, which lasted for less than a hundred years, witnessed the flourishing of Chinese drama and produced many talented playwrights. Among them, the names of over two hundred have come down to us. Most of these writers, such as Guan Hanqing, Ma Zhiyuan, Zheng Guangzu, Bai Pu, Wang Shifu, Li Wenwei, Wang Zhongwen, Gao Wenxiu, Zhang Shiqi and Xiao Dexiang, were men of humble origins, either Confucian scholars from impoverished families or physicians and magicians living by their wits and craft. Even a few actors, such as Hua Lilang and Hongzi Lier, are known to have engaged in writing scripts. Altogether, over seven hundred titles are known today, of which only two hundred have survived as complete texts.

Apart from their often ingenious plots, the extant Yuan plays cover a wide range of themes. There are, for instance, the trial plays, which often expose the atrocities committed by the privileged class and sometimes end with an unjust verdict.

1

Romantic themes are also popular, many related to the lives of courtesans. Some plays depict historical or legendary heroes, of which the most popular concern a group of noble outlaws based on Mount Liangshan in Shandong Province. There are also the mythical plays which sometimes have a strong note of morality.

Some trial plays openly rebuke the unscrupulous behavior of the rich and powerful. *Lord Bao Beheads Lu Zhailang*, for example, portrays a despot riding roughshod over the people in flagrant defiance of the law. Other trial plays are *The Riverside Pavilion*, included in this book, and *Lord Bao Deciphers the Butterfly Dream*, in which Lord Bao, a just official, manages to exculpate a poor scholar who had revenged his father by killing a member of the imperial clan. Lord Bao, the incarnation of law and justice, figures prominently in the trial plays, ten of which extant today have him as the hero. This volume contains two Lord Bao plays, *Case of the Chalk Circle* and *Grain Sale in Chenzhou*.

Some trial plays end in tragedy because of a miscarriage of justice, which was no unusual phenomenon considering the rampant corruption and malpractices such as bribery in the Yuan bureaucracy. Guan Hanqing's *Snow in Midsummer* is perhaps the best known of such plays. Dou E, a young widow, refuses to marry Donkey, a local loafer, who subsequently brings a trumped-up charge against her. With hardly any evidence, the judge extorts a confession from her by severe torture and sentences her to death. Three miracles, predicted by Dou E before her execution, then occur testifying to the sheer injustice of the case. Thus the story not only denounces the malpractice of officialdom but also accentuates the indomitable spirit of the underclass people and points to the existence of a higher order of justice. Also in this category are *Rescue of the Filial Son* and Yang Xianzhi's *Night Rain over the River*.

Romance and marriage is another major theme of Yuan plays such as the celebrated *Romance of the West Chamber* and *Over the Wall*. In the typical scenario, the young hero and heroine, both from respectable families, defy social conventions in the pursuit of true love, and in the process are often assisted by people of low social status such as maids or errand boys. The daring young couple are consistently portrayed in a positive light, applauded for their pursuit of marital happiness and their determination to take fate into their own hands instead of succumbing to the dictates of authority figures. In *Romance of the West Chamber*, the heroine, Yingying, finds her ideal mate in the person of Zhang Gong, a scholar yet to make his fortune, despite the disparity in their social status, on which grounds her mother strongly opposes the match. The name of Hong Niang, the cunning maid who acts as a go-between for her young mistress and the lovesick scholar, has entered everyday speech as a synonym for solicitous matchmakers. Free choice in the pursuit of love is also eulogized in *Over the Wall*. Li Qianjin, the heroine, falls in love with Pei Shaojun at first sight and elopes with him that very night. When her father-in-law repudiates her, she stands her ground and fights undauntedly to protect her family. In the final scene, when all ends well with a grand family reunion, she makes a strong case for her elopement by citing examples from history. Compared with Yingying, she was bolder in protecting her rights. In Yuan plays the marriage of widows such as Zhao Paner in *The Riverside Pavilion* is not frowned upon, a reflection of the more tolerant moral outlook of city residents of the time.

Closely related to romantic stories are the tales of courtesans who flourished mostly in cities where the Yuan plays were composed and performed. In spite of their low social status, the courtesans are often portrayed as talented and sincere, yearning to end their disreputable careers by finding

3

a lifelong mate, an effort which sometimes plunged them into even greater misery. Best known among these plays are *Rescue of a Courtesan*, *Golden String Pond* and *Qujiang Pond*.

Quite a few Yuan plays concern the adventures of a band of noble outlaws in Shandong Province. Living in misery, the common people not only wanted honest officials like Lord Bao to uphold justice on their behalf, but also longed for righteous champions of the good to weed out the wicked. Unlike the novel *Outlaws of the Marsh*, which gives a complete history of these Shandong desperados, the plays usually concentrate on episodic portrayls of their exploits in defeating despots and helping the people. Representative titles include *Li Kui Bears the Rod*, included in this book, *The Black Whirlwind Presents Heads*, and *Rescue of the Chief Clerk*.

These plays, based on historical events and people, lash out at the rulers of that time, express a longing for their native soul and eulogize local heroes. The *Zhao Orphan* is a representative work describing how Han Jue, Gongsun Chujiu and Cheng Ying rescued the orphan of the Zhang family in order to revenge the injustice done to his family. This play attacks the social system of the Yuan Dynasty. Other works of this kind are *Going to the Banquet Alone*, *Meeting of Shengchi* and *The Battle Against Fu Jian*.

The mythical plays are often presented in a very romantic vein, as represented by *Zhang Yu Boils the Sea* and *The Dragon King's Daughter*. In the former, Qionglian, the dragon king's daughter, offers her hand to Zhang Yu, a young scholar, as she becomes enamored of his exceptional talents and sincerity. Determined to be united with her, Zhang Yu lets nothing stand in his way and does not hesitate to boil the East Sea with his newly gained magic powers. This story was doubtless an inspiration to young lovers at the time. The play, adapted into a variety of local operas, is still very much alive on the stage all across China.

To understand why the short-lived Yuan Dynasty witnessed a proliferation of playwrights and the culmination of Chinese dramatic art, we must look at its social and cultural background.

The Yuan Dynasty was established by the Mongols in the mid-thirteenth century following their armed conquests of rival regimes including the Song Dynasty. Kublai Khan, the first Yuan emperor, gave priority to agriculture and encouraged the development of agricultural techniques. The vast expanse of this empire demanded the building of a network of post stations from central China to the border areas to enable the court to implement its edicts and get prompt news from everywhere. This resulted in improved facilities for communication and travel. Land and water routes to the West were also in their heyday. As the country recuperated from the aftermath of war, the growth of production and a highly developed transportation network promoted both inland and overseas trade, bringing wealth and prosperity to a large number of small- and medium-sized cities.

The emergence of cities with large populations was a vital factor in the development of urban culture. The entertainment needs of the city residents, including large numbers of handicraft workers, contributed directly to the growth and flourishing of drama during the Yuan Dynasty.

For eighty years after they took control of China, the Mongols discontinued the civil service recruitment examination in order to block the Han people from officialdom. Even after the examination was restored, discrimination against the Han persisted. A Han scholar had little chance of getting an official post through the examination; even if he succeeded, he would find it hard to get a subsequent promotion. This explains why a great many scholars steeped in classic learning chose to write plays aimed at the underclass.

The Yuan plays drew extensively from traditional enter-

5

tainment genres such as song and dance performances and the talking-and-singing shows, in which story telling was inter-mixed with singing to the accompaniment of musical instruments. On the other hand, classic and folk literature also offered a source of inspiration for playwrights, who could base their plots on short stories and oral tales from the Tang and Song dynasties, or enhance their work by adapting lines from classic poetry.

Another factor contributing to the flourishing of drama was the preference for song and dance performances by the Mongols and other nomadic peoples from the North. The Yuan plays, rich in song and dance, were thus able to secure a creditable position in society. In the Yuan bureaucracy, a court official of the third rank headed the Music Office, the ruling body for performers and official endorsement generally went a long way toward promoting the development of Yuan drama.

The Yuan plays hold a prominent position in the history of Chinese literature, marking the pinnacle of narrative art. Previously, Chinese literature was dominated by the lyric tradition represented by poetry and lyric prose. The Tang and Song dynasties preceding the Yuan saw the emergence of short stories written in classic style, and story-teller's scripts, as well as some short, immature plays. It was not until the Yuan that drama became a dominant literary genre with comprehensive plots and fully developed characters, exerting a far-reaching influence on the development of narrative art. *Romance of the Three Kingdoms*, *Outlaws of the Marsh* and *Journey to the West*, the three major novels of the Ming Dynasty, are all indebted to the Yuan plays to varying degrees. Many short stories of the Ming and Qing dynasties were also adapted from Yuan plays. For instance, *Tale of the Gold Lock* was based on *Snow in Midsummer*, and *The Eight Righteous Men*, on *The Zhao Orphan*. Yuan plays adapted into various styles of local operas remain part of the repertoire of theatrical troupes to this day, and characters such as Hong Niang and Dou E have become household names.

In the history of world literature the Yuan plays also lay claim to a place of honor. As early as 1735, the Frenchman R. P. De Premare published a translation of *The Zhao Orphan*, and an Englishman, J. F. Davis, translated *A Son Begotten in Old Age* and *Autumn Moon over the Han Palace* in 1817 and 1829 respectively. Other translated plays included *Romance of the West Chamber*, *Snow in Midsummer*, *Case of the Chalk Circle*, *Journey of Qiannu's Spirit*, and *The Street Vendor*.

It is not unusual for great dramatic works to be adapted into story form. Charles and Mary Lamb's *Tales from Shakesperean* is considered a masterpiece in its own right. The works of Moliere have also been adapted into stories. A well-adapted story can be a literary creation affording great delight to the reader, just as the original play is to an audience.

The Yuan plays lend themselves particularly well to literary adaptation because they have good story lines and interesting, true-to-life characters, the key elements in creating a good read. In selecting the fourteen titles for this book, which account for nearly one-tenth of the extant Yuan plays, the editor has tried to include works of different periods and themes from a dozen authors including, besides the four greatest Yuan playwrights (Guan Hanqing, Ma Zhiyuan, Zheng Guangzu and Bai Pu), several less famous but equally excellent writers as well as one anonymous author.

OVER THE WALL

*Bai Pu**

Li Zhi, known as Emperor Gaozong of the Tang Dynasty, ruled the empire in peace for over a dozen years after his ascension to the throne. He was able to spend his days drinking wine, watching flowers, and indulging in sensual pleasures. On a fine spring day in the third year of the Yifeng reign (A.D. 679) the emperor, accompanied by his entourage, went to the west imperial garden to enjoy the blooming flowers. To his disappointment, the flowers in the garden, though numerous, were too commonplace for imperial taste. When he held an audience the following day, the emperor ordered the Minister of Works to leave for the city of Luoyang, the homeland of peonies, to search the local gardens —either private or public—for strange and exotic flowers and bring them back to the capital, Chang'an. He was also to buy some seedlings of unusual species and cultivate them in Chang'an, so the emperor could have something to feast his eyes upon the next year.

The Minister of Works, Pei Xingjian, was married to Liu Shi, and the couple had a son named Pei Shaojun who learned to read and write at an early age. A handsome lad of twenty-one, he remained single and didn't seem to pay much

---

* Bai Pu (1226-c. 1306) is regarded as one of the four great playwrights of the Yuan Dynasty. He declined official appointments and chose to entertain himself in the country, drinking wine and composing poetry and plays. Of his sixteen plays, only three survive: *Over the Wall, Rain on Parasol Trees* and *Romance of the East Wall.*

attention to wine and women. Pei Xingjian was an old man unequal to the hardships of a long journey, so he asked the emperor to allow his son to take up the mission on his behalf. The emperor, taking pity on him, agreed. Thus Pei Shaojun set off for Luoyang accompanied by a servant named Zhang Qian, selected by Pei Xingjian for his capability.

At that time there lived in Luoyang a man named Li Shijie who was a member of the imperial clan. Formerly, while serving as governor of the imperial capital, he had offended the ruling empress, Wu Zetian, by his criticism and was demoted to supervisor of Luoyang. He and his wife, Zhang Shi, had a young daughter. Being a virtuous woman, Zhang Shi never complained about his demotion. Their daughter, Li Qianjin, was not only endowed with extremely good looks but also conversant with literature as well as needlework. At eighteen, she was still unbetrothed. It was not that her parents were not eager to secure her future; her father's unfortunate demotion and banishment was responsible for the delay. As the family settled down in Luoyang, Li found that his official duties did not take up much of his time, so he often went around visiting his fellow officials. In the meantime, mother and daughter stayed home behind a locked gate.

It is well said that "a full grown man should take a wife, and a full-grown girl should take a husband." Li Qianjin, coming of age in her secluded maiden's chamber, began to grow languid over her dim prospects for marriage. Fortunately her maid, Meixiang, was a smart and sympathetic girl who tried every means to comfort her, with partial success. Still, a fine spring morning or a moonlit night often found her lamenting the passing of time and the transience of her youth and beauty.

One spring holiday in the third lunar month, peonies were in full bloom all across the city of Luoyang. It was customary on this day for young people to take excursions to the hills and streams and enjoy the spring scenery. Forbidden to leave the house, Li Qianjin could only sit before her dressing table and stare at the decorated screen by the bed. One morning when Meixiang came into the room, Li Qianjin remarked, "Meixiang, look at the picture on this screen! These couples of young scholars and their pretty companions—what a fine sight they make!"

Meixiang had no trouble guessing what was on the young mistress's mind. "I know what you are thinking about," she said jokingly. "You are longing for a fine husband." Though brought up in an aristocratic family, Li Qianjin was a very forthright and independent-minded girl. To Meixiang's remark she responded unabashedly, "Yes! If only I had a fine husband, who loves me dearly and who spends his time by my side, I would not feel so lonely and deserted, nor would I have to endure such long, cold, sleepless nights!" Meixiang then suggested, "When the master comes back, we must ask him to arrange a marriage for you! You have grown so thin these days. Please take good care of yourself!" Li Qianjin knew only too well that her emaciation was not caused by any ailment and would not respond to any medicine. She found her daily meals tasteless, and would gladly find refuge in sleep, but sleep did not come easily to her. She seemed to be living in a daze, unable to concentrate on anything, and all because of uncertainties about her future! A few days earlier a matchmaker had called. Not knowing if the young man suited her, and too shy to inquire about him, she ended up turning down the proposal for fear of ruining her life by a wrong choice. The memory of this incident added to her melancholy. She heaved deep sighs as tears rolled down her cheeks.

Meixiang hastened to comfort her. "Mistress! It is a holiday today, and all the young people of the city are riding horses or carriages to the suburbs to enjoy the spring scenery. Though we can't leave the house, why don't we take a walk in the rear garden?" Urged by the well-meaning maid, Li Qianjin left the room with her and headed for the garden.

They walked down the winding veranda and came to the fish pond. At the sight of the dancing butterflies, mandarin ducks swimming in pairs, and bees and dragonflies flying and darting merrily all over the place, the young maiden felt more lonely than ever.

Suddenly she heard the neighing of a horse and someone shouting just outside the wall. Looking up, she saw a young man on horseback staring at her hungrily. This was Pei Shaojun. Since his arrival in Luoyang, he had visited many famous gardens and scenic spots in search of unusual flowers. He was passing Supervisor Li's rear garden when some apricot trees in blossom caught his eye, so he stopped by the wall to take a look. To his surprise the garden not only boasted flourishing flowers but also a ravishing beauty, who enchanted him so much that he could not take his eyes off her. She had eyes as bright as the stars and a face as pretty as spring flowers, appearing to be an immortal girl descended from heaven. "What a fine maiden!" he exclaimed. Hearing this, Meixiang whispered to Li Qianjin, "Someone's watching you over the wall!" Actually, Li Qianjin already saw the young man and did not mind his staring at her. He looked so handsome and elegant. "What does that matter?" she said defiantly. "Let him watch to his heart's content! I would not mind having such a fine young man for my lifelong companion and offering him everything I have! Why should I mind his watching me?" However, Meixiang thought it necessary to warn her young mistress. "You may cherish tender feelings for him, but does he feel the same for you?"

While the two girls were thus conversing in a whisper, Pei Shaojun kept staring at Qianjin as if glued to the spot. Afraid of getting into trouble, Zhang Qian tried to talk his young master into leaving. Lost in thought, Shaojun did not hear

Pei Shaojun has his eyes fixed on the beauty in the garden.

him. "By the way she looks at me, she must be thinking what I'm thinking," he said to himself. "If I just leave, both of us will be agonized!" Plucking up his courage, he wrote a note and told Zhang Qian to give it to the maid. Zhang Qian was to move his hand back and forth should the beauty be pleased, or from side to side if the maid scolded him.

Charged with this mission, Zhang Qian clambered over the wall into the garden, approached Meixiang, and struck up a conversation with her, saying he wanted to buy some flowers. Then he slipped her the note. Without looking at it, Meixiang handed it to Li Qianjin, who opened it and read the following quatrain:

> I find myself in the famed fairyland of Wuling,
> With peach blossoms blushing across the stream.
> Gazing over the wall, I am heartbroken with longing
> As the fairest of maidens bestows her smile on me.

Liu Qianjin had studied poetry herself, so she had no difficulty understanding the meaning of the verse, which pleased her not a little. She composed a quatrain on the spot and asked Meixiang to pass it over. Taking the note in her hand, Meixiang began to poke fun at her young mistress. Who should she give this note to? What does it say? What should she say to the young scholar? What if someone else is watching? She nearly drove the young mistress into a fit by threatening to show the note to her mother. Finally she went over to Shaojun with the note. Shaojun was so impatient that he actually snatched it from her. Opening the note, he read the following:

> I take a leisurely walk from my secluded abode,
> Twiddling a green plum to hide my shyness.
> Do not miss the appointment tonight
> When the moon climbs over the willows in the garden.

The verse was signed "Qianjin." Shaojun was thrilled with delight to find the maiden was not only beautiful but accomplished in letters. Now that a secret rendezvous was fixed for the night, Shaojun decided to take his leave. He would return at the appointed time to fulfill his dream, to cross the wall and be united with his love.

Back at the inn, Shaojun waited restlessly for the sun to go down.

Though a brave, forthright girl, Li Qianjin felt nervous over her first romantic appointment. When night fell, she sent the maid to find out what her mother was doing. It turned out that the old lady had already gone to bed. When Meixiang hastened back to inform Qianjin, she found the young maiden asleep, perhaps dreaming of a meeting with Shaojun.

To Shaojun's joy, the sun finally went down, and darkness fell. The moon then rose in the rear garden, bathing the houses in its silvery light. Li Qianjin made a few bows to the moon, beseeching it to withdraw its light and not ruin her plan for the night. Meixiang, following her young mistress to the garden, sighed on seeing this. "A good match is not easy to come by!" Since the maid already knew about the secret meeting, Qianjin asked her to help through to the end. For fear that Shaojun would startle the birds and dogs while stumbling his way through the rear garden and attract the attention of the old wet nurse, she sent Meixiang to wait by the wall and lead Shaojun to her chamber when he arrived.

Shaojun had been waiting anxiously outside the wall for some time when Meixiang came up. Telling Zhang Qian in a whisper to wait outside, he placed both hands on top of the wall and climbed over it into the garden. He bowed repeatedly to Meixiang, much to her amusement. Leading him to the room of the young mistress, she announced his arrival in a soft voice. Then she pushed him inside while she stood by the door to keep watch.

After greeting Qianjin with a few bows, Shaojun began pouring out his feelings for her. The young lady, her head lowered in abashment, admitted to sentiments of a similar vein. The two were thus absorbed in love talk when the old wet nurse, on her nightly patrol of the courtyard, approached the room. Despite her old age she still had strong legs, bright eyes, and good ears. The cooing of the love birds caught her attention from a long way off and made her quicken her steps. In a low voice Meixiang sent out a warning to her young mistress to blow out the oil-lamp, but even this did not escape the sharp ears of the old woman. "It's too late to blow out the lamp," she said, grabbing Meixiang by the hand. "I've listened for a long time already! Don't you try to get away!" Dragging Meixiang behind her, she pushed at the door of the young mistress's chamber.

Qianjin and Shaojun were startled by the wet nurse's voice and tried in vain to find a way of escape or a place to hide. They opened the door to let in the old woman and knelt before her, pleading for mercy. Fighting off her maidenly modesty, Qianjin announced that she and Shaojun were already husband and wife, but the marriage must be kept a secret from her parents. She asked the wet nurse to allow them to run away, saying she would always remember her for such a kindness. The wet nurse was naturally indignant on finding the young maiden thus seduced and demanded to know Shaojun's identity. When Qianjin replied that Shaojun was not an ordinary man off the street but the son of a minister on an official mission in Luoyang, the wet nurse insisted that they should not be married without parental consent. She then turned to Meixiang and accused her of leading the young mistress astray. Qianjin, however, being a brave and honest girl, declared there was no need to blame the maid. She had given her hand to Shaojun of her own accord, for she was in love with him, and he with her.

The wet nurse found the matter too grave to settle on the spot, so she seized Shaojun by the hand and threatened to take him to the yamen. As the son of a high official, Shaojun was unaccustomed to such treatment, but he had to swallow his pride and pleaded with the wet nurse in humble terms, fearing that a big quarrel might wake up the entire family and bring dishonor on the young maiden. When the wet nurse remained uncompromising, Shaojun changed his tactic and tried to intimidate her. He claimed to have bribed her into arranging the secret meeting with the young maiden. When the wet nurse tried to deny it, Meixiang joined in by testifying to Shaojun's words and blaming the wet nurse for taking a bribe and attempting to shift the blame on others. In the meantime Qianjin began to wail, saying the wet nurse was forcing her to kill herself. Besieged by the three young people, the old wet nurse found herself in a fix. I would die without a burial ground, she said to herself, if something bad happened to the young miss and the old lady blamed the thing on me. After thinking for a while, she came up with two solutions from which she asked Shaojun and Qianjin to choose. The first one was for Shaojun to leave at once and return to propose marriage to Qianjin once he became an official. Should he fail to achieve this, Qianjin would be free to marry someone else. The other alternative was for Shaojun and Qianjin to leave together and return to visit Qianjin's parents after Shaojun became an official. Without hesitation, Qianjin voted in favor of the second plan, for fear that if Shaojun should leave alone he might fall for some other girl and fail to return. As for Shaojun, he was too enamored of Qianjin to think of parting from her. Thus elopement seemed the best solution for both. It was then decided that the couple must leave that night, leaving the matter in the care of the wet nurse. Zhang Shi, they reckoned, would not raise a storm on finding out about it, as that would only publicize the family scandal. Before the two lovers left, the wet nurse wrung from Shaojun the promise to treat the young mistress well and return to acknowledge her parents as soon as he attained officialdom.

The young couple left Luoyang and headed for Chang'an, the imperial capital. As excitement over the elopement subsided, Shaojun began to worry over his future. What would his parents say when he abruptly brought home a bride without their consent? He brooded over the matter all along the way and finally, on his arrival in Chang'an, reached a solution. He sent Zhang Qian to go back to their house first and ask the old gardener to open the back gate and clean the studio in the garden ready to receive Qianjin. This, he explained to Qianjin, would only be a temporary arrangement. She would live in his studio in the rear garden for the time being. As soon as he found the chance to explain the matter to his parents, she would be moved into more suitable quarters. Considering the situation, Qianjin reluctantly agreed to this arrangement.

Acting on this plan, Pei Shaojun first moved Qianjin into the rear garden in secret, then came around and entered the house through the main entrance. He went to see his parents, reported his purchase of exotic flowers, and told his father of his decision to devote himself to studies in the rear garden in preparation for the civil recruitment examination. Therefore he would not come to greet his parents except on special occasions. Pei Xingjian readily gave his consent, much pleased with his son's ambition. Shaojun returned to the garden and tipped the old keeper handsomely, admonishing him not to let any strangers into the garden. When his parents were coming, he was to be informed beforehand. By this arrangement Shaojun was able to enjoy a happy, peaceful life together with his beloved wife, Qianjin.

The happy days passed very quickly. At the end of seven

years they had a son and a daughter. The son, Duanduan, was now six years old and the daughter, Chongyang, was four. Shaojun was so cowardly that he had not yet dared to reveal his marriage to his parents, but was resigned to letting his wife and children live like fugitives in the rear garden. Though highly displeased, Qianjin could not bring herself to go and present herself to her parents-in-law. She had to swallow her humiliation for the sake of her husband and adapt herself to living like a hermit. She had to worry constantly over her children, who did not know enough to restrain themselves and liked to roam the garden. It was all she could do, with the help of the old keeper, to keep the matter away from the master and mistress of the house.

On the festival of Pure Brightness, the family used to go and burn incense at the ancestral grave. This year, however, Pei Xingjian was so old and weak that he could not move without his walking stick. So Shaojun was told to accompany his mother to the graveyard.

Shaojun had no choice but to agree, knowing that his father attached great importance to ancestral worship. Before he left, he instructed the old gardener to watch over Duanduan and Chongyang carefully so they would not run around and cause trouble. He also promised the keeper a handsome bonus on his return from the grave, and the old keeper agreed to do his best. His mind at ease, Shaojun left home with his mother. The keeper then went in to tell Qianjin about the matter and ask her for some wine and fruit.

Confined to the garden with her children and unable to go out for an excursion even on a festival day, Qianjin could not help feeling sullen. The past seven years of her clandestine marriage felt to her like a dream. She had not heard from her parents in all these years and wondered if they were still in good health. Born and brought up in the best of families, she resented having to live with her husband in such secrecy.

19

While she was lamenting her fate like this, the old gardener burst in and began accusing her children of damaging the flowers on the wall and asking her to guard them more closely. Otherwise, he said, they might run into the old master and cause big trouble. Displeased, Qianjin berated the old man for failing to take good care of the children, as they had pricked their fingers while picking flowers. However, she did call them over and warn them not to leave the studio.

The old gardener, though scolded, managed to get some wine and fruit from the young mistress, so he went out into the garden and sat down to a few cups of wine. Feeling a little tipsy, he leaned against a rock to take a nap. As soon as he closed his eyes, Duanduan and Chongyang slipped out of the studio, hand in hand, and went up to stare at him. Finding him half asleep, Duanduan gave him a slap of his palm. The old man started and opened his eyes to see the two children. Muttering a curse, he told them to return to the studio, then closed his eyes again. But the children refused to listen to him. Chongyang came over and began to pound his leg with her small fist. Straining to open his eyes, the old keeper railed at her. "Why should a girl be so naughty!" Then he dozed off again.

It so happened that Pei Xingjian, having nothing better to do, came out for a walk in the garden accompanied by Zhang Qian. He wanted to find out for himself how Shanjun was doing in his studies. On entering the gate he caught sight of the old keeper nodding beside a rock, his face flushed with wine. Two small children were playing nearby, creating quite a racket. Displeased, Pei Xingjian went up and slapped the old man on the face. Thinking it was still the children, the old keeper, his eyes closed, grabbed a broom by his hand and hit back, muttering, "Take this, little rascal!" Pei Xingjian shouted angrily, "How dare you!" The old keeper, scared sober, sprang to his feet and stood respectfully before the old master. "To which family do these children belong? Why are they in my garden?" demanded Pei. Before the old keeper could come up with a plausible explanation, Duanduan chimed in, "We belong to the Pei family!" "Which Pei family?" Pei Xingjian asked in surprise. "The family of Minister Pei!" declared Chongyang, proud in her knowledge. The old keeper, in an attempt to save the situation, scolded the two children severely, accusing them of breaking into the garden and damaging flowers, and tried to drive them out of the garden. But the children, instead of being intimidated, pointed at him with their little fingers and threatened, "Wait till we tell papa and mama, and they'll break those old legs of yours!" Watching the scene, Pei Xingjian realized something was terribly wrong. Paying no more attention to the children, he headed straight for the studio, intending to find out the truth of the matter.

Hearing the noise outside, Qianjin stood up to look out of the window, and was horrified by what she saw. The children were walking toward the studio, panting with indignation, followed by old Minister Pei. She hastily dragged the children inside and closed the door, but the old minister already caught sight of her. He ordered the gardener to tell her to come to the lotus pavilion to meet him. Qianjin had no choice but to confront the old minister. Entering the lotus pavilion, she introduced herself as Pei Shaojun's wife. Dismayed and furious, Pei Xingjian retorted, "If you claim to be Shaojun's wife, tell me who the matchmaker was? What betrothal gift your family received? And who presided over the wedding ceremony?" Qianjin could answer none of these questions. Pei Xingjian, pointing to Duanduan and Chongyang, demanded to know which family they belonged to. At this the gardener, who was standing aside, suggested that he should be happy rather than angry over the matter. "Old Minister! Don't you see what a bargain this is for you? Without spending a cent, you have obtained for yourself such a heavenly daughter-in-law, and such a pair of lovable grandchildren. Why don't you throw a banquet to celebrate your good fortune?" Pei Xingjian hit the roof on hearing this. "Stop talking nonsense! How could this woman have come from a good family? Who can guarantee she was not a singing girl or something like that?" Pampered since childhood, Li Qianjin had never been insulted like this. Her eyes flashing with rage, she could not help answering back. "The woman standing before you comes from a noble family and is no person of lowly status!" "Shut up!" roared Pei Xingjian, outraged by her audacity. "A woman commits an unpardonable sin when she runs away with a man out of wantonness. How could such a woman come from a noble family? I can have you taken to the yamen and flogged!" Not to be browbeaten, Li Qianjin insisted that she was from a noble family and not a courtesan as he suspected. Even if taken to the yamen, this would still be her answer. Unable to bring her to submission, Pei Xingjian turned to the old gardener, charging him to tell the truth. Zhang Qian, afraid of being punished as an accomplice, took the chance to shift all the blame on the old keeper. Unfortunately for him, the old keeper suddenly remembered it was Zhang Qian who had accompanied Shaojun to Luoyang to purchase flowers. He told the old minister that Zhang Qian must have assisted Shaojun to marry Li Qianjin. Pei Xingjian turned to reprehend Zhang Qian, who claimed to be entirely innocent.

Just as the old minister were venting his anger at the two old servants, Pei Shaojun and his mother returned from their visit to the ancestral grave. The family gathered in the lotus pavilion. The old minister first blamed his wife for abetting her son and tarnishing the family name, then he rebuked Shaojun for the fruit of his seven years of 'study' in the rear garden. He ordered Shaojun to divorce Li Qianjin at once; otherwise, the young couple would be taken to the yamen for interrogation.

22

Much to Qianjin's indignation, Shaojun cowered before his father's outburst, so she had to confront the old minister on her own. Before he carried out his threat, she asked him to give his reason for breaking up the happy marriage. With no reason to offer, Pei Xingjian resorted to invective, describing Qianjin as a wanton woman who had changed husbands three times. "Pei Shaojun is my one and only husband!" Qianjin declared. Pei Xingjian then tried to demean her by quoting a common saying, "A woman married by engagement becomes the principal wife, but the one joining her man by elopement becomes a concubine." To this Qianjin responded, "What's the difference between an engagement and an elopement? The truth is we love each other, and this shows that the match has been made in heaven!"

At this, Pei Xingjian found a way to subdue Qianjin. A match made in heaven, he reasoned, should be able to create miracles, and he offered Qianjin the chance to perform two. First, she must rub her jade hairpin on a rock until it becomes a needle; second, she must fetch water from the well with a silver bottle hanging from a single thread. If she should succeed, he would accept her marriage as a heaven-made match; otherwise she must clear out straightaway and return to her own parents. Hoping against hope, Qianjin tried to perform the two demanding tasks. Unsurprisingly, she failed in both. Thereupon Pei Xingjian announced that her failure disproved once and for all her claim to a heavenly sanctified marriage. She must leave the Pei family and find someone else to marry. Qianjin found herself totally at the old minister's mercy. Shaojun was no help at all; succumbing to his father's wrath, he actually wrote his wife a divorce letter on the spot.

Filled with grief, Li Qianjin burst out crying. Unmoved, Pei Xingjian ordered Shaojun to return to his studio and get ready for the metropolitan examination that very year. Qianjin was forced to leave without her children, Duanduan and

Li Qianjin tries to fetch water from the well with a silver bottle
hanging on a single thread.

Chongyang. In vain she remonstrated against the old minister's cruelty and Shaojun's cowardice. Finally she asked Shaojun to escort her back to Luoyang. Even to this request Shaojun dared not agree openly, but had to find an excuse to take her back without his father's knowledge.

Li Qianjin found on her return to Luoyang that her parents had died grieving over the loss of their beloved daughter. The big house and large farmlands, along with the maids and servants, now belonged to her. She missed the children left behind in Chang'an, and not even the comforting words of Meixiang, the loyal maid, could relieve her deep longing. Sometimes she took a walk with Meixiang in the rear garden, where the apricot trees brought back to her that fateful meeting with Shaojun. She could find no way to assuage her sorrow.

Pei Shaojun, studying hard, finished first in the metropolitan examination and was appointed district governor of Luoyang. After taking office, he went straight to Supervisor Li's house in search of his wife. Coming before the entrance, he saw Meixiang standing by the second gate and went up to inquire after Qianjin. Acting as if she did not know him, Meixiang went in without a word. Pei Shaojun followed her into the house and, at the sight of Qianjin, greeted her with a thousand solicitous inquiries and offered to make up with her. The memory of his betrayal still fresh in her mind, Qianjin remarked caustically, "So you want to take me back as your wife? But I am afraid of another inquisition. Didn't your father call me a wanton woman who had brought disgrace on your family name? How can I join the Pei family again?" Time and again Shaojun begged her to forgive him. He did not fail to mention that he had been appointed governor of Luoyang; moreover, the old minister had retired from his post at the court and was staying home, unable to meddle in his son's affairs again. Hearing this, Qianjin said,

"What a joy it must be for him! Now he can fully indulge in his favorite pastime—breaking up other people's marriages!" When Shaojun said he wanted to move in that day, Qianjin refused to let him. He would not have divorced her, Shaojun explained, but for his father's command. Qianjin thought it a thin excuse and went on to denounce his father for his unjustified cruelty. "What a good minister he was! He seemed more interested in persecuting his daughter-in-law than attending to state affairs!"

When the result of the metropolitan examination came out, Shaojun's name as the Number One Scholar of the year spread far and wide in the empire. His parents, while rejoicing over their son's success, found out that their daughter-in-law was actually a member of imperial peerage, the only daughter of Supervisor Li. To make up with their son and also to avoid offending the imperial house, the old couple arrived in Luoyang with their grandchildren to call on their daughter-in-law.

Pei Xingjian walked in just as Shaojun was trying his best to placate Qianjin. At the sight of Qianjin he broke into a broad smile. "Oh, my dear child! How could I have guessed you are Li Shijie's daughter! I knew him well, and we even talked about marrying you to Shaojun on one occasion. Why didn't you tell me everything? I took you for a girl from a performer's family—something like that. Well, I have come with my wife and the grandchildren to offer you wine and mutton by way of apology!" The servants brought over the wine, and he filled a cup himself and offered it to Qianjin. "Yes!" the old lady chimed in. "Please acknowledge your parents-in-law, if only in return for our taking care of the children!" In spite of her lingering anger at the humiliation she had suffered, Qianjin gave in, mainly for the sake of Duanduan and Chongyang, who ran up to her, grabbed the hem of her dress, and wept piteously.

With Qianjin assenting to a family reunion, Pei Xingjian

raised the cup in celebration. Qianjin was compelled to bow to her parents-in-law in obeisance, but she declined the wine, saying, "This daughter-in-law has joined the Pei family by elopement! There is no need for her to drink the wine. She would be contented to be spared the jade hairpin, the silver bottle, and the divorce letter!" Pei Xingjian did not venture to reply. The rare humility displayed by the old man made Qianjin relent a little, and she took the proffered cup of wine by way of reconciliation. However, Pei Xingjian was so dull-witted that he began to mumble again. "My child, why didn't you wait for me to arrange a proper wedding? Why did you come to my house by elopement? When you arrived, why did you fail to mention you were Li Shijie's daughter?" Qianjin felt her anger surge up again. "Father! What is elopement, I pray? Am I the first woman in history to choose her husband herself? Have you never heard the story of the matchless beauty Zhuo Wenjun, who ran away with Sima Xiangru, that handsome and talented scholar, after listening to the amorous tune he played on the zither? Didn't the couple enjoy fame and prosperity afterwards, riding together in a four-horse chariot? Shaojun and I found each other over the wall, married in secret and are now reunited in glory. I don't think our match pales in comparison with that of the celebrated Sima Xiangru and Zhuo Wenjun! My only hope is that every marriage started this way have a happy ending!" Thus re-buked, Pei Xingjian realized he'd better hold his tongue.

This story illustrates the truth expressed in the following couplet:

To find your true love there is no need to watch from a decorated archway;
Sometimes a glance over the wall while riding on horseback will suffice.

SNOW IN MIDSUMMER

*Guan Hanqing**

In Chuzhou there lived an old widow named Cai. Thanks to the household property left by her husband, she was able to make a good living as a moneylender. There was no one else in the family except her eight-year-old son.

Dou Tianzhang, a poor scholar, lived in the same city. Though well versed in ancient poetry and the Confucian classics, he had yet to attain fame and honors. After his wife died of an illness, he brought up his daughter, Duanyun, alone and now she was seven years old. Under straitened circumstances, Dou Tianzhang was compelled to become one of Cai's clients, borrowing twenty taels of silver from her. The interest rate was so high that before long he found himself forty taels in debt to Cai. The old woman had come several times for the money, but Dou could not pay her.

Whenever Mistress Cai came to Dou's house, she would take Duanyun by the hand and ask her all sorts of questions, for she was such a cute, lovely child. Unable to get her money back, she hit upon an idea. Why not take the small girl as her son's child-bride? No sooner thought than done. She asked a neighbor to go as matchmaker and present Dou with the offer.

Dou Tianzhang could not find it in his heart to part with

---

* Guan Hanqing (c. 1210-c. 1310) is regarded as one of the four great playwrights of the Yuan Dynasty. Living a vagabond existence, he was familiar with the joys and sorrows of social underdogs. He wrote over sixty Yuan-style plays, eighteen of which have survived. His work not only reflects truthfully the harsh social reality of his times but, with a romantic twist, inspires hope through the final victory of light over darkness.

his only child. Though pestered by Mistress Cai to pay the debt and by her matchmaker, Dou refused to let go of his child. Then the imperial examination was drawing near and he must set out for the capital. To whose care could he consign his young daughter, Duanyun? As he was worrying over this matter, Cai's matchmaker called again. Pondering the situation, Dou Tianzhang concluded that the proposed match might not be all that bad. By agreeing to it, he would be cleared of the heavy debt, Duanyun would have a home, for better or worse, and he would also get some money to pay for his trip to the capital. Thus he said yes to the matchmaker and chose a lucky day for handing over Duanyun.

On the appointed date Dou Tianzhang got up early, called Duanyun to him, and exhorted her to be a good girl. In spite of her tender age, Duanyun somehow sensed the meaning of the event. Taking her father by the sleeve, she wept ruefully. With a heavy heart Dou Tianzhang left home with Duanyun, coaxing and persuading her all the way.

They came to Mistress Cai's house and were invited in. After taking his seat, Dou Tianzhang said, "I have brought my daughter to you today. I dare not expect you to take her as your daughter-in-law, but would be content if she can be of any service to you day and night. I am leaving for the capital to take the imperial examination. Please look after Duanyun for me." Pleased with Dou's humility, Cai replied graciously that they had become relatives by marriage. She handed Dou a piece of paper and a silver ingot. "Here is your promissory note back, and ten taels of silver for your traveling expenses. Please don't think the sum too small!" Taking the silver in his hands, Dou Tianzhang was seized with an intense heartache, feeling as if he were selling rather than marrying his daughter.

In spite of his sorrow, all he could do was to beg Cai to take good care of his daughter. "If Duanyun deserves a beating, for my sake please spare her the beating and just scold her. If she deserves to be scolded, for my sake please spare her the scolding and just give her a few words of instruction. As for the great kindness you showed toward me by returning the note and offering me money for the road, I can only repay you someday in the future!" Mistress Cai took pity on the poor scholar and promised to treat Duanyun like her own and never let her come to any harm.

Dou Tianzhang then pulled Duanyun aside and wiped away her tears. "My child," he whispered, "your father would not have done this if he had an alternative. You would not have enough to eat and wear if you should go on living with me. What's more, I am leaving for the capital to take the imperial examination; I have to entrust you to the old lady. My child, from now on you can no longer act willfully as at home. Don't be naughty, or you would be asking for trouble. On no account must you forget this! My child, I wouldn't have done this if I could help it!" As he said this, tears rolled down his cheeks. "Father," wailed Duanyun, "how can you leave me like this?" Dou Tianzhang knew there was no point staying any longer, so he freed himself from his daughter's grip and, without saying good-bye to Mistress Cai, walked out the door in a hurry.

Taking Duanyun by the hands, Cai pulled the child into her arms to console her. "My child, you have come into my house as my daughter-in-law, so we are a family now. There's no need to grieve, much less to weep. Follow me to the kitchen and see how you can make yourself helpful."

Thus Duanyun began her life as a child-bride. Mistress Cai and her son found the name Duanyun too difficult to pronounce, so they changed it to Dou E the first day she entered the house.

News never arrived from Dou Tianzhang after he left Chuzhou. Dou E worked hard in the Cai family, boiling tea, cooking meals, washing and bleaching clothes. Ten years later,

"How can you leave me like this, father?" wailed Duanyun.

she was a maiden of seventeen and Cai's son was eighteen. Now that they had both grown to adulthood, Cai selected an auspicious day, invited some neighbors to her house for a feast, and formally married the young couple.

The three of them made a harmonious family. Having grown up together, Dou E and her husband were comfortable in each other's company. But the happy days did not last. A weakling since childhood, Dou E's husband died of illness two years later. Dou E became a widow at a young age and had to dress in mourning for her husband for the next three years.

How forlorn the days must have felt for a young widow like Dou E those three years! She often counted the misfortunes that had befallen her: losing her mother at three, torn from her father at seven, and deprived of her husband at nineteen. Sometimes she blamed herself for all this, convinced she had been born under an evil star and was destined to suffer ill fortune all her life. Sometimes she blamed heaven and earth for being so callous to human misery. She was in such a melancholy mood that flowers in full bloom brought tears to her eyes, and the silvery light of the moon filled her heart with a painful longing. However, she tried her best to bear her misery and think of her oath to her husband and her duty to her mother-in-law. She decided to be true to her widowhood and serve Mistress Cai unfailingly.

One day Mistress Cai left home after saying to Dou E, "I am going out of the city to collect my money from Doctor Lu." This Doctor Lu lived outside the south gate of Chuzhou's Shanyang County, where he kept a drugstore and also practiced medicine. To describe his medical expertise, the local people composed this small verse:

He diagnoses all diseases with the utmost care,
And prescribes all medicines according to the Materia Medica.
No dead man has been brought back to life,

Though many live ones have died in his hands.

He took immense pride in his aptitude and considered himself superior to Bian Que, one of the best known physicians in Chinese history. However, not many people shared this opinion, so he had very few patients and could not make ends meet. On one occasion he borrowed ten taels of silver from Mistress Cai, and now he owed her twenty taels with interest. Cai had come several times to collect the debt, but he always managed to find an excuse to delay payment.

"Is Doctor Lu in?" Mistress Cai called out at the gate of the drugstore. Lu recognized her voice at once and hastily invited her in, for fear that the old woman would create a scene outside his shop.

Taking no notice of his obsequiousness, Cai asked him to pay his debt straightaway. Lu realized he would not be rid of her until she got the money, so he hit upon a plan. Smiling broadly, he said, "Old lady, I should have given back the money a long time ago. I am so sorry for making you come several times. I have the money ready today—twenty taels. Would you please come with me to the village to fetch it?" Eager to get the money, Cai agreed readily.

They left the drugstore and made their way to the village. When they came to a place with no one about, Lu looked around and called out, "Old woman, who is that person calling your name?" As Cai cocked her ears to listen, Lu slipped behind her and brought out a hemp rope he had taken with him, trying to strangle her with it. Cai dropped to the ground on her back.

"Help!" Cai screamed at the top of her lungs. Though a blackhearted scoundrel, Lu was scared by her shouting and hastily tightened the rope in his hands. However, two men emerged at the noise, and the younger one started running toward them. At this, Lu cursed his luck and took to his heels.

The young man helped Cai to her feet and turned to the old man. "Father, it's an old woman. She was nearly strangled to death." The old man came up and asked Cai what had happened. It took a long time for Cai to get her breath back. "My name is Cai," she said, "and I live in town with my widowed daughter-in-law. That murderer is Doctor Lu. He owes me twenty taels of silver. I went to his shop to collect the money today, but he lured me here and tried to strangle me. He wouldn't have to pay the money if I were dead, of course. Fortunately, you and that young man arrived in time to save me. Otherwise I would surely be dead by now."

Unfortunately for Cai, the two men were as bad as Doctor Lu. The young man's eyes lit up when Cai mentioned the widowed daughter-in-law living with her. Dragging his father aside, he whispered, "Father, didn't you hear that? Only she and her daughter-in-law are in her house. She must surely find a way to thank us for saving her life. Why don't you take her for a wife, and I will take the young one? We will make a happy family of four, don't you think? Go and propose to her now!"

The old man thought it a wonderful idea. He went up to Cai. "Old woman, my name is Zhang, and that is my son Donkey. Neither you nor your daughter-in-law has a husband, and neither I nor my son has a wife. Isn't it a good idea for me to marry you and my son to marry your daughter-in-law?" Cai, taken aback, refused. "What nonsense is this? You have saved my life, and when I go home I will give you a handsome sum to thank you. Don't ever talk like that again!"

Hearing this, Donkey's face fell, and he threatened her. "You won't do as I said? You think you can get rid of us with a little money?" He bent to pick up the hemp rope. "Well, this rope comes in handy. If you don't change your mind, I might as well strangle you." Cai was terrified. "Please don't rush me! Give me some time to think it over!" Donkey flourished the rope in his hand. "What is there to think about? Don't act like a fool—refusing a toast only to drink a forfeit." Afraid to be strangled again, Cai capitulated. "All right, the two of you can come home with me." Pleased, Donkey suddenly grew courteous, and even went up to support her. Together they returned to the city.

Arriving at her house, Cai grew hesitant. What could she say to her daughter-in-law if the three of them burst in like this? "Would you please wait outside the door?" she said. "Let me go in first to break the news to my daughter-in-law." Before the old man could speak, Donkey chimed, "A good idea for you to go in first, old woman! Tell your daughter-in-law her husband is waiting outside the door."

As Mistress Cai stepped into the house, Dou E came up and asked if she was tired or hungry and offered to cook some food for her. Faced with such a filial daughter-in-law, Cai could not bring herself to tell the bad news. Her head lowered, she began to weep silently. Alarmed, Dou E asked what was wrong. Entreated repeatedly, Cai at last came out with the story in a faltering voice. "I went to collect the debt from Lu, but he lured me to an out-of-the-way place and tried to strangle me. Fortunately I was rescued by an old man named Zhang and his son, Donkey. Then the old man Zhang wanted me to marry him. What a nuisance!"

Dou E found it too ludicrous to believe. "This would never do, mother! We have enough to eat and wear, and have no need for a man to support us. What's more, you are in your sixties. How can you get married at this age? It is really out of the question!" Cai knew Dou E was right, but she had already given her consent to Zhang. "My child, your words are reasonable, but these two men did save my life. They told me that since neither I nor my daughter-in-law has a husband, and neither of them has a wife, two heaven-bestowed marriages can be established. When I tried to refuse, they threatened to finish Doctor Lu's job and strangle me there and then. Well, I was so scared that I gave in. I promised I would marry Zhang, the old man, and you would marry his son, Donkey. My child, what else could I do?"

When she heard this, Dou E's face darkened. "Mother," she said, "this is outrageous! How can a sixty-year-old gray-haired woman like you marry again? People would laugh their heads off! Don't you remember how your husband worked hard all his life to earn this house and everything in it, which he left to you, so you don't have to worry for lack of food or clothing? How can you have the heart to marry someone else?" Finding Dou E's words hard to refute, Cai muttered that she did not know how to face the two Zhangs, who were waiting at the door, delighted with the prospect of marriage. "Mother," said Dou E, unmoved, "they may be delighted, but I cannot help worrying about you. You seem too old to drink the wedding wine, and you may not be able to tie the love-knot due to your poor eyesight. Can't you imagine how the neighbors would laugh at us?" Shamed into anger, Cai declared there was no alternative but for each of them to marry a new husband. Dou E flatly refused. "If you really want to take a husband, go ahead and do it. As for me, forget it!"

While they were thus debating in the house, the two Zhangs grew impatient waiting outside. Donkey, grabbing his father by the hand, burst into the room. Delighted by the good looks of the young woman, Donkey assumed such a dandified air as he could muster and chanted in an oily voice, "With a narrow-brimmed hat on my head and a tight-sleeved robe on my back, don't I look like a bridegroom today! Well, the two of you are damned lucky to marry such fine husbands like us." Pushing his father toward Mistress Cai, he edged his way to Dou E. Before he could say anything, Dou E cried out, "Keep away from me, you ruffian! Keep your distance!"

Faced with the two repellent men, Dou E tried again to

"Keep away from me!" shouted Dou E.

dissuade her mother-in-law. "Mother, how can you bring into our house such a crude old man and his shameless thug of a son?"

Mistress Cai was at a loss what to say to her daughter-in-law. Donkey, however, was not put off by Dou E's words. Walking up to her, he seized her by the hand and tried to make her bow to heaven with him, as newlyweds were supposed to do at the wedding ceremony. Seething with rage, Dou E pushed him away forcefully, sending him sprawling, then went back to her room. Filled with shame and anger, Donkey pointed at her back and cursed loudly. "How dare a slut like you give herself airs like this? Even a virgin should not have been so offended merely because I touched her. Don't think you can get away with this! I won't be a man if I cannot take you as my wife!" A timid woman, Cai tried her best to comfort the two men, offering wine and preparing fine food for them, with a promise to bring her daughter-in-law around. After that, the father and son settled down in Cai's house. They acted as if they were the heads of the family, constantly asking for food and wine and demanding to be waited on all day.

Mistress Cai tried to argue Dou E into submission, but Dou E advised her in return to guard her moral integrity. Due to her father's instruction, Dou E was convinced that a woman should remain faithful to her only husband all her life. She held in high esteem the couples well-known in history for their mutual devotion. One of her heroines was Zhuo Wenjun of the Western Han Dynasty who left her well-to-do family to join her husband, Sima Xiangru, and for the next few years made a living by selling wine. Then there was Meng Guang of the Eastern Han Dynasty who treated her husband, Liang Hong, with such great courtesy that she raised the tray to the level of her eyebrows when serving him a meal. There was also Meng Jiangnu, back in the time of the First Emperor of the Qin Dynasty, who traveled a thousand miles in search of her husband Fan Qiliang. Failing to find him, she wept so bitterly that a section of the Great Wall collapsed to reveal his remains buried underneath. Such were the paragons of virtue that Dou E had been taught to admire. For her to remarry was utterly unthinkable.

As Dou E showed no sign of submission, the Zhangs grew more and more irritated with her. Finally Donkey came up with a vicious plan.

Badly shaken by Doctor Lu's murder attempt and the constant intimidation of the Zhangs, Mistress Cai fell ill and became bedridden. It was then that Donkey decided to poison her. Left alone, Dou E would be defenseless against him. But where could he get poison? It suddenly occurred to him that they had walked past a drugstore the day they followed Cai into the city. Why not get some poison there? He left the city and made his way to the drugstore. At the sight of Dcotor Lu, he realized to his delight that this was the very man who had tried to murder Cai. Walking up to the counter, he shouted, "Doctor, good pal, get some medicine for me." "What medicine do you want?" asked Lu. "Give me a dose of poison." "What a bold man! I dare not sell that kind of thing!"

"You dare not sell poison?" sneered Donkey. "I happen to know what you dared to do! Didn't you try to strangle the old woman, Cai, a few days ago?" He grabbed Doctor Lu, threatening to take him to the yamen. Lu was scared cold and numb. "Good brother, please spare me," he pleaded in a shaking voice. "I have the medicine you want." He pulled out a drawer, wrapped some poison into a small packet, and shoved it at Donkey, who walked away well satisfied. "That thug is up to no good with the poison," Lu thought to himself. "If something bad happens, I will be implicated if I stay here." He decided he had better get away without delay. Wrapping up some rat poison to sell, he left for Zhuozhou, a neighboring prefecture.

Returning with the poison, Donkey met his father who suggested they go and inquire after Cai's illness. Donkey readily agreed.

When they entered Cai's room, the old man tried to show his concern by asking about her illness and offering to get her any dish she fancied. Cai said she would like some mutton tripe soup. Old Zhang turned to pass on the message to Donkey, who went out and told Dou E to cook a bowl of mutton tripe soup for her mother-in-law.

When Dou E brought over the bowl of soup, Donkey tasted it, saying a little more salt was needed. As soon as Dou E turned her back, he took out the poison and poured it into the bowl. When Dou E returned with the salt, Donkey found an excuse to go out, and it was old Zhang who took the bowl to Mistress Cai. Dou E helped Cai sit up in bed to drink the soup. Suddenly Cai felt sick in the stomach and dizzy in the head, and indicated that she did not want the soup anymore, so Dou E helped her lie down in bed again. The smell of the soup brought water to old Zhang's mouth. Seeing the covetous look on his face, Cai said he could help himself to the soup. "Oh no," protested Old Zhang, "the soup is for you!" Dou E turned her back to him with disgust.

After a proper display of modesty, old Zhang took the bowl and drank up the soup in no time. No sooner had he emptied the bowl than his head began to swim, an intense pain piercing his stomach. "Something's wrong with the soup!" he screamed. Then he just dropped dead to the ground.

Terrified, Cai broke into tears. Donkey, who had been lingering near the house, rushed in at the noise, expecting to find Cai dead in bed. Instead, he saw his father's body on the ground. Without a moment's hesitation, he caught hold of Dou E and yelled angrily, "Hey! You've poisoned my father! Don't think I will spare you!" Cai was totally stupefied, trembling all over. Dou E, however, was not in the least intimidated, as she had nothing to do with the murder. "Where could I have got the poison?" she retorted. "You put the poison into the soup when you sent me away to fetch salt. You forced my mother-in-law to let you stay, and now you have poisoned your father to blackmail us. Don't try to scare me in this way!"

Unable to browbeat Dou E, Donkey turned to threaten Cai. "Did you hear that, old woman? She accuses me of poisoning my own father! Would anyone believe her?" He went to the door and shouted, "Listen, neighbors all around! Dou E has poisoned my father!" Scared out of her senses, Cai waved her hands frantically, begging him to stop. Donkey went back to her bed and scowled at her savagely. "Are you afraid or not?" "I am afraid!" "Do you want me to keep quiet?" "Yes, please!"

Having Cai at his mercy, Donkey said, "If you really want me to spare you, what you need to do is very simple. Just tell Dou E to address me as her dear, sweet husband, and I will spare both of you." Broken down completely, Cai asked Dou E to gratify his wish. But Dou E remained unyielding. "Mother, how can you make such a thoughtless remark? It's impossible for me to marry this scoundrel!" "All right, Dou E!" said Donkey. "You have poisoned my father, that's for sure! Now do you want to settle this in public or in private? If you want a public settlement, I will take you to the yamen, to be flogged and birched until you confess to your crime, and what can you expect then but a death sentence? If you want it settled in private, you simply become my wife, and what a good bargain for you!" Dou E refused to accept the "private settlement," saying she had committed no crime and the last thing she wanted was to marry him. At this, Donkey dragged both women out of the house, heading for the yamen to lodge a complaint against Dou E.

41

The governor of Chuzhou, Tao Wu, was quite famous for his stupidity and greed. His unique golden rule of officialdom ran like this:

As an official I am smarter than most of my peers.
When accusers come, I ask them for gold and silver.
But when my superiors come to inspect,
I plead illness and stay home.

Each day he held court at the yamen, and when someone came to lodge a complaint, he always knelt to the accuser before returning to his seat to receive the other's salute. When asked the reason for this, he explained, "Well, people coming with lawsuits provide me with food and clothing just as my parents did. Why shouldn't I show my respect for them?"

On this day Tao Wu was sitting in the main hall when Donkey arrived with Dou E to file his suit. As usual, Tao Wu knelt before Donkey before going back to his seat. Banging a wooden slab on the desk, he charged the plaintiff to speak first. Donkey, a local bully who was wont to sue others for nothing, knew the procedures quite well. He stepped forth, fell on his knees, and kowtowed. "Your humble subject, Donkey, is the plaintiff. I accuse this young woman, Dou E, of murdering my father by poisoning a bowl of mutton tripe soup. This old woman, named Cai, is my stepmother. What an injustice I have suffered, your excellency! Please help me in the name of the law!" "All right," said Tao Wu. "Whoever among you poisoned the soup, speak up now!" Both Dou E and Mistress Cai denied having anything to do with the matter. Donkey, of course, claimed that he had not poisoned the soup. Thereupon Tao Wu burst into a rage. Pointing to his nose with his finger, he bellowed, "If none of you poisoned the soup, do you suppose I did it?" He ordered the runners to torture the young woman into confession.

Dou E stepped forth and knelt. "Your excellency, please

calm your anger, and listen to me. My mother-in-law is not his stepmother. He is named Zhang, but she is named Cai. When my mother-in-law went to Doctor Lu to collect a debt, he led her to a secluded place outside the city and tried to strangle her. Donkey and his father happened to pass by and saved her life. That's why my mother-in-law let them stay in our house and promised to support them in return for their help. Then they began to have this evil plan against us. His father wanted my mother-in-law for his wife, and this scoundrel here wanted me for his. I have not yet finished mourning for my newly deceased husband; how could I have submitted to his coercion? That is why he hated me and my mother-in-law and wanted to do us harm. My mother-in-law happened to fall ill and wanted me to cook mutton tripe soup for her. I don't know how Donkey got his poison, but when he sent me away to fetch salt, he poisoned the soup. Thanks to heaven, my mother-in-law suddenly belched and no longer wanted the soup, so she let old Zhang drink it. After drinking the soup, the old man dropped dead. Neither my mother-in-law nor myself had anything to do with the murder. I hope your excellency, being a wise official, will give us a just verdict!"

Dou E's speech was so eloquent and well-founded that Donkey panicked and decided to change tactics. Kowtowing to Tao Wu repeatedly, he said, "Your excellency can no doubt see the truth very clearly. The old woman is named Cai, and I am named Zhang. Why should she have kept us in her house if she did not want to marry my father? This young woman is extremely bullheaded; you cannot make her confess without a beating!"

It would not take much reasoning to detect the truth of the matter, but unfortunately Tao Wu did not believe in reasoning. Instead, he held the view that truth always came out after a sound beating. His interest was aroused when

Donkey described Dou E as extremely bullheaded, so he ordered the runners to use a big stick to beat her.

The runners responsible for beating people at court were all strong and hefty fellows picked out by Tao Wu himself. Soon Dou E was covered with blood stains and bruises all over her body. Several times she fainted, then woke up when the runners splashed her with cold water. In spite of all this, Dou E insisted on her innocence. Tao Wu felt quite frustrated, then he hit upon what he thought was a brilliant idea. "Give that old woman a good beating!" he ordered. Dou E was truly scared when she heard this, for Cai was an old woman still weak from her illness; how would she be able to bear physical torture? But what could Dou E do to save her mother-in-law? "There's nothing else I can do," Dou E sighed to herself. "Stop! Stop, please!" she called out. "Don't beat my mother-in-law. I will confess! I poisoned the old man; my mother-in-law had nothing to do with it!"

So long as he obtained a confession, Tao Wu did not care to look further into the case. He had the scribe wrote down Dou E's confession, made her sign it, and ordered the runners to place her in shackles and throw her into prison, to be beheaded the following day. Deeply grieved, Mistress Cai crawled up to Dou E, leaned on her, and wept bitterly, regretting that she had cost her daughter-in-law's life. In the meantime the vicious ruffian, Donkey, kowtowed his thanks to Tao Wu. "What an upright judge! My injustice will be avenged tomorrow, when Dou E gets the punishment she deserves!" Tao Wu, immensely pleased to be called an "upright judge," ordered forthwith the release of Donkey and Mistress Cai.

Dou E did not have a wink of sleep that night in the death house. Try as she might, she could not recall having ever done anything to deserve such a cruel end to her life, and wondered how the gods in heaven could allow her to be treated in this way. At daybreak, she heard three rounds of drum beats followed by three rounds of the gongs. The prison guard unlocked the door, and two executioners walked in, broadsword in hand. Dou E realized she was at death's door. With no one to listen to the injustices visited upon her, she began to curse heaven and earth. "Oh heaven! You have the sun and the moon to shine both in the day and at night, and you have gods and ghosts to preside over the destiny of man. You should be able to tell right from wrong, but why do you take black for white, and good for evil? Why do you let the good live in poverty and die young, and the wicked enjoy wealth and longevity? Heaven and earth, you bully the good people and are scared of the wicked! What earth is this that does not discriminate between good and bad? What heaven is this that confuses the kind with the wicked?"

The executioners, not interested in Dou E's complaint, urged her to hurry up to the execution ground, which had been cleared, with guards posted at the four corners. The official in charge of the execution had already taken his seat awaiting the arrival of the convict. The passers-by in the street all stopped to watch; some shed tears of pity, while a few openly condemned Donkey, the ruffian who got away with murder, and Tao Wu, the befuddled governor. Coming to the main street, Dou E stopped to speak to the executioners. "Brothers, I have a favor to ask. Please do not turn me down!" Then she explained that she would prefer not to take the main road for fear that her mother-in-law would catch sight of her and become inordinately grieved. Touched by her filial devotion, the two executioners led her down a bypass toward the execution ground.

Failing to see Dou E on the main road, Cai followed the crowd to the execution ground, where she met her daughter-in-law escorted by the executioners. "My child!" Cai wailed. "How can I take the pain to see you come to this end?"

Sobbing, Dou E spoke to Cai of her last wishes. "Mother-in-law, don't cry for me. For fear of getting you into trouble, I was compelled to make a false confession. If you pity me for a motherless child and remember the years when I waited on you, please make sure to pour some leftover food on my grave on the first and fifteenth days of each month, and burn some paper money if you can spare it. For the sake of your child, please promise to do as I tell you!" Choked with tears, Cai nodded her head repeatedly. Dou E added that from then on Cai would have to take care of herself, for she would be left alone in the world.

The heartrending scene of Dou E bidding farewell to her mother-in-law brought tears to the eyes of many onlookers. At the appointed hour, the supervising official ordered the executioners to get on with the job. Cai was told to step back as the executioners removed the shackles from Dou E. "Your excellency," Dou E suddenly cried, "If you do me one last favor, I will die without regret." She then asked for a clean mat to be placed under her feet, and a piece of white cloth to be put up on the flag pole. "When my head is cut off," she said, "my blood will spurt up to the white cloth, without a single drop falling to the ground. This will be a sign to prove my innocence." Considering it was her last wish, the official gave his consent, convinced that her prediction was unlikely to come true.

When the executioners brought the mat and put up the white cloth, Dou E stepped on the mat, and in a voice choked with grief, she said, "In the Zhou Dynasty there was a loyal minister named Chang Hong, who was falsely accused and put to death. His blood, when collected and stored, turned into fresh green precious stones, and they remind later generations of the injustice he suffered. Because I, Dou E, have also suffered an injustice as deep as the ocean, I want my blood to spurt high into the sky and not flow down to the earth!" The executioners, moved to sympathy, allowed her to go on, since it was her last chance to speak.

"Your excellency," cried Dou E, "on this day in midsummer, I want snow to fall until it is three *chi* thick on the ground to cover my body and prove my innocence." The supervising official regarded her words as the ravings of a dying person. "What nonsense are you talking about!" he said. "Whatever injustice you have suffered, you won't be able to get a single snowflake in midsummer, much less a heavy snow three *chi* deep!" Dou E, who had studied history and literature with her father, knew quite well what she was talking about. "Are you saying it is impossible to snow in summer?" she asked. "Haven't you heard the story about Zou Yan, the faithful minister of Yan, who was locked up in prison because someone slandered him to the prince? It was a hot summer day in the fifth month, but he wept so bitterly in prison that large snowflakes fell from the sky. With three *chi* of snow on the ground, I would not need a burial place!"

With the supervising official silenced, Dou E went on, "Your excellency, after my death, Chuzhou will suffer from drought for three years because of the injustice I have suffered!" The official angrily ordered her to shut up. "You deserve to be slapped for such a remark! What you just said is utterly blasphemous!" Undaunted, Dou E retorted, "You can't be so sure that the officials can bully people like this without incurring the wrath of heaven! Haven't you heard the story of Zhou Qing, a filial woman of the Han Dynasty, who was wrongly put to death by the governor of Donghai? For three years afterwards, Donghai did not have a single drop of rain. Now it is Chuzhou's turn to suffer this fate, all because officials have no sense of justice and treat the common people like dirt!"

As Dou E was thus airing her grievances, dark clouds suddenly gathered over the execution ground, and a cold wind began howling. "Come, dark clouds!" cried Dou E. "Blow, fierce wind! Let my three wishes come true to prove my innocence!"

The supervising official shuddered in the cold wind and urged the executioners to get the job done. When the broadsword was brought down, her blood, as she had predicted, instead of flowing down to the ground, spurted onto the white cloth hanging high above. At the same time it began to snow heavily. "This must be an unjust case!" remarked the onlookers. The supervising official, ignoring these comments, got up and hurried away with the runners.

After Dou E's father, Dou Tianzhang, left Chuzhou sixteen years before, he passed the imperial examination and became an official in the capital. He rose steadily in rank until he was made assistant administrator of the imperial court. However, the servant he sent to Chuzhou to look for Mistress Cai and Duanyun returned with the news that Cai had moved away. Dou Tianzhang was deeply distressed. The thought of his daughter sold as a child bride always brought tears to his eyes, and because of this he had poor eyesight in his old age. Nevertheless, he was a diligent, conscientious official and carried out his duty with honesty and distinction, thereby gaining the trust of the imperial court. Recently he had been promoted to surveillance commissioner of the south and north Huaihe River regions and dispatched on a tour to check and examine cases and uncover corrupt officials in local governments. A gold plate and an imperial sword empowered him to execute criminals without obtaining prior consent of the court.

In the third year after Dou E's death, Dou Tianzhang arrived in Chuzhou, where he learned to his surprise and anxiety that the place had been suffering from crop failures for three years because of a severe drought. He decided to find out the cause of this problem.

As Dou E was shouting her grievances, dark clouds gathered over the execution ground, and a cold wind began to blow.

The day he arrived in Shanyang County all the officials in Chuzhou came to pay their respects. However, he declined all guests and confined himself to the studio, intending to look through all the cases tried in the past few years.

The files piled up high on his desk. He took the file on the top and opened it. "Convict named Dou E, charged with poisoning her father-in-law to death...." He felt a bit uneasy. Why should the convict bear the family name of Dou? Furthermore, she had committed an inexcusable offense, and the case was already closed. Unwilling to read the file, he slipped it to the bottom of the stack.

Tired after a day's travel, Dou Tianzhang grew sleepy in the quiet of his studio and yawned repeatedly. Bending over the desk, he closed his eyes to take a nap.

After her death, Dou E's spirit was bent on revenge. Learning of her father's arrival in Chuzhou, she came to the yamen and, finding her father asleep in his chair, slipped into his dream. Dou Tianzhang was overjoyed to see his daughter standing at the door, but as soon as he went up to meet her, he woke up from the dream. The lamp was flickering, so he went over to prick the snuff. Taking this chance, Dou E's spirit took her file and placed it back on top of the stack. Dou Tianzhang returned to his seat, picked up a file from the stack, and saw to his amazement that it was the same one he had slipped to the bottom. Could there be a ghost in the office? Or was it the sign of an unjust verdict? Badly shaken, he shouted for his servants.

Dou Tianzhang was terrified when, in answer to his call, there appeared before him a weeping spirit. "Father, don't be afraid!" said the spirit. "I am your child, Dou E." Dou Tianzhang opened his eyes wide and recognized his daughter, Duanyun, who explained that Mistress Cai had changed her name to Dou E after she entered Cai's house. Dou Tianzhang was about to go and take her by the hand when he suddenly recalled the file he had just read. In an instant his joy turned to fury. "So you have murdered your father-in-law! How could I have expected you to commit such a crime? You have disgraced your family and shamed the good virtues of your ancestors. Now confess to what you did. If you try to conceal anything, I will have you escorted to the temple of the town god and sentenced to be a starving ghost with no chance of rebirth!"

Dou E, cowering under her father's outburst, waited for him to vent his anger, then began to describe in detail how she had been wronged, and how her three wishes had come true. In the end she asked, her voice charged with emotion, "Father, don't you see I was wronged? I was taken to the execution ground just because I refused to marry a scoundrel! I was put to death just because I refused to disgrace my ancestors! Will such an injustice never be redressed? Father, now you have the power over people's life and death. Please find out the truth of this case and have Donkey cut to pieces to avenge your child!" Listening to his daughter's tearful tale, Dou Tianzhang was overcome with dismay and pity. After the spirit left, he sat up all night brooding over the matter.

The next morning Dou Tianzhang went to the main hall of the yamen to meet the officials of Chuzhou. "Why hasn't it rained for three years here in Chuzhou?" he asked the governor. "It has nothing to do with your humble servant," replied the governor. "There is nothing one can do about bad weather, and the people of Chuzhou simply have to accept it as bad luck." Dou Tianzhang raised his voice in anger. "Don't you try to fool me! A filial woman named Dou E was wrongly executed. At her death she invoked heaven to give Chuzhou no rain for three years so that not even a stalk of grass would grow. Do you deny this?" The governor replied, "The case was tried by my predecessor, Tao Wu. He left Chuzhou after receiving a promotion." Dou Tianzhang found it incredible that a fatuous official like Tao Wu should have been promoted. As the governor knew nothing about the case, Dou sent runners to seize Donkey and Doctor Lu and summon Cai. He decided to retry the case himself.

Donkey, having gone unpunished for the murder, went on staying in Cai's house and extorting food and clothing. The runners seized him and brought him to the yamen along with Cai. Dou Tianzhang had him taken to the main hall at once for interrogation. Instead of pleading guilty, Donkey insisted that Dou E had concocted the poison. "Cut it out, you rascal! Dou E was a young widow who never left her house. Where could she have gotten the poison?" Ignoring the question, Donkey answered back, "Your excellency, if I had added the poison, why should I have chosen to poison my own father instead of someone else?" Dou Tianzhang was quite upset, not knowing how to answer the question. At this moment Dou E's spirit emerged in front of Donkey, to his great terror. Pointing at him, Dou E gave a detailed account of what had happened on that particular day. Even then Donkey still pleaded not guilty, counting on Doctor Lu's absence to enable him to get away for lack of witnesses. Unluckily for him, Lu was found and brought to the yamen.

The moment he stepped into the hall, Doctor Lu realized it was no use pleading ignorance. To save himself from a beating, he confessed to everything, recounting how his attempt to murder Mistress Cai had been thwarted by the arrival of Donkey and his father, and how Donkey had come afterwards to get poison, and how he had fled to Zhuozhou. With all the evidence against him, Donkey was finally made to confess his crime and the case was thus cleared. Dou Tianzhang meted out punishment to all the offenders based on the gravity of their offences. Donkey was sentenced to death by torture, to be cut into pieces in public. Lu was sent into exile. Tao Wu, the former governor, was seized and given a hundred strokes of the birch and barred from any official post for the rest of his life. Dou E's spirit emerged for the last time to bid her father farewell. "Father," she sobbed, "the injustice I suffered is redressed at last. But injustices like mine have been far from rare since ancient times. Please eliminate corrupt and evil officials to protect the common people!" Choked with emotion, Dou Tianzhang could not say a single word. Dou E's spirit turned to leave, then paused. "Father, I almost forgot. My mother-in-law is old and has no one to attend to her. Please take pity on her and take her home. Then my mind will be at ease." Dou Tianzhang nodded repeatedly, and Dou E's spirit left the yamen. So this is the story of Dou E, who suffered such a gross injustice and brought down snow in midsummer as heaven and earth mourned for her tragic end.

THE RESCUE OF A COURTESAN

Guan Hanqing

In the suburbs of Luoyang lived a scholar, An Xiushi, who studied ancient books assiduously from childhood and became quite versed in Confucian classics. Due to bad fortune he did not get above the county level in the imperial examination, meaning he could not obtain an official post. Of a sanguine disposition, he was content enough to enjoy his leisure.

One year he came to Bianliang, a prosperous city famous for, among other things, its many brothels. The young scholar became a frequent visitor to these places.

Among the many courtesans of Bianliang there was a young girl named Song Yinzhang who came from a respectable family. Her father died early without leaving any money. To save her mother and herself from starvation, she was forced to take up the oldest profession in the world.

Apart from her youth and beauty, Song was well-cultured, and if somewhat naive about worldly affairs, that only added to her charm. An Xiushi took to her the first time they met, and began to devote all his attention to her. When he mentioned his wish to marry her, Song intimated that she was willing.

A few months later, An Xiushi found himself short of money. All courtesans judged their patrons in terms of money, and Song Yinzhang was no exception. As An's presents became less and less frequent, her passion for him waned considerably.

At this juncture Zhou She, the son of a vice-prefect of

Zhengzhou, also arrived in Bianliang. In his hometown, Zhou was a well-known patron of the brothels. He even composed a verse to extoll his exploits with women:

For thirty years I've stuffed myself with fine food,
For twenty I've enjoyed the company of flower-like girls.
I never know the price of rice or firewood,
But I do worry for want of money for women and wine.

Presumably he had come to Bianliang on business, but all he did was hang around in the bawdy houses. He cut a very handsome figure in the eyes of naive young girls, and virtually twisted them around his fingers. Once a girl fell into his trap, he never failed to make her regret it by suddenly turning into a sadistic monster and mistreating her in myriad ways. It was not easy to tell how many hapless courtesans fell victim to his deceptive wiles.

Zhou She took a liking to Song Yinzhang, who appeared to possess a unique charm. By lavishing presents on her with the money he had brought for doing business, he impressed her quite favorably. His generosity brought An Xiushi's destitution into sharp relief, so Song began to give An Xiushi the cold shoulder. Deeply hurt, An hardly ever came to visit her anymore.

Seizing the chance, Zhou She continued to put himself in the good graces of Song Yinzhang and also tried to ingratiate himself with her mother. He went to visit her every day, the epitome of tenderness and solicitude, fanning her in summer and warming the quilt for her in winter. When Song went out to visit or received guests at home, Zhou made himself helpful by offering his opinion about which robe most suited the occasion, or what jewelry should be worn for the night. When Song finished her toilet, he made a point of looking at her from different angles, and would not let her leave without smoothing her collar or adjusting her hairpin. Sure enough, his pains were duly rewarded. Song became deeply attached to him.

Song's mother, however, was not so easily taken in. Despite Zhou's apparent openhandedness and humility, she sensed something unctuous in his manner and had doubts about his character. Not trusting him with her daughter's future, she found excuses to delay their marriage. But Song Yinzhang, who had no idea of what her mother really thought of Zhou She, kept urging her to consent to the match. "My child," her mother finally said, "I don't think Zhou She is an honest and kindhearted man. I am worried that you will plunge yourself into misery by marrying him!" Song Yinzhang was too enamored with Zhou to listen. "Mother, don't worry about this. Zhou She is very good to me, and I am determined to marry him." Unable to dissuade her, her mother gave her reluctant consent.

Just then Zhou She was heard calling Yinzhang's name outside the door. Song Yinzhang started as if hearing a clarion call and hastened out to greet him in her sugary voice. "Oh, Zhou She, my darling, you have finally come." Taking her by the arm, Zhou She asked, "How is your mother? Has she agreed? I have come specially to find out about this." Song Yinzhang told him the good news and led him to meet her mother.

Song's mother had to accept the situation. Acknowledging Zhou's salute, she said, "I have agreed to the match between you and Yinzhang, but there is one point I must make clear today. After she enters your house, you must not maltreat her!" Zhou She would agree to anything to get Yinzhang to marry him. Nodding his head, an obsequious smile on his face, he pledged, "Trust me, mother. I will never dare maltreat your daughter." He asked the mother and daughter to prepare a banquet for friends and relatives, while he went away to get his betrothal gifts.

It happened that An Xiushi, after many days' absence, came at last to call on Song Yinzhang, only to be informed of her upcoming marriage to Zhou She. For the first moment he was dazed. With neither a ready tongue nor a full purse, he knew he would be unable to persuade Yinzhang to part with that dandy. He decided to pay a visit to Zhao Pan'er, Song's sworn sister, and ask for her help.

Though herself a courtesan, Zhao Pan'er had a strong sense of justice and was always ready to help those in distress. A good judge of character, she often gave Song Yinzhang advice. Among Song's patrons she liked An the best and Zhou the least. As they happened to come from the same village, she felt a natural affinity for An and always had an affable chat with him when she met him at Song's place.

When An Xiushi found Zhao at home, he said anxiously, "Sister, I have come today to ask you a favor. Please go and speak to Yinzhang. Some time ago you advised her to marry me, but now she is planning to marry Zhou She. Why should such a thing happen? Please talk some sense into her and make her change her mind."

Zhao Pan'er hesitated, knowing Yinzhang would be unlikely to change her mind. "She can choose to marry whomever she likes," she said, "so what can we possibly do about it? What girl does not want to find a fine husband? What girl does not hesitate a great many times before making the final choice?"

The topic of marriage reminded Zhao Pan'er of her own grievances, about which she had no one to confide in. She told An that many young courtesans, eager to quit their profession, married in haste only to find themselves the victim of insult and torment a few days later. What could they do but blame themselves for the misfortune, and shed silent tears? "At the thought of such prospects, I tell myself I might as well spend my life all alone!"

An Xiushi asks Zhao Pan'er to stop Yinzhang
from marrying Zhou She.

An Xiushi, an honest and sincere man, was genuinely concerned and asked if she really had no plans to get married. "It's not that I don't want to marry," Zhao Pan'er said. "It's simply too hard to find the right man. Look, among the frequent visitors, very few are honest men like you, most of them are playboys with no sense of shame or morality. Should I marry such a man, even if I am faithful, he would still accuse me of dishonesty and inconstancy. Even if I abide by all the womanly virtues, he would still regard me as a former courtesan, a woman with a past. I knew someone who married into a family as a concubine and worked her fingers to the bone in the house, but in the end she was sent to the yamen on a trumped-up charge and suffered a dire fate. If Yinzhang marries Zhou She, I'm afraid she will fall into the same trap!"

Having vented her complaints, Zhao Pan'er began to consider the problem at hand. "Go back and wait for my message," she told An Xiushi. "I will go at once to persuade her. Don't be too happy if I succeed, and don't grieve too much if I fail." Delighted, An Xiushi thanked her repeatedly, then took his leave.

Zhao Pan'er changed her clothes, adjusted her hair adornments, and then headed for Song Yinzhang's house. On entering the room she found Yinzhang busy with her toilet in front of the mirror. "Sister," Zhao asked deliberately. "Who are you going to visit today dressed up as pretty as a flower?" "Sister, I am not visiting anyone!" Yingzhang replied merrily. "I am going to get married!"

"Really? That's fantastic! I've just come to propose a match!"

"Who are you talking about?" asked Song Yinzhang in surprise.

"A young scholar by the name of An Xiushi," replied Zhao Pan'er with a straight face.

"Sister, you can really tell a joke! If I should marry An,

the newlywedded couple would have to chant the beggar's rhyme and roam from door to door asking for leftovers!"

"Well then, who do you want to marry?"

"I am marrying Zhou She!" came the definite reply.

Zhao Pan'er tried a different tactic. "Isn't it a bit too early for you to get married?" To this Song replied that she had already become tired of her life as a courtesan and longed to put an end to it by getting married. After that, even if she should die young, at least she would become a decent ghost.

Judging by the determination and bitterness in Yingzhang's words, Zhao Pan'er knew she had to be more frank. "Younger sister, you are still at a tender age. If you don't consider An your ideal mate, wait till I find someone else for you. Please listen to my warning. Think about it carefully and don't rush into any decision." When Song showed no signs of relenting, Zhao Pan'er went on in a more agitated voice. "Listen, sister. A habitual brothel goer like him will never make a good husband. What sort of a man is he, really? He does nothing all day except fool around with women. Though he cuts a handsome figure when dressed in fine clothes, he has no sense at all of morality or reason."

Irritated, Song Yinzhang rejoined, "At least he knows enough to treat me with civility!"

Zhao Pan'er talked until her lips were dry and her mouth parched, but Song Yingzhang remained stubborn. Stamping her feet in frustration, Zhao said, "All right, sister, you can refuse to listen to me. When you find yourself in big trouble, don't come to me for help!" "Don't worry about that," Song countered. "I won't come to disturb you even if I find myself living in hell!"

Just as the two women were engaged in this bitter quarrel, Zhou She arrived at the house. He made a big show of ordering the servants to lay out the betrothal gifts he had brought. Disgusted with his airs, Zhao Pan'er was on the point of giving him a good dressing down when he approached her with a smile. "Isn't this my dear sister, Zhao Pan'er? Come and enjoy some food and wine! I am the host today!" Disgusted with his unctous manner, Zhao Pan'er remarked sarcastically, "You are the host? And you invite me to a banquet? You don't suppose I am on the brink of starvation, do you?"

Zhou She, barefaced as he was, ignored her caustic tone. "Sister, whether or not you choose to eat this meal, I need you to do something for me. I need you to vouch for my marriage!"

"Your marriage to whom?"

"With Song Yinzhang!"

"Really?" Zhao Pan'er took this chance to scold him. "What do you want me to vouch for? Shall I vouch for her make-up, or her embroidery, or her sewing, or her bearing sons and daughters for you?"

Rebuffed, Zhou She began to swear. "What a sharp tongue you have, you stinking bitch! The marriage has been settled, with or without you to vouch for it. I don't need to ask any favor from you!"

Ignoring this, Zhao Pan'er left to look for An Xiushi and tell him the news. Sorely disappointed, An wanted to leave Bianliang at once. Zhao Pan'er, however, advised him to stay at the inn, convinced they would not have to wait long for a change in the situation.

Zhou She then threw a banquet at Song's house to celebrate the wedding, and the following day the new couple left for Zhengzhou, she sitting in a hired sedan chair and he riding horseback.

As they approached Zhengzhou, Zhou She's spirits began to fall. "How people will laugh at me, the famed playboy, when they learn I have married a prostitute and brought her home!" he thought to himself. "How will I be able to keep my dignity among my buddies?" Thereupon he decided to keep his marriage a secret. The servants were ordered to carry the

Zhao Pan'er, unable to make Yinzhang change her mind,
gives Zhou She a good talking-to.

sedan chair into the house by the back door, while he galloped ahead and entered the house through the main entrance.

The moment she stepped into Zhou's house, Song Yinzhang was determined to mend her ways and be a good wife. What she did not expect was the metamorphosis occurring in Zhou She. No longer the tender lover she used to know, he now displayed his true colors and began showering her with both verbal and physical abuse. The day she entered the house, she was given fifty strokes of the stick "to reduce her airs." Song Yinzhang tried in vain to reason with him. Zhou intimated that once a woman fell into his hands, he would beat her to death rather than divorce her. After eating and drinking his fill each day, he never failed to beat her up for his amusement.

Song Yinzhang realized, if a bit too late, what a grave mistake she had made. If only she had listened to the good counsel of her friend! Zhou She was a barbarous womanizer; how could she go on living with him? Would she not die at his hands eventually? The only way to save her life, she concluded, was to get away. But where could she find help? Her mother, away in Bianliang, was too old and decrepit to be of much assistance. Her sworn sister, Zhao Pan'er, was warmhearted and always ready to lend a hand; besides, she was an astute, resourceful woman. But Song Yingzhang hesitated when she remembered the unpleasant conversation with her sworn sister at their last meeting. When several days passed and she could think of no alternative, she decided to swallow her pride and ask her sworn sister for help.

Zhou She's house was adjacent to a grocery store. The store keeper, Wang, often heard Song crying when she was beaten and therefore took pity on her. One day he was going to Bianliang to purchase some goods. After Zhou She left for the wineshop, Song Yinzhang wrote a short note and asked Wang to take it to her mother.

Song's mother burst into tears on reading the note, which described how Song had received fifty strokes of the stick the first day she entered Zhou's house, and how she had been beaten in the morning and abused at night. Song Yingzhang said she was dying of torture and humiliation, and begged her mother to hurry to her elder sister, Zhao Pan'er, and ask her to come to the rescue. Song's mother took the note and, leaning on her walking stick, set out straightaway for Zhao's house.

Ever since Song had left for Zhengzhou, her fate was on the mind of Zhao Pan'er. The thought of Song's marriage never failed to remind her of her own bitterness and grievances. When Song's mother came, she immediately sensed what had happened. On reading the note, she said, "Mother, remember what I told you? Zhou She must not be trusted and will never make a husband. But Yinzhang was taken in by his sweet words and fancied she had found her lifelong mate. Now look at what has happened! Scarcely a few days after the wedding, and she finds herself at his mercy! Don't say I didn't warn you!"

The old lady still tried to defend her daughter. "We cannot blame Yinzhang for all this," she sighed. "Zhou She promised under oath that he would always treat her kindly!"

Her eyes widening in disbelief, Zhao Pan'er said, "How can the two of you be so naive! What whoremaster would hesitate to swear an oath in the name of heaven and earth, vowing he will die a miserable death should he break his promise? Such an oath is just like a gust of autumn wind whistling across one's ears, to be forgotten the moment it is uttered. How can you take it as real?"

Song's mother was rendered speechless. Concerned for her daughter, she again appealed to Zhao Pan'er for help. "You were right about Zhou She, and Yinzhang has paid dearly for her mistake. But the two of you are sworn sisters, aren't you?

Are you going to stand by and watch her suffer? Please find a way to save her life!"

Zhao Pan'er, of course, would not refuse to save her sister from ruin, though she was still mad with her. Taking out two silver ingots, she handed them to the old lady. "This is my private money," she said. "You can go and bail Yinzhang out."

"That won't do! Yinzhang said in her letter that Zhou She would rather beat her to death than divorce her. We have to find another way to rescue her."

Zhao Pan'er felt at a loss. She picked up the note and read it over again. An image of Song Yinzhang, beaten black and blue, emerged before her eyes. "How can I sit here doing nothing while my sworn sister is in great danger?" she thought to herself. "Besides, if that scoundrel Zhou She gets away with all this, no one knows what he will do next to the likes of us!" She thought long and hard. As a courtesan, what could she possibly do to rescue Yinzhang?

An idea finally came to her. Since Zhou She was wont to frequent the brothels in search of his victims, she could make use of this and beat him at his own game. She went over to her dressing table and, looking in the mirror, found herself as lovely as ever. She adjusted her hairpins and earrings, put on a few pieces of fine clothing, and took a few steps about the room. She was still a voluptuous woman with an alluring walk.

Song's mother was disappointed to find Zhao Pan'er so absorbed in her toilet. "What can we do?" she whimpered.

With a smile, Zhao Pan'er whispered a few words in her ear. "Do you really think this will work?" asked the old woman doubtfully. Zhao Pan'er scribbled a note and had it given to Wang to take back to Song Yinzhang. Turning to the old woman, she said, "Take it easy! No need to knit your brows or shed tears. I promise to bring Yinzhang safely back."

Having sent Song's mother away, Zhao Pan'er packed up

two large cases of clothing and sent for Zhang Xiaoxian, a bellboy running errands for the brothels. With Zhang carrying the cases for her, she mounted a horse and set out for Zhengzhou.

Two days later they arrived in Zhengzhou. Walking down the main road bustling with traffic, they saw numerous shops with servants standing at the gate of every inn to solicit customers. Before entering the city, Zhao Pan'er put on a new dress and applied make-up to look her best. A sharp-eyed inn waiter caught sight of her, rushed over to stop her horse, and led her into the inn.

The proprietor of the inn was none other than Zhou She, who used it not so much to make money as to enable him to sight pretty women. All the waiters in the inn had instructions to report to him immediately whenever a nice-looking woman turned up.

It was hard to find another courtesan, even among the best brothels in Zhengzhou, to equal Zhao Pan'er with her ravishing looks and enchanting figure. Every man at the inn became instantly enthralled by her beauty. The waiter was about to rush away to inform Zhou She when Zhao Pan'er stopped him and told him to get Zhou She to meet her. "Yes," the waiter answered. "I'll tell him to come at once."

The waiter hunted among many brothels and gambling houses until he finally found Zhou She. An invitation from a gorgeous woman sounded too good to be true, and Zhou dashed to the inn as fast as his legs could carry him.

Entering the hall, he caught a glimpse of a young woman in one of the main rooms gazing out of the window. When he walked into the room, the woman turned and cried, "Oh, Zhou She, you are here at last! How smart for my sister to catch you, and how fortunate she must be to have such a handsome man as her husband! How come you are looking even younger than before?"

Only then did Zhou She recognize her. His first impulse was to snub her, but her sweet words left him much mollified, and he pretended not to know her. "Oh well, you look quite familiar to me. We must have met somewhere.... Oh yes, I remember now. Once I stayed at an inn and you played the zither for me. I made you the gift of a piece of silk, didn't I?"

Amused, Zhao Pan'er turned to Zhang Xiaoxian, the bellboy. "Xiaoxian, do you remember that?"

"No, I never saw him giving you any silk."

Zhou She was not the least perturbed. "Oh well, I have it wrong. Last time I gave a feast in a restaurant, you were among the guests, weren't you?"

"Xiaoxian, did you see me there?"

"No, I didn't."

Zhou She went on to invent another story, but Zhao Pan'er lost patience and cut him short. "Zhou She, how can you turn your back on an old friend when you find someone new! You and I are old acquaintances, and you pretend not to know me!"

Unable to play the buffoon anymore, Zhou She pulled a long face. "Yes," he said coldly, "now I remember. You are perhaps Zhao Pan'er?" "Yes, I am she." Zhou She's voice suddenly turned harsh. "So you are Zhao Pan'er! It is you who tried to destroy my marriage! Now that you have come into my inn, I will settle accounts with you!" He bade the waiter close the door, as now he was going to teach her a good lesson. When Zhang Xiaoxian went up to stop him, Zhou She slapped him harshly across the face, leaving five finger marks. "Hey you!" Xiaoxian cried out painfully. "How can you beat me like this when my sister has come all this way with her clothes and private savings to marry you?"

Zhou She was staggered. As he stepped back puzzling over the matter, Zhao Pan'er began to talk in a leisurely voice. "Sit down, Zhou She, and listen to me." With Zhou She back in his seat, she went on. "Why should you be so insensitive, Zhou She? When you came to Bianliang, everyone began to talk about you—how handsome you are, and what fine qualities you have for making a woman happy. My mind was full of your image and my heart filled with longing even before I set eyes on you. However, when I finally made your acquaintance, you seldom came to visit me, leaving me to pine away with a broken heart. You were totally unaware of my feelings. How could you ask me to vouch for you and Song Yinzhang when I wanted you for myself? How could I help getting angry with you?" Zhou She's heart began pounding wildly at these words, and he could hardly stay seated.

His change of attitude did not escape Zhao Pan'er. Taking a sip of the tea served by the waiter, she went on. "After you left, I missed you. I thought for a long time and finally decided to take everything I had and followed you here. Well, what have I got from you in return but abuse? Xiaoxian, saddle the horse. Let's go home," and she stood up to leave.

Zhou She, totally convinced by this time, hurriedly got up and blocked her way. "If I had known your intention to marry me, how could I have beaten your brother?" He apologied profusely to Xiaoxian.

"You really didn't know I want to marry you? Well, in that case, I should not blame you. But from now on, since I am to marry you, I want you to go nowhere, and stay here with me day after day."

This was a request Zhou She had no intention of rejecting. "Nothing could be easier! With you by my side, I can stay here year after year, not just day after day!" Disgusted with his buffoonery, Zhao Pan'er nevertheless had to befriend him with forced smiles.

Zhou She stayed at the inn for three days, during which time Zhao Pan'er kept him from stepping outside the gate.

At the end of three days, a racket was suddenly heard

outside. Brushing off the waiter who was trying to stop her, Song Yinzhang stormed into the room and found Zhou She and Zhao Pan'er chatting away by the bed. Song pointed her finger at Zhao Pan'er and began to curse and swear at her. "You old, shameless, stinking whore! No one would take you, so you have come here to steal my husband! Shame on you!" When Zhou She tried to drive her away, Song turned her invective toward him. "Zhou She, you don't need to come home! If you return, you'd better carry a knife with you, for I will wait for you with mine! If you can't kill me, I will kill you!"

Zhou She was furious that Song Yinzhang, who used to cower under his constant beatings, should suddenly grow so bold. He took a long, thick stick from under the bed and raised it to strike Song, but just then Zhao Pan'er caught him by the arm. "I have been trapped by the two of you!" she wailed. "You deceived me with your sweet words, then sent your wife to insult me!" By this time Song had stepped outside the door. Zhou She did not know whether to pursue Song with the stick or offer an explanation to Zhao. Blocking his path, Zhao said, "What do you want to do with such a thick stick? If you should beat her to death, who would I have to depend on?" "A man won't lose his life just for beating his wife to death!" "Is that what you said? You don't mind beating your wife to death? Who dares marry you then? Xiaoxian, saddle the horse and bring it here! Let's go home!"

Zhou She clasped his hands in front of his chest and made several bows. "My dear sweetheart, please listen to me. I really didn't know this slut was coming, I swear. If I had anything to do with this, I should die a cruel death!"

"You really didn't know about it? Well, that slut has no virtue to speak of, and her tongue is so vicious! If you really don't want her, divorce her and I will marry you at once!"

Zhou She hesitated. "It's easy enough to divorce Song," he

thought to himself. "But what if Zhao Pan'er breaks her promise to marry me afterwards? I would be left empty-handed!" He rolled his eyes and broke into an unctuous smile. "Good sister, don't blame me for being too cautious. Suppose, after I divorce Song Yinzhang, you close your eyes and pretend not to know me, and will not marry me, wouldn't I be in a pretty fix? Here, if you make an oath, I will go and divorce Song."

"All right! If that's what you are worried about, listen to this: Let me die a cruel death if I refuse to marry you after you have divorced Song Yinzhang!"

The oath convinced Zhou She that Zhao really wanted to marry him. "Strike while the iron's hot," he said to himself, and decided to celebrate the marriage that very night. He went out, called the waiter over, and started telling him to buy sheep, wine and red silk.

Taking him by the arm, Zhao Pan'er said sweetly, "Oh, why do you make a distinction between what's yours and what's mine? I have brought ten bottles of good wine, a sheep, and a pair of red silk gowns. When we become husband and wife, yours will be mine, and mine will be yours!" Zhou She danced with joy on hearing this. He sent away the waiter and returned to the room, taking Zhao in his arms.

Zhao Pan'er decided to prod him further to ensure the success of her scheme. Sitting in front of him, her hands on his shoulders, she said, "Zhou She, I will marry you with everything I have. Aren't you lucky to get a beautiful wife without spending a cent? We will live ever happy together. If you should become poor, I will stay with you. If you should get rich, please don't desert me." Zhou She was tickled pink to receive such compliments, as she went on. "Zhou She, you will find me a much better wife than Song Yinzhang. I am infinitely superior to that slut in just about everything, be it needlework or make-up, sewing or embroidering, cleaning or bleaching—you name it. Why not divorce her now so I can marry you at once?"

Cajoled by her honeyed words, Zhou She downed several cups of wine in high spirits and grew quite tipsy. He promised to divorce Song Yinzhang the minute he returned home.

On her return from the inn, Song Yinzhang had just enough time to pack up her valuables when Zhou She burst into the house, seething with wrath and smelling strongly of liquor. He scribbled a few lines on a piece of paper and handed it to Song. "This is a divorce letter for you. Now get out of my house as soon as possible!" "Oh, Zhou She, what have I done to deserve a divorce?" Song Yinzhang wailed and broke into tears.

"Why don't you move it? If you don't clear out at once, I'll break your legs!" "What? You heartless, treacherous phoney! You want me to leave, but I won't!" She acted as if she were determined to stay, so that Zhou She had to push and shove her out of the house.

Stepping through the gate, Song Yinzhang continued to mutter curses. When the gate was slammed shut, she glanced back to make sure that Zhou was not following her, then wiped off her tears and hastened to the inn to meet Zhao Pan'er.

Zhao Pan'er already had her luggage packed and sat up waiting with Zhang Xiaoxian. When the two sisters met, they first cuddled in tears, then burst out laughing together. Zhao Pan'er asked to have a look at the divorce letter, so Song handed it to her. While Song was chatting with Zhang Xiaoxian, Zhao Pan'er tucked away the letter and took another piece of paper, which she handed to Song, telling her to keep it in a safe place. The three of them dared not linger at the inn, so they checked out and left for Bianliang in great haste.

Zhou She ordered his servants to clean up the house in order to receive his new bride. Dressed resplendently, he went to the inn to fetch Zhao Pan'er, only to find to his dismay that the room was empty. When the waiter was sent for, he said, "A short moment after you left, the woman checked out, saying she was going to your house for the wedding, so I dared not stop her." With no time to spare for scolding the waiter, Zhou She leapt onto a horse and galloped down the main road leading to the city gate.

Whipping the horse furiously, Zhou caught up with Zhao Pan'er and Song Yinzhang a short distance outside the city. Reining in the horse, he called out, "Where are you going, you petty slut? Song Yinzhang, you are my wife. How dare you run away with someone else?"

"My good man, didn't you give me a divorce letter and send me away? I am no longer your wife, and you have no power over me!"

Zhou She realized to his consternation that a nasty trick had been played on him by the two women. A habitual trickster himself, it took just a blink of his eyes to come up with a solution. Moving close to Song Yinzhang, he said, "Did you read carefully? The letter I gave you is invalid. It only has four of my five finger marks. I meant it to be a joke, you know."

Stupefied, Song Yinzhang took out the letter without thought in order to take a close look, but at that moment Zhou She lunged from his horse, snatched it from her hand and put it into his mouth, biting it into shreds. "Well," he cackled, "where is the divorce letter? Aren't you still my wife?" Song Yinzhang was so distressed that she burst into tears. "What shall I do, sister?" she lamented to Zhao Pan'er. At this, Zhou She shifted his attention to Zhao. Cocking his head, he shouted, "You are also my wife!"

"You must be joking! How come I am your wife?"

"You drank my wine, ate my mutton, and received my red silk as a wedding gift. Of course you have become my wife!"

"What nonsense is this? The wine was mine, the mutton was mine, and the red silk was also mine. Which of these was paid for by you?"

Zhou She was struck speechless. Then, rolling his eyes, he thought of something else. "Sister, didn't you take an oath to marry me?"

"Ha! You are tickling me to death! No one but an idiot like you would believe the oath of a courtesan! You should have known better, you imbecile! Didn't you also take an oath to treat Yinzhang well?"

Zhou She found himself at his wits' end under the verbal thrusts of Zhao Pan'er, so he turned to Song Yinzhang to force her to return with him. Trembling in fear, Song tried to hide herself behind Zhao Pan'er. Zhou She moved close and stretched his arm to grab her. At this Zhao Pan'er remarked, "Sister, why are you so afraid of him? You may return with him if that's what you want, but you are surely not his wife anymore! What he chewed and swallowed just now was just a piece of paper—I have tucked away the divorce letter in a safe place. What is there for you to be afraid of?"

Zhou She was furious. He eyed Zhao Pan'er closely, and would have leaped over to seize the divorce letter if only he had known where she had put it. Seeing this, Zhao Pan'er broke into a smile. "For your information, I have hidden it well. You wouldn't be able to get it back even if you had the strength of nine oxen!"

Unwilling to admit defeat, Zhou She remembered that his father was the vice prefect of Zhengzhou. "No one can disobey the law laid down by the emperor," he muttered. "Let's go to the yamen to fight this out."

The three of them returned to the city. Arriving at the yamen, Zhou She was the first to cry "injustice!" Li Gongbi, the prefect, then had the trio brought into the main hall.

"Your excellency, please restore justice to me! Someone

abducted my wife!"

"Who abducted your wife?"

"My wife, named Song Yinzhang, was abducted by this woman by the name of Zhao Pan'er!"

Li Gongbi turned to Zhao Pan'er. "What do you have to say?"

Encouraged by the mildness of his voice, so unusual among officials, Zhao Pan'er stepped forward and knelt. "Your excellency, Song Yinzhang was already a married woman when this rascal, Zhou She, forced her to be his wife. How he makes my teeth gnash in hatred! Relying on the wealth and power of his family, he throws his weight around bullying innocent people. Furthermore, he gave Song Yinzhang a divorce letter today. How can he accuse me of abducting his wife?"

Before Li Gongbi could ask more questions, An Xiushi arrived in time to lodge a suit against Zhou She on a charge of abuducting Song Yinzhang, his lawful wife.

Li Gongbi accepted An's complaint and asked who was the witness for the marriage. It was Zhao Pan'er, replied An. "Were you the witness for the marriage?" Li turned to her and asked.

"Yes, your excellency! This young scholar, An Xiushi, has studied ancient classics since childhood and is very honest and upright in character. He has sent hairpins, earrings, and other betrothal gifts to Song, and Song's mother has formally married her daughter to him. They are husband and wife in the sight of the law. Zhou She not only threw morals to the winds by abducting another man's wife, but tried to bring a false charge against his victim. Your excellency, please uphold law and justice and let this couple be reunited today!"

Li Gongbi happened to be an upright official. Having interrogated all witnesses and examined the evidence, and not entirely ignorant of Zhou She's reputation, he made his verdict. Banging the desk with a wooden slab, he called out harshly, "Zhou She! How dare you force Song Yinzhang, who already has a husband, to be your wife? I would have you punished severely but for the sake of your father, who happens to be my colleague. As it is, you only get sixty strokes of the birch, and your exemption from labor conscription is henceforth revoked! From now on you have to behave yourself and put an end to your infamous conduct!"

Song Yinzhang was declared to be An Xiushi's lawful wife by the court, so the old lovers were finally reunited. Having rescued Song Yinzhang and taught Zhou She a good lesson, Zhao Pan'er left the yamen of Zhengzhou and returned to Bianliang in high spirits.

THE RIVERSIDE PAVILION

Guan Hanqing

Sister Bai took her vows in the Qing'an Convent as a small girl and for dozens of years did nothing but worship the Buddha and chant Buddhist scriptures, with crude tea to drink and coarse meals to eat everyday. By the time she was made abbess of the nunnery, she had become quite resigned to a dull monastic life.

Near the nunnery there lived the Li family. The head of the family, Li Xiyan, had died recently, leaving his young and beautiful wife, Tan Jier, alone in the house. To get over her sorrow, she came to the nunnery every day to have a chat with Abbess Bai. A kind-hearted woman, Abbess Bai treated her very well. However, as a beautiful young widow, Tan became the target of the dandies and hooligans of the area; they swarmed around her like flies to honey. Abbess Bai kept worrying that some indecent incident might eventually take place.

Abbess Bai had left home early and had no relatives except for a nephew named Bai Shizhong who had recently been appointed magistrate of Tanzhou. On his trip to Tanzhou to take office, he came to the convent especially to call on his aunt. Abbess Bai was delighted to find that, after many years, her nephew had grown into a handsome man and become an official, and she had all sorts of questions for him. When she inquired after his wife, he replied sadly that she had died several years before. After a moment of silence, an idea occurred to Abbess Bai. Tan Jier was a widow, and Bai

Shizhong a widower; she was young and beautiful, and he was handsome and talented. Wouldn't that be a nice match? The more she thought about it, the more she was convinced that it was a marvelous idea. "Nephew," she said, "stop grieving. The dead cannot come back to life, whereas the living have to live on. I know a woman named Tan Jier who has exceptional beauty and talent. I intend to be the matchmaker for the two of you. What do you say?" Bai Shizhong said he was willing, but doubted if it could be settled in such haste. Abbess Bai was confident, for she learned in her daily chats with Tan that she did not object to remarrying; the only problem was to find the right mate.

Just then Tan Jier came to the convent as usual. Abbess Bai told Bai Shizhong to hide behind the curtain and come out to meet Tan when he heard a cough. Then she invited Tan Jier to come in.

To Abbess Bai's surprise, Tan Jier announced her decision to become a nun. The night before, Tan had not had a wink of sleep. Having finished her three-year mourning period, she could hardly bear the loneliness anymore. If she wanted to marry again, where could she find another man to cherish her as much as her deceased husband? She would rather take the vows and find some peace and quiet in the convent. Abbess Bai was stupefied when Tan announced her decision to be a nun; but after hearing her out, she realized that Tan was simply not coping well as a single woman. "How can a person like you take the vows!" she said. "A nun has nothing but plain clothes to wear and vegetables to eat; was that what you were used to as the wife of an academician? And how would you put up with the loneliness when evening comes?" Tan Jier faltered, but put on a determined look. "I can bear all that, Abbess Bai! I am not afraid!" When the abbess went on to describe in detail the hardships of monastic life, Tan Jier lowered her head and fell silent.

Observing the look on Tan's face, Abbess Bai knew her words had struck home. "Young lady!" she said, "Why don't you find a suitable man to marry? Won't that be far better than being a nun?" "Where can I possibly find a man who will love me as much as my late husband?" questioned Tan Jier. At this, the abbess thought the time had come to play matchmaker, so she coughed repeatedly.

Hiding behind the cloth curtain, Bai Shizhong not only eavesdropped on the conversation between his aunt and Tan Jier, but also caught a few glimpses of Tan's beautiful features. Hearing the cough, he rushed out to greet her, bowing with clasped hands. Startled, Tan hastily returned his greetings, then turned to Abbess Bai. "Since you have a guest here, I am going home." "Don't go yet," said the abbess. "He is the suitable man for you to marry." Tan blushed profusely. "What are you talking about, Abbess? What makes a Buddha-chanting nun suddenly turn into a go-between?" Abbess Bai told Tan to drop her pretenses, and went over to shut the door. "Abbess!" cried Tan in shame and rage. "We've known each other for many years and enjoyed each other's company. How can you do this to me today? Hiding a man in your room —it's disgusting. From now on I will never set my foot in your room again!"

Though Tan worked up a rage and declared she was leaving, she did not take a single step toward the door. The observant Abbess Bai knew Tan was just trying to find a way out of the situation without appearing immodest, so she tried to appease her. "Don't be angry. In my opinion, you are as fair as he is talented. Why don't you become united as husband and wife right away?" When Tan Jier kept protesting, Sister Bai tried another tactic. Pulling a long face, she asked Bai Shizhong, "Hey, young man! Who invited you to come to this convent?" Taking the cue, Bai Shizhong replied, "This young lady here asked me to come and meet her." "What

Startled, Tan Jier returns his greeting and turns to leave.

nonsense!" Tan Jier exclaimed angrily. "So the two of you plotted together to trap me! I won't put up with this!"

Abbess Bai believed a little more threatening might do the trick, so she demanded, "Young madam, do you want to settle this in court or in private?" "What do you mean by this?" asked Tan in puzzlement. "Well," the abbess said, "if you want a settlement in court, I will go to the yamen and accuse you of having a secret meeting with a man in the convent instead of staying home like a decent woman. You will be interrogated and beaten up, all for nothing. But if you agree to a private settlement, things will be entirely different. You are a young woman as pretty as a picture, and he is a handsome young man with a bright future ahead of him. Everything will be fine if you allow me to arrange this perfect match for the two of you."

Tan Jier was torn by conflicting emotions. "He is a fine-looking man indeed," she thought to herself, "but how can one tell whether he has a kind heart?" She turned to Abbess Bai. "Abbess, if he promises to treat me with respect and concern, I will marry him and spend the rest of my life with him. However, if he just wants to seek pleasure for the moment, and plans to desert me afterwards, I won't have anything to do with him!"

Bai Shizhong was exhilarated. "I promise!" he cried out eagerly. "I swear!" Well pleased with his earnestness, Tan Jier turned to Abbess Bai. "Abbess, don't you describe the Qing'an Convent as a quiet place for worshipping Buddha? It turns out to be a fine place to find a mate! Don't you often express willingness to do good deeds? Well, you certainly can be of great help to love-sick maidens and lonely young men!" Abbess Bai, happy to have found a mate for her nephew, did not mind Tan's scoffing in the least.

Bai Shizhong and Tan Jier were thus happily married. As Bai had to hasten to Tanzhou to take office, and Tan was without a tie in the world, they bade Abbess Bai good-bye and set out for Tanzhou at once in a light boat.

This fine match aroused envy and jealousy among the local hooligans. One villainous man named Yang was especially outraged. An official from a powerful family, he styled himself Lord Yang and was the worst of the local bullies, robbing innocent people of their money and possessions and assaulting other men's wives. It would have been impossible for Tan Jier, a beautiful young widow, to escape his attention. In fact, he had been planning to take her as a concubine. News of her marriage to Bai Shizhong thus filled him with rage. As he still wanted to get Tan Jier for himself, he decided to get rid of Bai Shizhong first. Acting on his motto "No true man is without venom," he went to see the emperor to speak ill of Bai Shizhong, accusing him of indulging in wine and pleasure, raping women, neglecting his official duties, and provoking widespread complaints among the common people. Enraged, the emperor ordered Bai beheaded. "Your Majesty," Yang said, "Bai Shizhong is a very cunning man. Your humble subject volunteers to go to Tanzhou and bring back his head." The emperor agreed. Taking two servants, Li Qian and Zhao Shao, Yang set out for Tanzhou at once on board an official boat. On his way he could think of nothing but getting the job done quickly so he could have Tan Jier to himself.

After Bai Shizhong took office in Tanzhou, his mother stayed on in the imperial capital. As soon as she learned that the emperor had sent Yang to Tanzhou to execute Shizhong, she summoned her steward and bade him get to Tanzhou before Yang and warn her son to take precautions.

In the meantime, Bai Shizhong was immersed in conjugal bliss. With a gentle and virtuous wife at home, he was able to devote much of his attention to official duties, thus gaining widespread support among the local people of Tanzhou. He was seated in the front hall of his house one morning when the steward arrived with his mother's letter. Upon reading it, he was filled with anxiety. How would he cope with Yang armed with an imperial edict? Preoccupied with this problem, he did not go to the rear hall to chat with his wife.

In that rear hall, Tan Jier grew impatient waiting for her husband, so she walked over to look for him. She found him pacing up and down the room, wearing a worried look on his face and holding a piece of paper in his hand. She suddenly suspected that he had another wife in his hometown who had sent him a letter to vent her anger. "Why are you here?" asked Bai Shizhong at the sight of her. "Why haven't you come to me?" asked Tan Jier. "Have you gotten a letter from your former wife?" "What? I don't have a former wife! Well, these are just a couple of official documents that need to be handled!" Unconvinced, Tan Jier went on to cross-examine him until he finally came out with the true story. "Believe me, a former wife really doesn't exist! That infamous knave, Yang, wants to seize you. He slandered me in front of the emperor, who sent him to Tanzhou with an imperial sword and a gold tablet to behead me. My dear wife, I just learned the news from this letter written by my mother and brought to me by our family's old steward. The worry is killing me!"

Instead of being scared, Tan Jier felt a great sense of relief. She was content as long as Bai Shizhong was true to her. As for a knave like Yang, she was confident that she could deal with him. "Why should you be afraid of him!" she said. "I would like to have a test of strength with that rogue. In the end he will surely return home empty-handed, like the proverbial fool who tries to fetch water with a bamboo basket!" Her voice lowered to a whisper as she described what she was going to do. Though a bit apprehensive, Bai Shizhong admitted the plan was ingenious. While she went out to execute her scheme he stayed home to await good news.

Accompanied by Li Qian and Zhang Shao, the two trusted

servants, Yang headed for Tanzhou by boat. Li Qian and Zhang Shao, both drunkards and sycophants, tried their best to make sure their master enjoyed the trip.

After a few days, the boat was sailing in the middle of the river at dusk when a full moon rose to shed its light on the water's surface. It suddenly occurred to Zhang Shao and Li Qian that it was the Midautumn Festival. So they moored the boat by a riverside pavilion and went to buy some wine and fruit. "Your excellency," they said to Yang with a bow, "it is the Midautumn Festival today. We have prepared some food so you can drink the wine while watching the moon." Going without wine for some days, Yang was only too glad to down a few cups, but he feared that the servants would get drunk and neglect their duties. So he pulled a long face and tried to look indigant. "You two scoundrels, what nonsense are you talking? I am here on important official business, to carry out an imperial edict! What do you mean by asking me to drink wine?" Fully aware that Yang was only putting up a show, Li Qian and Zhang Shao responded, "Your excellency, we mean well, really! We are only trying to show our filial respect to you. You may drink to your heart's content, but we will definitely not ruin your business by drinking too much." At this, Yang agreed with seeming reluctance, so the three of them sat down to enjoy their small feast.

Just as their faces became flushed with wine, a small boat sailing down the river approached the pavilion. It had a young woman on board, a net full of fish laying at her feet. Anchoring the boat, the woman stepped ashore and called out, "Fresh fish for sale! Fresh fish just out of the river!"

When Li Qian stuck out his neck to look, he was greeted by a very sweet voice. "Greetings, brother!" Tickled by the seductive tone, Li Qian broke into a cheeky grin. "Oh! Don't I know you? Are you not Mrs Zhang?" "Oh yes," replied the young woman. "Of course I am Mrs Zhang! Can't you recognize me?" Thus encouraged, Li Qian began to smile and grimace and assail her with obscenities. "How sweet you are!" said the fisherwoman. "Now go and tell your master that I'm going to cook this fish for him. If I can make some money this way, I will be nice to you."

Li Qian hastily passed on the message to Yang, who was delighted to hear that a beautiful young fisherwoman offered to cook him a fish. When the woman was brought into the boat, Yang looked her up and down admiringly. "Why have you come here, little woman?" he asked. "Your excellency, I have just caught a golden carp and would like to offer it to you." Greatly pleased, Yang said, "That is very nice of you indeed! I will take the fish then. Li Qian, take the fish away and fry it. Add plenty of ginger and pepper! Little woman, sit down and drink some wine with me!"

When Zhang Shao placed some more fruit and other dishes on the table, Yang had him pour a cup of wine for the fisherwoman. She declined, saying she could not drink. However, she proposed toasts to them repeatedly, paying compliments and chatting away merrily.

After a while, the three men were all a bit drunk. "Your excellency," asked the fisherwoman, "What has brought you to the pavilion this evening?" A very wily man, Yang remained alert although his head was swimming. He replied that he was heading for Tanzhou on official business, but would not say anything further. At this, Li Qian found a chance to show off his knowledge. "To tell you the truth, Mrs Zhang, we have accompanied his excellency to Tanzhou to execute Bai Shizhong!" This enraged Yang, who told Li Qian sharply to hold his tongue. The fisherwoman sighed deeply. "Oh, your excellency! If you have really come to seize Bai Shizhong, the people here will be rid of a scourge!" Much relieved, Yang nevertheless did not pursue topic, but only urged her to drink some wine. But the fisherwoman kept prying. "Your excellency, since you have come on official business, why is there nobody from Tanzhou to receive you?" "Little woman, of course you wouldn't understand. I did not tell the local officials because I don't want the news to leak out."

As Yang and the fisherwoman were thus chatting away, Li Qian and Zhang Shao helped themselves generously to the wine, downing one cup after another. Infatuated with the woman, Yang called Li Qian over and whispered, "Li Qian, why don't you be a matchmaker for me? Tell Mrs Zhang I already have a wife at home, so I'll make her my second wife. She will be given everything my first wife has—shawls, robes and embroidered handkerchiefs." Li Qian was eager to comply, knowing he would be duly rewarded for his trouble. "Leave it to me, your excellency." Turning to the fisherwoman, he said, "Mrs Zhang, you are blessed with good fortune! His excellency has taken a fancy to you! Though you cannot be his first wife, he will make you his second!" The fisherwoman looked flattered. "Your excellency," she went over to ask Yang, "Was Li Qian telling the truth? Do you really mean that?" "Yes!" Yang responded hastily. "I mean every word of it!" "Who am I, a humble fisherwoman, to deserve the attention of your excellency!" Yang's face lit up with pleasure and he grinned from ear to ear.

When Yang bade the fisherwoman sit next to him, she declined, saying, "How can a humble woman like me sit by your side? Your excellency, promise to eliminate that wicked official to save the common people, and ... and be faithful to me till we are both old and grey!" As she said this, she flashed a dazzling smile at Yang. Yang was dizzy with delight, while Li Qian and Zhang Shao joined in the merry-making, doing everything they could to please their master. Suddenly the fisherwoman's face turned serious. "Your excellency, don't forget your promise to get me everything your first wife has —like pearl-decorated hats, rosy silk scarves, and pretty three-

85

brim umbrellas!" Yang swore he would gratify all her wishes. "Of course I will honor my promise! Little woman, while we drink the wine, let's compose some couplets together." Then he read out the first half of a couplet: "Her silk sleeve knocks over the parrot cup." Immediately the fisherwoman came out with a second half: "My jade hand tucks in the phoenix quilt." Yang banged the table with joy. "Wonderful! Wonderful! Little woman, you can read and write, can't you?" The fisherwoman replied that she was not entirely uneducated. Downing several cups in his excitement, Yang composed another line: "No chicken-head seed can stretch its neck." Again the fisherwoman came out with a matching line in a flash: "No dragon-eye fruit can turn its glance." As Yang exclaimed his admiration, Li Qian and Zhang Zhao, though they knew nothing about poetry, joined in by doing their share of shouting, toasting, and drinking.

"Your excelleny," the fisherwoman said in a sugary voice, "I've never met a man as talented as you. Would you please compose a poem for me to mark this happy occasion?" Delighted by the compliment, Yang readily agreed and had Li Qian bring paper, ink, and a writing brush. Racking his brains, he finally scribbled down a poem titled "Moonlight Over the West River." In a surge of pride he read it aloud:

> The moon shines through the autumn dew;
> A cool breeze sweeps over the river.
> I have a deep longing not to be disclosed
> For the lovely maiden standing by the flowers,
> Like an immortal sailing down the moon,
> Or a fairy descending from the clouds.
> In a hurry I dedicate this crude verse
> To her who knows my heart's desires.

The fisherwoman clapped her hands and smacked her lips in admiration. "Wonderful! What exceptional talent and learning you have! Let me make up a few lines in reciprocation!" She took hold of the brush and started writing. "Now listen to this poem of mine, 'Night-Sailing Boat,' dedicated especially to you!"

Couples of swallows and orioles, twittering amid flowers,
Are better off than lonesome phoenixes.
A fleeting moment of love,
Consummated in a flash of bliss,
Is predestined in past lives.
Heaven has promised me to you,
For a life full of harmony.
Over the cool river,
Under the full moon,
Together we ride in the night-sailing boat.

Yang was greatly pleased on hearing the poem, in which the fisherwoman seemed to express the wish to enjoy everlasting happiness with him. "Wonderful!" he exclaimed. "Excellent! Little woman, come over and have some wine!"

The fisherwoman still declined to drink, but kept offering wine to Yang. "Your excellency," she asked, "how will you be able to execute Bai Shizhong?" Though tipsy, Yang brushed the question aside and urged her to drink and enjoy herself. But Li Qian would not give up the chance to impress the woman. "Mrs Zhang, our master has the imperial sword bestowed by His Majesty!" Before Yang could stop him, he took out the sword and handed it to the fisherwoman. "Is this the imperial sword?" she asked in disbelief. "It doesn't look much different from my fishing knife. Your excellency, if you really enjoy my company, why don't you lend it to me for three days? I can use it to kill and slice fish for you. At least it looks much sharper than my fishing knife." Unwilling to be left in the cold, Zhang Shao took out the gold tablet and handed it to the fisherwoman. "Look, here is the gold tablet!"

The woman looked at it with interest. "Is this genuine gold? Your excellency, if you really enjoy my company, why don't you use it to make a few gold rings for me?" Not to be outdone, Li Qian took out the imperial document. "Here!" He handed it to the fisherwoman. "I have the imperial document!" But she did not look much impressed. "What imperial document? To me it looks like a business contract." At this time Yang was hunching over the table, too drunk to speak. While the two servants were falling over each other to curry favor with her, the fisherwoman tucked the document into her sleeve. Then she brushed them aside, went up to Yang, and poured another cup of wine for him. "Your excellency, drink one more cup!" Dead drunk, Yang could hardly speak. "Little woman," he mumbled, "I've had enough wine. Now you sing us a tune...." No sooner had he said these words than he fell with a thud onto the deck.

Li Qian and Zhang Shao were already giddy with drink. The moment Yang fell asleep, they also dropped to the ground. Soon the boat was filled with snoring.

When the fisherwoman went up to shove and kick at each of them, they neither opened their eyes nor made the slightest response. The fisherwoman was none other than Tan Jier in disguise. Making sure the document was secure in her sleeve, she picked up the pieces of paper with the poems on them and slipped them into Yang's sleeve. With the imperial sword in one hand and the gold tablet in the other, she leaped into her boat and left the pavilion, heading for Tanzhou. The moon was shining brightly over the river. Tan Jier felt fearful when she realized the danger she had put herself in just then, but she was thrilled at the thought that Yang would no longer be able to harm her or her husband.

It was almost dawn when Yang finally woke up. His eyes still closed, he murmured in a wheedling tone, "Little woman, little woman, come here!" When no one answered him, he

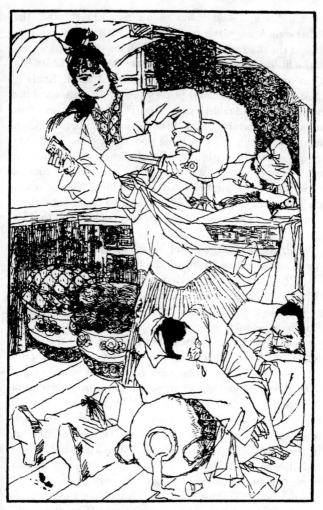

With the three men dead drunk, Tan Jier makes away
with the imperial sword and gold placard.

opened his eyes and found to his astonishment that the fisherwoman was nowhere in the boat. Alarmed, he began to kick at the two servants furiously. "You idiots! Get up! Where is the little woman? And where are my sword and tablet?" Li Qian and Zhang Shao were quickly jostled sober. Rubbing their eyes, they scrambled to their feet and began searching for the sword and tablet, but in vain. The three of them began cursing and swearing, and blaming one another. Li Qian suddenly thought of something and slipped his hand into Yang's sleeve. "Everything is all right!" he cried, taking out two pieces of paper. "We still have the imperial document here! With this alone we can kill Bai Shizhong!" Nevertheless, the loss of the imperial sword and the gold tablet made them quite upset. There was nothing else they could do, so they set out for Tanzhou at once.

Arriving in Tanzhou, they headed straight for the magistrate's yamen. They burst into the hall to find Bai Shizhong sitting behind his desk. "Hey!" Yang called out. "Bai Shizhong! What an impudent man! Li Qian and Zhang Shao, seize this rogue of an official!" Before Li and Zhang could take a step, Bai Shizhong stood up calmly and demanded harshly, "Who are you? Who gives you the right to arrest me?" Yang smiled coldly. "You don't know who I am? I am none other than Lord Yang—everybody knows me, and everybody is scared of me! Who gives me the right to arrest you? I am in possession of an imperial edict! Now listen to this!" He took out a piece of paper from his sleeve and began to read aloud. "Moonlight over the West River—Oh no, this is the wrong one!" Before he could tuck it away, Bai Shizhong snatched it from his hand and glanced at it. "Do you call this an imperial edict? It looks to me like an obscene verse!" "Don't be too sure of yourself," sneered Yang. "Now listen to this!" He took out another piece of paper and read, "The Night-Sailing Boat—What the devil!" Bai Shizhong again snatched the paper and looked at it. "I begin to know you, Lord Yang!" he said in a harsh voice. "Another obscene verse! Are you aware of the heinous crime you have committed by trying to pass off such vulgarities for an imperial edict?"

With the imperial document missing, Yang became quite crestfallen. However, he did not lose his presence of mind, thinking he had no reason to be afraid of Bai Shizhong, who could not produce any formal charge against him. This thought was interrupted by a woman's voice crying out, "Your excellency! Take pity on a poor woman! Your excellency! Uphold justice for a poor woman! I was fishing on the river when a certain Lord Yang accosted me and insulted me in all manners. Please avenge the injustice I suffered!" Startled, Yang looked up and saw Mrs Zhang kneeling in the hall.

"I can't believe such a thing could have happened in Tanzhou!" Bai Shizhong remarked. "Tell me the details!" The woman said she was married and made her living by fishing in the river. The evening before, she ran into a man who styled himself Lord Yang. He tricked her into his boat by offering to buy her fish, then started to make advances at her, even forcing her to agree to be his concubine. "Your excellency!" the woman cried piteously. "You must help a poor woman by punishing that villain!" The woman's tearful complaint sent Bai Shizhong into a rage. He told the woman to go back and prepare a written complaint, then he turned to Yang, a cold smile on his face. "I really know you now, Lord Yang! You face a serious charge here! It seems you are capable of all sorts of monstrosities! How shall I deal with you?"

Even as the woman was speaking, Yang made up his mind to make a deal with Bai Shizhong. When Bai thus berated him, he replied cheekily, "Good sir, I will overlook your trespasses if you don't press charges against me. Is this a deal?" Bai Shizhong considered. For lack of evidence, he could not bring formal charges against Yang; what's more, the accuser

91

was actually his own wife. Since he did not have the power to bring Yang into total submission, it was expedient to let him off. "All right," he said finally, "it's a deal. I will not arrest you this time, if you promise not to play any tricks against me in the future!"

With the case thus concluded, Yang still felt reluctant to leave without a glimpse of Tan Jier. Since he was in Tanzhou already, he had to take a look at her if only to feast his eyes. Putting on a brassy smile, he said to Bai Shizhong, "Your excellency, from what I heard, you have married a ravishing beauty. Could you ask her to come out and meet me?" Bai Shizhong felt a surge of anger, then he thought to himself, "It would teach Yang a lesson to let him know how my wife has outsmarted him, so he will give up his improper craving once and for all." So he said to Yang, "All right, if you really want to meet my wife, I will ask her to come out."

Tan Jier, back in her usual dress, walked into the hall with deliberate steps. "Lord Yang," she said with a sarcastic smile. "Forgive me for not coming out to greet you earlier." Yang looked up and stared at her in bewilderment. "You look so familiar to me! Where possibly could we have met before?" Li Qian walked up and whispered into his ear, "She is the fisherwoman, Mrs Zhang!" "What!" Yang jumped, incredulous. "You are the fisherwoman? That fisherwoman was you in disguise? Oh, fair lady, you do have powerful means at hand! Imagine to have me fooled and twisted around you little finger! What a formidable lady!" Showing no sign of excitement, Tan Jier said, "Thank you for everything, Lord Yang. If not for your kind attention to me last night, my husband would have been taken away and beheaded, and I would have been seized by you. To you we owe the safety of our family, don't we?" Listening to her ridicule, Yang was too stupefied to utter a single word.

The story spread very quickly. The imperial court dispatched a minister named Li Binzhong to Tanzhou to look into the case. An honest and impartial official, Li conducted a thorough investigation and returned with an accurate report. The emperor, though reluctant, deprived Yang of his post and sent him home. Thus Tan Jier and Bai Shizhong were able to enjoy their conjugal bliss into a ripe old age.

ROMANCE OF THE WEST CHAMBER

*Wang Shifu**

During the Tang Dynasty there lived in the city of Luoyang a young scholar whose family name was Zhang, given name Gong, and styled name Junrui. His father, who had served in the imperial court as Minister of Rites, died at fifty. The following year his mother passed away. With no official post, no family and no relatives, Zhang Gong left home and traveled around. One year the imperial court announced its decision to hold a metropolitan examination in the capital and invited scholars from all across the empire to participate. Zhang Gong decided to go. On his way to Chang'an, the imperial capital, he would pass the Hezhong Prefecture where he planned to visit his sworn brother, Du Que, stationed at Puguan Pass. He and Du Que had been born in the same village and gone to the same school. Laying down the pen for the sword, Du Que took the military recruitment examination, came out first, and was appointed Admiral for Pacifying the West in command of a hundred thousand troops garrisoned at Puguan.

After a day's travel, Zhang Gong reached Hezhong at dusk and stayed the night at a local inn.

Hezhong was strategically located at the Yellow River

---

* We know very little about the life of Wang Shifu, a contemporary of Guan Hanqing. Of the fourteen plays he composed, three are extant. *Romance in the West Chamber* has been called the "best play ever written under heaven."

bend. Zhang thought he might as well take the chance to see the sights, so he asked the waiter if there were any famous mountains or well-known temples worth visiting. The waiter replied that nearby was the Monastery of Universal Salvation. Built in honor of the late Empress Wu Zetian, the monastery boasted high pagodas and spacious halls. No traveler to Hezhong, regardless of his religious belief or academic doctrine, failed to visit this monastery.

The following day Zhang Gong went to the monastery. Arriving at the gate, he was greeted by a young monk responsible for receiving guests. Zhang bowed with clasped hands. "I am a young scholar from Luoyang. Someone told me your honorable temple is very quiet and serene, so I have come to worship the Buddha and pay my respects to the abbot. Is he in?" The young monk, finding Zhang a scholar, was very courteous in his reply. "My master is not in. My name is Fa Chong. Please come to my master's room for a cup of tea." Saying he could do without the tea, Zhang asked the monk to take the keys and unlock the Buddha's hall, the bell tower, the pagoda court, the hall of the arhats, and the kitchen. He wanted to climb the pagoda, count the arhats, pray to the Buddha, and take a look around and enjoy himself.

After a visit to the Buddha's hall, he was about to step out when he caught sight of two girls who seemed to be a young mistress and her maid. The breathtaking beauty of the young lady left him transfixed on the spot as he stood admiring her delicate and graceful demeanor. Her waist was slender and soft like willow twigs, and her voice sweet and melodious like the singing of an oriole. The maid saw the avid look on his face and urged the young lady to move on, but the beauty did not appear offended. Before stepping out of the hall she even turned and threw a glance at him.

It took a long while after the two girls departed for Zhang Gong to regain his senses. "Monk," he said to Fa Chong, "did you see the Goddess of Mercy showing her presence just now?"

"Watch your tongue," admonished the monk. "That young mistress is from the late Chief Minister Cui's family! You'd better keep yourself out of trouble!"

Zhang Gong urged the monk to tell him why the chief minister's daughter might have come to the monastery. With some reluctance Fa Chong came out with the story. The monastery was first built by Empress Wu Zetian but it later collapsed. The renovation was sponsored by Cui Jue, the late Chief Minister. Even the abbot, Fa Ben, received his tonsure from Chief Minister Cui. When Cui died of illness his wife, Lady Zheng, was left with their daughter, Yingying, and their son, Huanlang. While Huanlang was still a small boy, Yingying was already nineteen. Accompanied by their family maid Hong Niang, Lady Zheng was carrying her husband's remains back to his hometown of Boling for burial when their path was blocked and they were compelled to stay at the monastery. Lady Zheng had already written asking the help of Zheng Heng, the son of a court minister to whom Yingying was engaged. They had stayed in the west chamber of the monastery for many days. For fear that Yingying would grow languid in the secluded quarters of the monastery, Hong Niang was told to take the young mistress out for a walk whenever there were no visitors in the monastery.

.   Zhang Gong forgot all about going to the capital for the imperial examination. "Please tell the abbot," he said to Fa Chong, "that I would like to have a room here where I can study the classics. I will pay the rent without fail. Tomorrow, I'll move in."

The next morning, Zhang Gong washed his face, combed his hair, and put on his best clothes. Checking out of the inn, he went to the monastery. This time the abbot, Fa Ben, was there to receive him. After an exchange of greetings, Zhang offered a tael of silver to the abbot, saying the inn was too noisy a place for studying the classics, and that he would like to have a room near the west chamber where he could read his books in quiet and enter and leave the monastery unobtrusively. Taking the silver, Fa Ben agreed readily.

They were thus chatting when Hong Niang was sent over by Lady Zheng to ask the abbot when he planned to hold the Buddhist service for the late chief minister. Zhang Gong, stepping aside, kept peering at the pretty maid with her lovely face and graceful manners. Now and then she threw him a glance with her beautiful eyes, setting Zhang Gong's heart on fire. When Hong Niang said she was going to the Buddha's hall to see the preparations for the service, Zhang Gong hastily told the abbot that he would also like to go there. The abbot could not but agree.

Walking down the Buddha's hall, the abbot said to Hong Niang, "Everything is ready for the service. Lady Zheng and young mistress can come on the fifteenth of this month to burn incense." As soon as he heard this, Zhang Gong hit upon an idea. All of a sudden he burst out crying, much to the dismay of the abbot. After howling for a while, Zhang told the abbot that he had never burnt paper money for his parents after their demise, and he was put to shame by the filial piety displayed by the daughter of Minister Cui. He would be very grateful if the abbot, acting on the Buddhist principle of infinite compassion, allowed him to join in the service and offer five thousand coins as a belated sacrifice to his parents. His compassion inspired, the abbot agreed and bade Fa Chong prepare some more incense and candles for the day.

When the three returned to the abbot's room, Zhang Gong found an excuse to leave first, then stood waiting by the path leading to the west chamber. Hong Niang, eager to return and report to Lady Zheng, bade the abbot good-bye soon afterwards and headed for the west chamber. At the sight of her, Zhang Gong went up and bowed deeply. "Please accept my salute!" Hong Niang hastily returned his greetings.

"Are you the maid to Yingying, the young mistress of Minister Cui's family?"

"Yes, but I don't consider myself worthy of your attention, sir."

"My family name is Zhang, my given name Gong, and my styled name Junrui. I am a native of Luoyang, twenty-three years old, and the seventeenth of the first lunar month is my birthday. I am yet unmarried...."

More amused than offended, Hong Niang snapped, "Who cares to know all this stuff?"

Unabashed, Zhang Gong asked, "Does the young lady come out often?"

"Watch your tongue, sir!" Hong Niang said severely. "Mrs. Cui maintains firm discipline over the house; no outsider is allowed to transgress. Since you appear to be a scholar, sir, don't you know what questions are appropriate and what are not? Don't take liberties like this anymore!" She turned and went away without waiting for a reply.

The maid's response threw a wet blanket over Zhang Gong who stood there torn with conflicting thoughts. He was convinced that Yingying was the ideal mate for him, and lamented that she should have a harsh and unreasonable lady for a mother. Then he muttered to himself that Yingying was to blame for driving him almost crazy with the glance she gave him before she left. It was in great agitation that he returned to his room.

Hong Niang went to see Mrs. Cui and told her that Fa Ben, the abbot, had gotten everything ready for the Buddhist service on the fifteenth. Then, tucking at Yingying by the sleeve, she returned with the young lady to her room. "You won't be able to guess what a funny thing happened to me!" She began to giggle. Yingying asked the maid what was so funny. Hong Niang replied that on her way back she was accosted by the young scholar they had run into in the Buddha's hall the day before. "As soon as he saw me, he said, 'My family name is Zhang, my given name Gong, and my styled name Junrui. I am a native of Luoyang, twenty-three years old, and the seventeenth of the first month is my birthday. I am yet unmarried.' Then he went on to ask if you often come out, and of course I gave him a severe thrashing." Hong Niang threw the young lady a quizzical look. "What was on his mind, I wonder? What a thickheaded fellow he is!" Yingying found it easy to surmise what was on the young man's mind. She told Hong Niang not to talk about the incident anymore lest her mother would hear of it. Then, with Hong Niang carrying some candles and joss sticks, they went to the garden to burn incense, as they did every night at the monastery.

Having wrung the information from Fa Chong, Zhang Gong slipped into the garden before moonrise and hid himself behind a rock, ready to feast his eyes on the beautiful maiden when she came out.

Late in the night the garden was a mixture of silvery moonlight and dusky bushes. A side door leading to the west chamber suddenly creaked open, and a puff of fragrance was carried over by a gentle breeze. Yingying entered with light steps accompanied by her maid, Hong Niang.

In the Buddha's hall Zhang Gong had been able to steal a quick glance at the young maiden, but now he could finally gaze at her to his heart's content. With an air of innocence around her, she appeared to him like an immortal girl just descended from the moon. She lit some joss-sticks and began to pray lightly. "The first stick is devoted to my father; I wish him a quick ascension to heaven and enternal bliss. The second is devoted to my mother; I wish her health and longevity. The third one is devoted to ... to ..." she faltered, pausing for a long while. Suddenly Hong Niang was heard to

Yingying whispers her wishes before the incense burner.

remark, "Sister, let me say the wish on your behalf: May you find an ideal husband as soon as possible!" Yingying did not comment, but merely made a few light sighs. Listening with rapt attention, Zhang Gong thought to himself, "The young lady is certainly equal to Zhuo Wenjun in beauty, and she seems to be longing for a talented young scholar like Sima Xiangru. Though lacking in talent, why don't I compose a poem to test the water?" He had the words in an instant and began to intone the following:

On a moonlit night in spring,
Flowers bloom unnoticed in the dark.
Looking up into the bright moon,
Why do I find the fairy girl missing?

Yingying started and turned to Hong Niang. "Did you hear that? There's someone at the corner chanting a poem!" Hong Niang said she had heard it clearly. "It's the voice of that thickheaded fellow who is yet unmarried at twenty-three," she added. Ignoring the remark, Yingying began to intone a poem by way of response:

The perfumed chamber is a forlorn place
To spend long days of the fragrant spring.
The poet's compassion must be aroused,
When my deep sighs reach his ears.

"What a quick-witted young lady!" Zhang Gong exclaimed admiringly, realizing that Yingying was well endowed not only with looks but with brains as well. Since the message of her poem was rather straightforward, he decided to take a chance by walking up to her then and there and finding out how she would treat him. Straightening his robe, he left the rock and headed for the table bearing the incense burner.

Hearing his footsteps, Yingying turned to look. Hong Niang, who had been instructed by Mrs. Cui to keep her

101

young mistress away from strangers, whispered to Yingying, "Sister, let's go back! Otherwise your mother will be displeased!"

Though reluctant, Yingying meekly complied. Zhang Gong's smile froze and his jaws dropped in dismay as he found himself alone in the garden. Sinking into a gloomy mood, he muttered to himself, "Oh, young maiden! Why should you have walked away from me like this? What shall I do without you?" He returned crestfallen to his room, where nothing awaited him but an oil-lamp. The sound of the wind rustling the leaves added to his melancholy. Unable to put the young lady out of his mind, he spent many a sleepless night in his room.

When the fifteenth day finally arrived, the abbot sent Fa Chong to invite Zhang Gong to enter the Buddha's hall and burn incense before the arrival of Mrs. Cui and Yingying. Zhang Gong was all prepared for this invitation. He followed Fa Chong into the Buddha's hall and, failing to see Yingying, kept asking about her. The abbot, however, urged him to burn his incense. Reluctantly he picked up three joss sticks and placed them before the Buddha, praying in a whisper, "I wish the living long, prosperous lives, and the dead a good time in heaven. Hopefully, Hong Niang will hold her lashing tongue, the mother will not stand in the way, and the dogs remain quiet. O Buddha! Please bless me with a tryst with the young maiden at the earliest opportunity!"

After saying his prayer, he lingered in the hall until Lady Zheng and Yingying arrived. At this, Fa Chong joked under his voice, "Look, your prayer is instantly answered by the gods!" Zhang Gong's face lit up with pleasure as all his sorrows instantly dispersed.

At the sight of a young man in the hall, Mrs. Cui frowned with disapproval. The abbot hastily explained, "Your Ladyship, I have a relative who is a very learned scholar. When he heard about the service today, he asked me to let him join in so he could pray for the Buddha's blessing for his parents, and I really did not have the heart to turn him down. Please do not be offended!"

Hearing this, Mrs. Cui said she did not mind. Since the young man was a relative of the abbot, she added, she would regard him as one of her family and would like to be introduced to him.

In the meantime the monks, whether old or young, were transfixed by the astonishing beauty of the young lady and the comeliness of her maid. Staring agape, a monk missed the inverted bell he was beating and landed the mallet on another monk's head. A monk going to light the joss stick ended up burning his hand. Suddenly all the oil-lamps went out in a gust of wind, but the monks were too preoccupied to notice it. "The lamps have blown out!" cried the abbot. Zhang Gong was glad to have a chance to attract the young lady's attention. "I'll go and light them!" he responded.

Taking it all in, Yingying whispered to Hong Niang, "That young scholar is so handsome, and very talented also, judging by the poem he composed that night. Look, how he bustles around trying to impress us!"

Zhang Gong kept stealing furtive glances at Yingying, and found to his delight that his attention did not go unnoticed. His spirits soared, and he brimmed with confidence and energy.

Late into the night, the abbot finally announced the service was concluded. Mrs. Cui returned to the west chamber, taking Yingying with her. Zhang Gong grumbled to himself about the brevity of the service, walked back to his room, and sank back into melancholy.

After the meeting, Yingying was gripped with longing. It was late spring. The sight of the rain washing pear blossoms to the ground added to her dejection, and she began to lose

103

weight as her spirits fell. Like Zhang Gong, she grew languid day by day, unable to sleep at night. She even began to grow tired of Hong Niang, who followed her like a chaperon wherever she went. Sensing the young lady's silent displeasure, Hong Niang found it necessary to explain that she was under strict orders from the mother to keep her from going astray.

The two young lovers were jostled out of their lassitude when a certain incident took place. During her stay at the monastery Yingying's beauty and talent began to be known, and finally attracted the attention of Sun Feihu, commander of the troops guarding Heqiao a short distance from the monastery. Though an officer of the imperial army, Sun was wont to harass the local people like a chief desperado. Leading five thousand troops under his command, he laid siege to the monastery, demanding that Yingying be handed over.

After hearing the report, the abbot hastened to inform Mrs. Cui, who became speechless with fright. The soldiers were heard shouting outside, "Listen, people of the temple! We will give you three days to hand over Yingying for marriage to our general. Otherwise we will burn the temple to the ground and kill everyone inside, monk or no monk!"

By this time Yingying and Hong Niang had come out at the news. Standing by Mrs. Cui, they waited anxiously for her to think of some solution. But the old lady just rubbed her hands helplessly. "Why should this happen to me, an old woman of sixty?" she wailed. "What can we do? What can we do?" Yingying realized to her dismay that she had no one to depend on for her safety: her mother was old, her brother was small, and Hong Niang was just a maid. There seemed no alternative but to sacrifice herself. She suggested to her mother that she would marry that rogue of a general to save the family and the lives of the monks in the temple. Mrs. Cui refused to consider it, saying such a marriage would be a gross disgrace to the family. Yingying thought for a moment, then said, "Mother, you have to let go of me one way or another. I have an idea. Why don't you promise my hand to whoever can relieve the monastery of the siege? That would be better for me than being carried away by the rebel general." Mrs. Cui reluctantly agreed to the plan. She asked Fa Ben, the abbot, to inform everyone in the monastery of the reward for repulsing the rebel troops. No sooner had Fa Ben finished his words than Zhang Gong clapped his hands and stepped forward. "I can send the rebels to their heels. Why doesn't anyone ask me?" The abbot turned to Mrs. Cui. "This is the young scholar who joined in the service the other day."

When Mrs. Cui asked how he proposed to drive away the rebels, Zhang Gong did not answer promptly. "Since whoever dispels the rebels will marry the young mistress, please let her return to her room, because I don't want my wife frightened. I promise to put an end to this siege." At this, the old lady told Hong Niang to escort Yingying back to her room. Taking Hong Niang by the arm, Yingying murmured, "Thank heaven for the young scholar's offer to help! I wish him success in dispelling the rebel troops." After the two young women had left, Zhang Gong asked the abbot to go out and deliver a message. "Tell them that Mrs. Cui is willing to give her daughter's hand to the general, but unfortunately the young lady is still mourning for her father. At the end of three days, when the mourning ceremony is completed, she will be able to put away her mourning dress and marry the general. If the general should be unwilling to wait and attempt to take her by force, the young lady would most probably die of fright, and the general would return empty-handed." The abbot went out and repeated the words to Sun Feihu, who agreed to wait for three days. Then Zhang Gong described what he planned to do. He told the abbot that he had a sworn brother, Du Que, who was the famed White-Horse General in command of a hundred thousand troops at Puguan Pass, a mere forty-five *li* from the monastery. If he sent a letter to Du Que, the general would surely come to his rescue. But who could be trusted with the letter? The abbot sighed with great relief. "If the White-Horse General can come," he said, " we don't have to be afraid of Sun Feihu! As for sending the letter, I recommend a disciple named Hui Ming. He never chants the scriptures or sits in meditation, but enjoys drinking wine and picking fights. However, he is always willing to lend a helping hand to those in distress. He will volunteer to deliver the letter if you know how to goad him."

Acting on the abbot's advice, Zhang Gong went out and shouted, "Someone is needed to take this letter to the White-Horse General to ask for help. Who can do it? Who dares do it?" Sure enough, Hui Ming volunteered to go. After downing an entire pot of wine, he tucked the letter away in his bosom, tightened his belt, and dashed out of the temple, a dagger in each hand. Taking the rebels by surprise, he broke out of the encirclement and headed for Puguan.

The White-Horse General, Du Que, learning of Zhang Gong's arrival in the Monastery of Universal Salvation, had sent someone to fetch him, but Zhang failed to come. When Hui Ming came with the letter, he hastily opened it. After greeting his sworn brother, Zhang Gong went on to describe how people in the monastery, himself included, were put in grave danger by Sun Feihu's rebel troops, and begged Du to come to the rescue. Du Que bade Hui Ming return to the monastery first, saying he would summon the troops and set out without delay.

Mrs. Cui and Fa Ben waited in the monastery anxiously. Finally, on the third day, a monk came in to report a commotion among enemy ranks. Then they heard loud battle-cries. "My brother must have come with his troops!" remarked Zhang Gong. Shortly afterwards Du Que walked into the room. "Where is my brother, Zhang Gong?" he called out. Zhang Gong went up to greet him. Mrs. Cui also exchanged greetings and expressed her gratitude.

Zhang Gong explained to Du Que that he had failed to call on him because of illness. He thanked Du profusely for coming to the rescue, as Mrs. Cui had to keep her promise and marry her daughter to him. Delighted at the news, Du Que offered his congratulations. Mrs. Cui, evading the topic, ordered the table laid out and invited the general to a feast. Having yet cleared up the battleground, Du Que declined. "The rebels have been repelled due to Zhang Gong's help," he said to Mrs. Cui. "I hope you will keep your promise to marry the fair maiden to the talented gentleman. I will come and offer my congratulations some other day." He saluted with joined hands and took his leave. Mrs Cai turned to Zhang Gong. "I dare not forget our indebtedness to you. You can move into our compound today. Tomorrow I will have some food and wine prepared and send Hong Niang over to invite you. There is something we must discuss, so please do come."

The following day Zhang Gong rose much earlier than usual and used up two pails of water to wash himself. He brushed his silk hat until it was spotlessly clean, then sat down to wait for Hong Niang. After what felt like a long time, there came a knock on the door. Rushing over to open it, he was so excited at the sight of Hong Niang that he blurted out "Yes, I will go at once" even before she had time to deliver the invitation. Walking about excitedly, he bombarded Hong Niang with questions, begging her to tell him if he looked neatly dressed, since he did not have a mirror in the room, then asking if Yingying would keep her word, if it would be all right for him to go without any betrothal gifts, and if other guests were invited. Hong Niang placed her hand over her mouth to smother a giggle. "What a nuisance you poor pedants are! How can the young mistress go back on her word? You are the only guest today. Doesn't your exploit in dispelling the rebels make the best gift for a wedding?"

These words sent Zhang Gong into raptures. He left eagerly with Hong Niang, convinced that he would soon be celebrating his wedding with Yingying.

At the banquet, Mrs. Cui offered Zhang Gong a toast to express her thanks. Then she told Hong Niang to invite Yingying to the table. Yingying arrived in high spirits, thinking the banquet in honor of Zhang Gong meant the end of her pining. "Yingying, come here!" ordered the august lady. "Salute your elder brother!" At the word "brother," Zhang Gong knew at once that something was terribly wrong. Yingying also realized to her dismay that her mother intended to break her promise. Their spirits sagging, the two lovers sat with lowered heads, unable to say a word. Ignoring all this, Mrs. Cui said, "Yingying, offer a toast to your elder brother!" Reluctantly Yingying took up the wine cup, but Zhang Gong changed countenance and declined, saying he had no capacity for liquor. At this, Yingying handed the cup back to Hong Niang. However, Mrs. Cui urged Yingying to offer her toast once more, but again Zhang Gong declined. They were both too downcast to drink wine or enjoy the food. Finally, Mrs. Cui bade Hong Niang take Yingying back to her room. On the way Yingying poured out her complaints against her mother's faithless conduct. The dispirited look on Zhang Gong's face filled Hong Niang with pity and distress.

After taking Yingying to her room, Hong Niang returned to serve at the table, and Zhang Gong stood up to face Mrs. Cui. "Forgive me for being a little drunk, but I have a question to ask. Previously, you promised to marry Yingying to whomever could save the monastery from the siege. I offered my humble services and fulfilled the task. When I received an invitation to come today, I expected it to be a wedding celebration. Instead, you want me and Yingying to treat each other like brother and sister. Why?" Groping for an excuse, Mrs. Cui said Yingying had been engaged to Zheng Heng, her nephew, and therefore could not marry him. She offered to reward him with a handsome sum of money to purchase gifts for his future bride. Zhang Gong was highly displeased. "Even if you regret your decision, there is no reason for you to suppose I did everything for money. Since there is no wedding for me here, I will take my leave today." Mrs. Cui, however, was a bit worried about the White-Horse General, who knew of the match and might come to offer his congratulations someday. How would she answer his query? After a moment's consideration, she asked Zhang Gong to stay so they could discuss the matter later.

As Zhang Gong was giddy from wine, Mrs Cui told Hong Niang to support him back to his room. Closing the door behind him, Zhang Gong dropped to his knees, giving Hong Niang quite a start. He told Hong Niang how he had longed for Yingying and expected to be united with her in marriage that very day; the blow was too much for him to take, so he did not want to go on living. As he spoke, he proceeded to untie his belt, as if he would hang himself with it, but Hong Niang made him stop. Dissatisfied with Mrs. Cui's breach of faith, Hong Niang finally decided to help the lovers. Zhang Gong was told to get his zither ready that night. When Yingying came out to the garden to burn incense, he would be alerted by a cough from Hong Niang. Then he should start playing the zither and see what happens next. With this, Hong Niang departed at once without waiting to hear Zhang Gong's profuse thanks, as Mrs. Cui was expecting her.

Zhang Gong took out his zither and wiped it until it was shining. Now he placed all his hope on the zither, with which he would convey his heartfelt longings and arouse his beloved.

At nightfall the clouds dispersed, the bright moon rising over the garden. As usual, Hong Niang laid out the incense burner on the table in the garden and urged Yingying to go. But after the unhappy events of the day, Yingying was in an apathetic mood. "What's the use of burning incense?" she grumbled. "What difference would it make?" Nevertheless, after some prodding she followed Hong Niang into the garden.

Upon entering the garden, Hong Niang coughed as if caught in a gust of wind. At this signal, Zhang Gong began to play his zither. Yingying was caught by the music at once. It reminded her of tingling bracelets, the ringing of bells hung along the eaves, a breeze rustling through a bamboo curtain, or the chiming of the giant bell in the Buddha's hall. Tracing the sound to Zhang Gong's room, she walked over and listened in rapt attention. The zither was pouring out all the player's emotions: first it was in a heroic vein, conjuring up the image of horsemen charging forth, clashing spears and swords; now it became mild and soft, like fallen flowers dirfting away on the surface of a stream; now it was cool and clear, reminding one of a moonlit night, or an autumn breeze; now it was tender and sweet, like two lovers billing and cooing. Yingying became completely enraptured.

"Sister," said Hong Niang, "you can stay here and listen while I go back to see your mother. I'll return in a minute." Thus informed of Yingying's presence outside the window, Zhang Gong turned the strings and started on a new tune, "The Phoenix Looking for a Mate," while chanting the love song written by Sima Xiangru for Zhuo Wenjun. This love story was familiar to Yingying, who was well versed in classical literature and poetry. Moved to tears by the heartache in the music, she whispered, "I know all about what you feel. You are high in my regard and close to my bosom!" Zhang Gong heaved a long sigh. "Her Ladyship was ungrateful, but why did you also betray me, young maiden?" "You blame me unjustly! It was all my mother's idea, I did not betray you. If

I were in control of my own life, I would not stay away from you. Now my mother wants me to do needlework all day. If I had any time at my disposal I would not let you miss me in vain. Though we have just the window paper between us, it is like a high mountain keeping us apart! How can I hear anything from you, or you from me, this way?"

Just then they heard quickening steps coming toward them. "Sister," Hong Niang said, "let's go back! Your mother's waiting for you." Yingying turned with a start, as if caught in the act. Observing the look on Yingying's face, Hong Niang recognized her attachment to Zhang Gong and decided to test how deep it was. "Sister, what's the use of listening to the zither? Zhang just asked me to tell you he is leaving."

Startled, Yingying grabbed Hong Niang by the hand and blurted out, "Good sister, please ask him to stay for a while!"

"What shall I tell him?"

Yingying was too agitated to mince words. "Tell him I am trying to make the old woman come around! Tell him to ignore the false words of my cold-hearted mother! I won't let him yearn for me in vain, and I won't give up on a steadfast and faithful man like him!"

For the next few days the two lovers had no chance to meet again or even exchange messages. Zhang Gong, weighed down by pent-up feelings of sadness and distress, decided to take to his bed, pretending to be more sick than he really was. As news of his illness would be passed around, Yingying might find an excuse to visit him.

Learning of Zhang's illness but unable to visit him herself Yingying, in a faltering voice, asked Hong Niang to go on her behalf. When Hong Niang refused, saying Mrs. Cui would be furious, Yingying became so worried she actually bowed to the maid and begged her. Hong Niang was in fact quite willing to help. After poking fun at her young mistress, she agreed to go.

111

Once in the studio, she wet the window paper and cut a small hole to peer into the room. Zhang Gong was lying in bed all dressed up, heaving one deep sigh after another and looking quite thin and pale. Taking a gold pin from her hair, Hong Niang tapped on the door. At the sight of Hong Niang, Zhang Hong eagerly invited her in. "I am sent by the young lady to inquire after your illness," said Hong Niang.

"Do you have a message for me?" asked Zhang Gong anxiously.

"For the past few days the young lady has neglected her toilet and keeps calling your name," said Hong Niang. Zhang Gong was excited to learn that Yingying missed him so much, and he begged Hong Niang to take a short letter to her. Hong Niang looked reluctant, saying she feared the consequences should the young lady be offended. When Zhang Gong hastily offered to reward her with gold and silver, she was affronted. "What a poor pedant! Do you consider youself a rich man? Do you think I have come to see you because of your money? What a snob! What impertinence! Don't you know how to ask for a favor? Well, at least you can ask me to take pity on you because of your loneliness!" Zhang Gong apologized to her with contrition and begged her to take pity on him. "That's a bit better!" Hong Niang seemed appeased. "Jot it down, and I will deliver it for you."

Zhang Gong took up his writing brush and wrote the letter on a piece of fancy paper, pouring out his longings for Yingying and dedicating another poem to her. Folding the paper into a square, he handed it to Hong Niang. "Please take it to your mistress without fail!"

On her way back, Hong Niang was summoned by the old lady. In the meantime Yingying was waiting impatiently for Hong Niang to return with a message about Zhang Gong. When Hong Niang failed to show up, Yingying grew drowsy and dozed off in her bed.

Having tended to the old lady, Hong Niang returned to Yingying's room and found her lying in bed. If she handed the letter directly to Yingying, the young lady would surely scold her to keep up the pretence of filial obedience. So Hong Niang placed the letter on the dressing table instead.

Yingying was already awake, rubbing her ears and sighing deep sighs. At Hong Niang's footsteps, she sat up in bed and looked at the maid inquisitively. But Hong Niang merely remarked that her hair was loose and needed combing. Disappointed, Yingying sat down in front of the dressing table where she found the letter folded in a square. She quickly picked it up and opened it. Over and over she read the letter, her eyes lighting up with joy. Hong Niang was about to joke with her when her expression changed abruptly. "Hong Niang," she demanded harshly, "tell me where you got this, you slut! Who had the nerve to deride me like this, the daughter of Chief Minister Cui? Do you think I am used to such treatment? If I go and tell my mother about it, you will receive a good thrashing on your bottom!"

The young lady's pretended anger completely failed to intimidate the maid. "It was you who sent me to see him," she argued, "and he asked me to take this to you. You well know I can't read—how should I know what it's about? It was you who started everything, yet you try to make a scapegoat of me! There is no need to frighten me, sister, by saying you will go and tell your mother—I will take this letter and report everything to her myself." Scared, Yingying caught hold of her maid and begged her to stop. "I was only joking!" But Hong Niang kept a straight face. "Take your hand off! Don't think you can escape a good thrashing on your bottom!"

After exchanging a few more verbal barbs with her maid, the young lady asked how Zhang Gong was doing. Hong Niang replied that after the night he played the zither for her, he missed her so much he couldn't eat but only gazed at her room and shed silent tears. He was virtually withering away.

"Why doesn't he send for a good doctor?"

"He said his illness will not respond to any medicine, and the only cure is sweat from an amorous night."

Embarrassed by the blunt expression, Yingying turned away. "Hong Niang, but for your sake, I would show this letter to my mother, and he would have to suffer the consequences. We have to treat each other like brother and sister now; any transgression would be unthinkable. Fortunately you don't have a loose tongue, otherwise the others would learn about this and start spreading all kinds of rumors!"

"Who are you trying to fool?" Hong Niang retorted. "He's pining away for your sake. What do you propose to do next? You gave him high hopes, but you want to back out now, leaving him dangling in the air!"

Keeping a stiff face, Yingying wrote a short note and told Hong Niang to give it to Zhang Gong and warn him not to write to her like that again if he didn't want Mrs. Cui to learn of his indecent behavior.

Perplexed, Hong Niang picked up the note and thought for a moment. In sympathy with Zhang Gong, she did not want to bring him bad news, yet she had to obey her young mistress and deliver the letter. Before she left, however, she made a few caustic remarks to Yingying. "Why weren't you afraid of the cold the night you listened to him playing the zither? You went up to seduce him yourself, and now you try to shift the blame on me? Though you look prim and proper and talk like a prude, you knit your brows in distress and wear a woeful appearance when alone. What deceit!"

Hong Niang came to Zhang Gong's room and found him standing and waiting at the door. "Sweet maid!" he cried out on seeing her, you are the pillar of my heaven! What news do you have for me?" When Hong Niang told him there was no good news, he blamed her for not trying hard enough. Hong

Niang claimed to have done her best, saying it was his letter that ruined everything. "It is natural that you should suffer because of this," she said, "but what have I done to deserve her criticism? From now on, don't bother me anymore. No more pitiful appeals from you. Now I will take leave, the old lady may need me."

Zhang Gong, driven to the verge of despair, felt cold from head to toe. Grabbing Hong Niang by the hand, he fell on his knees. "Sweet maid, who can I rely on if you walk away from me like this? Please think of somthing to save my life!" Hong Niang said she wanted to have nothing more to do with it. "Since you are a scholar, you should know better than to keep hoping when there is no hope at all." Zhang Gong, still on his knees, begged Hong Niang to take pity on him. Only then did Hong Niang remember the note from Yingying. She took it out and handed it to him.

Zhang Gong hurriedly opened the note. After a quick glance, he exclaimed with delight. "Wonderful news! I should have burnt some incense and made deep bows before opening this letter! Sweet maid, are you not pleased for my sake?"

"What do you mean? What's this all about?"

"I am telling you, Hong Niang. Your young mistress was just putting on a show when she scolded me. In this letter she invites me to meet her in the garden tonight!"

Bewildered, Hong Niang asked him what the letter said. "Listen to this poem," replied Zhang Gong.

With the moon ready to rise over the west chamber,
The gate to the garden opens ajar in the breeze.
On the other side of the wall flowers begin to sway,
Heralding, perhaps, the arrival of the fair maiden.

While Hong Niang felt annoyed at Yingying's deceitfulness, Zhang Gong began to ponder how he could get into the garden that night. He could hardly wait for the rendezvous and wished he were like a legendary hero capable of shooting down the sun with his powerful bow.

On her return, Hong Niang did not speak to Yingying but kept a watchful eye on her, waiting to see how she would treat Zhang Gong that night.

The sun went down, and the moon rose in the east over a clear sky. As usual, Hong Niang escorted Yingying to the garden to burn incense. While Yingying stood by a rock whispering her secret wishes, Hong Niang went over and opened the gate to peer around. Zhang Gong, who had been waiting outside, burst in and took Hong Niang into his arms. "You have finally come, my fair lady!"

"Take a better look to see who I am!" snapped Hong Niang. "You would be in big trouble if it had been the old lady instead of me!"

Zhang Gong, realizing his mistake, apologized profusely. After telling him Yingying was standing by the rock, Hong Niang warned him to be gentle in his advances so as not to scare her.

In spite of Hong Niang's admonition, Zhang Gong was so thrilled at the sight of Yingying that he just went over and grabbed her into his arms. Her heart pounding wildly, Yingying asked, "Who is this? Who is this?"

"It's me."

"Well, so it's you," said Yingying. "What sort of a man are you then? Why do you burst in on me like this as I am burning incense and offering my prayer to the Buddha? What would you say to my mother if I should tell her about this?" Zhang Gong groaned inwardly. Yingying had changed her mind again!

"Hong Niang," Yingying called out. "We have a thief here!" Hong Niang, who had heard the exchange between Yingying and Zhang Gong, asked who the thief could be. When Zhang Gong replied that there was no thief but him,

Hong Niang demanded to know why he had come. Yingying urged her to take him to Mrs. Cui, but Hong Niang disagreed. "Wouldn't he lose his face if we take him to the old lady? Instead, let me scold him on your behalf." Without waiting for a reply, Hong Niang turned to address Zhang Gong. "Come here and kneel! Since you have studied the Confucian classics, you cannot be ignorant of the rules of propriety. What do you intend to do by creeping into the garden so late at night? Are you aware of your guilt?" Choked with rage, Zhang Gong replied that he was not. Hong Niang then turned to persuade Yingying, who agreed to forgive Zhang Gong. "I am indebted to you," she said, "because you saved my life. Since you are my brother now, how can you cherish improper thoughts about me anymore? How would you explain yourself if my mother should learn of your behavior? Please stop acting in this way. I won't let you off if you make the same mistake again!" She then left the garden alone.

Zhang Gong could do nothing but vent his grievances to Hong Niang. "I have come at her invitation, and what do I get in return? Utter nonsense!" When he wanted to write Yingying a letter demanding an explanation, Hong Niang refused to deliver it for him, and advised him to have no more illusions and give up the whole idea once and for all.

It was getting late, so Hong Niang took her leave. Zhang Gong returned to his room in great distress. Filled with humiliation and despair, and besieged by the cold night air, he soon succumbed to a severe headache and high fever. When he was too ill to get up the next morning, the abbot was informed. Mrs. Cui, hearing about this from the abbot, asked him to send for a doctor. She also sent Hong Niang to call on Zhang Gong.

Hong Niang first went to inform Yingying of what had happened. Apparently, she said, the young scholar was not accustomed to the harsh rebuke he had received the night

117

before, and broke down under the humiliation. "Good lady, you have ruined him." Badly shaken by the news, Yingying sat thinking for a while, then wrote a few words on a piece of decorated paper and handed it to Hong Niang, saying the letter spelled out the recipe for saving Zhang Gong's life. "Don't play the same old trick again," said Hong Niang with suspicion. "The first time was quite enough, don't you think?" After Yingying assured her that the recipe was genuine and would surely work this time, Hong Niang agreed to play messenger again.

Zhang Gong was lying in bed, his face pale and emaciated, heaving deep sighs. Hong Niang entered the room and told him her young mistress had prepared a recipe for him. Taking a look at the letter, Zhang Gong sat up abruptly and began waving his hands in joy. "If I had known you have such a letter for me, I would have come out to receive you. Oh, sweet maid—" "Not again!" Hong Niang interrupted him. "You don't understand," said Zhang Gong eagerly, "your young mistress has invited me to—" "What does she say in the letter? Tell me!" Zhang Gong said it was an eight-line poem. "You only have to look at the last line to know what the poem means: 'Tonight at last there will be an amorous moment.' This poem is quite different from the last one. She will definitely come to my room tonight."

Hong Niang was surprised to learn that Yingying had offered to stay the night in Zhang Gong's room. Glancing around, she could see only a cotton quilt and the zither for a pillow, so she asked him how he would keep the young lady from the cold of night. Zhang Gong, growing anxious, took out ten taels of silver and offered to rent a bedding set from her. Hong Niang replied jokingly that she had no bedding to spare.

By this time Zhang Gong seemed to have fully recovered from his illness. He thanked Hong Niang for her kind help, expressed his worry about Mrs. Cui, and wondered whether Yingying would change her mind again. Hong Niang, both amused and touched by his sincerity, promised to bring Yingying to him as long as the young lady was willing to come. Zhang Gong again showered her with words of gratitude.

Hong Niang returned to find Yingying wearing a straight face as if nothing unusual were to take place. Late at night, she bade Hong Niang prepare the bed, saying she was going to sleep. Hong Niang was not to be tricked as before. "If you go to bed like this, how about that young man?" "What young man are you talking about?" "Oh no, not again, sister! Don't treat it as a game, for it may cost the young man's life. If you go back on your word once more, I will go and make a full confession to your mother. I will tell her that you asked me to take a letter to Zhang Gong and arrange a secret meeting with him." "What a sly girl!" muttered Yingying, her face flushed with embarrassment. "How can I bring myself to go? I would be dying of shame!" "What's there to be ashamed of? You can just close your eyes once you get there." Hong Niang went out and returned in a minute to assure Yingying that Mrs. Cui had gone to bed. Yingying, while still professing reluctance, headed eagerly for the door, much to Hong Niang's amusement.

Escorted by Hong Niang, Yingying slipped out of her room, walked down the veranda, and came before Zhang Gong's room. Hong Niang went up to knock on the door. At the sight of Hong Niang, Zhang Gong asked if her young mistress had arrived. Without replying, Hong Niang shoved a bedding set into his arms. "How are you going to thank me?" "With heaven for a witness, I will always cherish you in my heart!" "All right. Be gentle with the young mistress. Otherwise you may scare her." Hong Niang turned back, pushed Yingying into the room, and closed the door, remaining outside to keep watch.

Zhang Gong knelt to receive Yingying into the room, then helped her onto his bed. He expressed his longing for her, saying he was so grateful to her that he would turn into a dog or a horse in his next life to serve her. Yingying mentioned her worry that, by giving herself up to him, she would be deserted by him someday. "I will never dare!" exclaimed Zhang Gong repeatedly.

Their long-hoped-for union finally consummated, the young couple were still murmuring sweet nothings to each other at daybreak. Afraid to be discovered by the old lady, Hong Niang tapped on the window and urged Yingying to leave. Zhang Gong walked Yingying to the door and begged her to come to him again that night.

After that, Yingying enjoyed her secret rendezvous with Zhang Gong at every opportunity. For them, there were no more feelings of despair, lovesickness, or uncertainty. Zhang Gong, his mind entirely free of worry, regained his health with miraculous speed. In the meantime Yingying's figure grew supple and well-rounded, and there began to be a sensual sway in her posture. Sometimes, lost in thought, she looked absent-minded and said things that did not make sense. Such abnormality did not escape the experienced eye of her mother. One day, when Hong Niang had just left after offering her morning greetings, Mrs. Cui muttered to herself, "I wonder what the two of them have been up to?" Huanlang, standing by her side, thought he was asked a question, so he said, "A few days ago, while you were already in bed, I saw Hong Niang and my sister go to the garden to burn incense. When I went to bed a long time afterwards, they had not yet returned." Hearing this, Mrs. Cui told the boy to bring Hong Niang to her at once. Huanlang gloated when he found Hong Niang. "Mother knows about you and my sister going out at midnight. She wants to see you now to give you a good beating!"

When Hong Niang turned to blame Yingying for not

covering up her track carefully, Yingying begged her to try to explain it away in front of her mother. But Hong Niang was aware that it would no longer be possible to conceal the matter from the old lady. Having decided on her strategy, she went calmly to confront Mrs. Cui.

"Little slut, why don't you kneel and repent? Do you admit your guilt?" Mrs. Cui's voice was trembling with fury.

"I don't admit any guilt!"

"How dare you be so stubborn! By telling the truth, you might be spared. If you don't, I will have you beaten to death! Who gave you permission to take Yingying to the garden late at night?"

"We didn't go. Who said we did?"

"Huanlang saw you, and he told me everything!" responded Mrs. Cui. She left her seat and raised her hand to strike at Hong Niang.

Hong Niang was not at all scared. She told the old lady to put down her hand, restrain her anger, and lend a ear. "One night," she said, "Yingying and I were chatting over our needlework, when we decided to visit Zhang Gong in his illness. We went to his room, where he complained that Your Ladyship had gone back on your word and had repaid kindness with ingratitude. After a while, Zhang told me to leave first and said Yingying would stay a little longer. Since that night, the two of them have been spending every night together. What's done cannot be undone. There is no need for you to make a big fuss about this."

Mrs. Cui was mad with fury. She rebuked Hong Niang in harsh words, saying she was responsible for what had happened. Undaunted, Hong Niang argued that the culprit responsible was neither Zhang Gong, nor Yingying, nor Hong Niang, but Mrs. Cui herself. Mrs. Cui could hardly believe her own ears. "All right, you slut," she said in a voice choked with rage, "tell me why I am the person responsible for all

In her anger the old lady raised her hand to hit Hong Niang.

this!"

Ignoring the old lady's wrath, Hong Niang spoke her mind in a leisurely manner. "Trust, I hear, is the foundation of human relationships. Previously, you promised to marry the young mistress to whomever could dispel the rebels. Zhang Gong succeeded in eliminating the rebels, so that your family was saved from catastrophe. But then you changed your mind and broke your promise. Given the circumstances, the least you could have done was to reward him handsomely and send him away. Instead, you have allowed him to move in and stay with us, giving the two young people the chance to get together on their own. Can you deny it was all your own doing?"

Mrs. Cui was struck speechless, not knowing how to reply. At this, Hong Niang proposed a solution. It was inexpedient, she argued, to pursue the matter further. In the first place, the honor of the Cui family was at steak. By taking the matter to the yamen, Mrs. Cui would be blamed for failing to discipline her own child. If the magistrate should look further into the case, he would discover the ungrateful manner in which Mrs. Cui had treated Zhang Gong. Moreover, it was not at all unlikely that Zhang Gong would succeed in the upcoming imperial examination and become an official some-day. "If you listen to the words of your humble maid, it would be in everyone's best interest for you to overlook their mistake and give your blessing to their marriage." Mrs. Cui conceded that Hong Niang's words were reasonable. There seemed no alternative, she said, but to marry her daughter to that knave, since cooked rice could not go back to being raw again. She told Hong Niang to bring the two trespassers to see her.

After telling Yingying, Hong Niang went to find Zhang Gong. "The old lady knows what you and Yingying have done," she said, "but fortunately I have persvaded her to let Yingying marry you." Zhang Gong was both startled and delighted, saying he was too shamefaced to meet Mrs. Cui. "Come on," urged Hong Niang, "don't be such a coward trying evade responsibility for what you've done!" Thus Zhang Gong went to see Mrs. Cui, who gave him a strong reprimand. "What a scholar you are to have acted in total disregard of moral principles! I would have you escorted to the yamen but for the disgrace it would bring to my family name. Oh well, I give you my consent to marry Yingying. However, for many generations our family has not had an unranked scholar for a son-in-law. You will leave for the capital tomorrow while Yingying stays behind. Come back to see us after you are made an official. Should you fail in the examination, don't show up anymore!"

The following day Mrs. Cui had a farewell feast prepared for Zhang Gong at an inn.

It was a day in late autumn, with clouds floating high in the azure sky and the ground covered with fallen chrysanthemums. In the strong autumn wind wild geese were flying south on their homeward journey. Yingying awoke early in a dispirited mood. She sat up in her bed, brooding gloomily, with no intention of combing her hair or applying makeup. However, Hong Niang urged her to get dressed, for they would soon set out for the inn where the old lady was waiting. Arriving there by carriage, Yingying saw Zhang Gong together with Fa Ben, the abbot, and her mother. Mrs. Cui bade Yingying sit down by her side, while Zhang Gong and Fa Ben took seats across the table and Hong Niang came up and filled the cups with wine. "Today I formally betroth to you my daughter, Yingying," Mrs. Cui announced to Zhang Gong. "Don't let her down. Go to the capital and distinguish yourself in the imperial examination." Zhang Gong pledged to do just that. Fa Ben remarked that he expected nothing but good news. Yingying, however, lowered her head with tears in her eyes. The thought that she would soon be separated from her

Yingying offered a cup of wine to Zhang Gong
to send him on his journey.

beloved by a thousand rivers and hills, and that many things could happen to keep them apart, filled her heart with distress. Unable to pour out her mind at the table, she could only sigh deeply. Mrs. Cui, as ever unmindful of her daughter's mood, pressed her to offer a toast to Zhang Gong. Hong Niang tried to get Yingying to eat a little food, as she had not had even a drop of water that morning. With a sigh Yingying whispered to Hong Niang, "How can you make me eat when I am filled up with sorrow and distress? Why should he leave me behind like this merely for the sake of vain glory?"

A while later Mrs. Cui took her leave along with Fa Ben, telling Yingying to stay a short moment longer, then return home. When her mother turned her back, Yingying told Zhang Gong that he must return immediately whether he succeeded in getting an official post or not. Zhang Gong, however, was very confident, saying he would surely come out first in the imperial examination. Her worries unappeased, Yingying composed a poem for him:

Where is the maiden you left behind?
Are old-time affections forgotten?
What made you cut off your old ties,
And devote your love to another?

Listening to the poem, Zhang Gong knew at once what was on Yingying's mind. "I will be devoted to you all my life," he pledged. "I will never set my eyes on another woman." Thereupon he composed a poem for her in return:

For the traveler on a long journey,
Who is closest to his heart,
Who took pity on him in distress,
If not his one and only bosom friend?

Zhang Gong was about to mount his horse, but Yingying took him by the hand and told him to take care of himself on the journey. He must eat with restraint, get plenty of sleep and, on his arrival in the capital, take his time and get used to the climate. Zhang Gong, touched by her solicitude, asked what else she had to say. "I have no doubt that your talents will be recognized," she said. "But I do fear that you may desert your betrothed in favor of another. Promise to send me letters, and I will send mine to you. Whether or not you pass the examination, come back to me. Bear this in mind especially: do not fall for another woman. Promise this to me!" Zhang Gong again pledged his loyalty. "You may set your mind at ease in that respect. No one can possibly attract me like you do!"

It was getting late, the sun about to sink behind the distant hills. With Hong Niang urging Yingying to return, and Zhang Gong ready to begin his journey, the two lovers parted tears fully.

Zhang Gong galloped for thirty *li*, arriving at dusk at a place called Caoqiao, where he put up at an inn. Without eating supper, he went to bed. The memory of the sweet tenderness the night before, with the beauty in his arms, contrasted sharply with his present lonely state. The disconsolate chirping of insects in the autumn breeze accentuated the gloomy atmosphere in the room. Worn by the day's journey, he gradually drifted into a dream.

He was soon awakened by a sudden knock on the door. Opening the door, he found to his astonishment Yingying standing before him. Panting heavily, Yingying told him she had slipped out and followed him there without her mother's knowledge, as she could not bear the long separation and wanted to accompany him to the capital. Delighted, Zhang Gong received her into the room. No sooner had they sat down than they heard a loud knock at the door. When he opened it, a group of soldiers burst in, clamoring for Yingying's arrest. Alarmed, Zhang Gong woke up. Unable to fall asleep again, he walked out to the court. The air was heavy with fog, and the ground covered in dew. Looking up, he saw the morning star and the fading moon. After a while, he heard a cockcrow. Early in the morning he paid the waiter and left the inn. Several days later he arrived at the imperial capital.

Zhang Gong came to the capital in late autumn, and in early spring the following year took the metropolitan examination. His articles were so excellent that he came out first in the examination, gaining the title Number One Scholar. He was put up in an official guesthouse awaiting an appointment from the emperor. To set Yingying's mind at ease, he wrote a letter and dispatched a servant to take it to her at the Monastery of Universal Salvation.

In the meantime Yingying was pining away, lovesick. A few months of longing and sorrow had left her wan and thin. Sometimes she climbed the stairs to gaze into the distance, but the chilly mists and fading plants only served to aggravate her melancholy. One night, however, she found the lamp wick burst into a flower-like shape. The next morning she heard magpies chirping merrily in the trees. These two unmistakable signs of good fortune were followed by the arrival of Zhang Gong's servant with his letter.

All sorts of feelings welled up in her heart when Yingying took the letter she had been expecting for half a year. Opening it, she read the following: "I arrived safely in the capital. Thanks to my ancestors' blessing and my dear wife's grace, I won the first place in the metropolitan examination. Now I am staying in the official guesthouse awaiting His Majesty's appointment. I have sent my servant with this letter to keep you from worrying about me. After I receive an appointment and take office, I will return immediately to celebrate our wedding." The letter ended with a poem:

From the scholar residing in the jade house of the capital,
Comes this message to the lovely maiden living east of Puguan:
The day will come when he gets a brocade robe from the
* emperor,*
Then she will no more stand waiting for him at the gate.

After reading the letter, Yingying went into raptures, all her sorrows and worries completely gone. She bade Hong Niang take the servants away to eat and rest while she went to her room to write a reply.

After a while she came out and handed the servant a letter and a packet, along with ten taels of silver for traveling expenses. The servant was made to promise to tuck the letter away in a safe place and keep it from the rain, handle the packet with great care and not use it for a pillow, and take both the letter and the packet safely to his master. When the servant got up to leave, Yingying stopped him again and told him to pass on a message. Zhang Gong had stayed in the capital too long already, she said, and should hasten back at the very first opportunity.

After Zhang Gong had waited in the guesthouse for many days, the imperial edict finally came, appointing him as compiler of the Imperial Academy to work on the national history. But Zhang Gong was not at all interested in compiling national history at the Imperial Academy. What he wanted was a post in Hezhong Prefecture where he could be reunited with Yingying. He did not sleep well, lost his appetite, and at last fell ill. An imperial physician was sent for, but he had no cure for the lovesick.

At this juncture the servant returned. His heart throbbing, Zhang Gong opened Yingying's tear-stained letter in which she described her worries, her longing, and her joy at receiving good news from him. The letter ended with a poem in response to his:

I lean across the railing, gazing into the distance,
Wondering if the talented man is beguiled by a wench in the
  capital.
The good news brings me up from my sick bed;
Sitting by the window, I try a new makeup before the mirror.

The effect of the letter proved miraculous, for it brought
Zhang Gong up from his sick bed at once. He opened the
packet and looked over the gifts, surmising the message each
of them conveyed. With this neatly stitched undershirt she
must be reminding him of her tenderness. With this zither
she must be advising him to quiet his heart and cultivate his
virtue. With a pair of socks she must be warning him against
visiting indecent places. With the jade hairpin she must be
admonishing him not to set her aside to the back of his mind.
With a wide belt she was probably asking him to keep her
always at heart. With a flute made of tear-stained bamboo she
must be revealing her deep longing for him. So Zhang Gong
had no difficulty at all deciphering Yingying's messages. All
her doubts, he knew, orginated from her profound love of
him. He vowed to himself that he would always remain true
to her in return for such love and devotion.

He stroked the gifts lovingly, then told the servant to
empty a rattan case, line it with several lays of paper, then
place the gifts inside with the utmost care.

As a common saying goes, the road to happiness is strewn with
setbacks. Zheng Heng, Mrs. Cui's nephew, had previously
received her letter asking him to come to the monastery and
help her escort his uncle's coffin back to Fuling. After a long
delay, he arrived in Hezhong, only to learn that Yingying had
been betrothed to Zhang Gong, who had saved her from the
rebels with the help of the White-Horse General. Filled with
remorse and frustration, Zheng Heng did not know what to

do. When he failed to show up in a few days, Mrs. Cui, who had learned of his arrival, sent Hong Niang to visit him. After saluting him, Hong Niang asked bluntly, "Her Ladyship wants to know why you failed to visit her after you came." Ignoring the question, Zheng Heng asked Hong Niang to do him a favor. "It is my uncle who had Yingying betrothed to me. At his death, our wedding was postponed. Now that the mourning period is over, I beg you ask my aunt to name the day for my marriage to Yingying. Afterwards I can accompany my bride to her hometown to bury her father's remains. Otherwise, it would be inconvenient for the two of us to travel together along the way." He promised to reward Hong Niang handsomely after the wedding.

"I am afraid the subject is closed," said Hong Niang. "Yingying is going to marry someone else!"

Enraged, Zheng Heng retorted, "A woman cannot be engaged twice. Why should my aunt break her promise after my uncle's death? How can she do this?"

"Of course she can," said Hong Niang. "Where were you when Sun Feihu besieged the monastery with his rebel troops? How could my family have lived to this day but for Zhang's rescue? What effrontery for you to come vying for the fruit after the danger is over! If Yingying had been taken away by those bandits, what chance would you have to win her?" Zheng Heng became tongue-tied under Hong Niang's eloquent rebuke. After a moment he muttered, "Well, I wouldn't complain if she were to marry into a wealthy family; but to marry a poor wretch of a scholar! In what respect am I not superior to him? I have so many things he doesn't have—a noble origin, a close kinship with your family, and her father's blessing!"

"Hold your tongue!" Hong Niang cried out, angered by his slanderous remark about Zhang Gong. "Don't brag about your background, and don't even mention your kin. You are a rascal—that's what you are, whereas Zhang Gong is a gentleman. You cannot be mentioned in the same breath with him! Because you have a minister for a father, you always go around bullying others, but Zhang Gong has studied the classics and treats other people with respect. You are infinitely inferior to him, just as the pitiful light of the firefly cannot compare with the moon!"

Shamed into anger, Zheng Heng, showing the true colors of a bully, declared he would send two dozen strong men to carry Yingying off in a sedan chair. "She will leave home a girl," he threatened, "and return a woman!" Hong Niang did not hesitate to hit back. "You, the son of the Minister of Rites, talk like one of those bandits commanded by Sun Feihu! If you do not mend your filthy ways, you will come to a miserable end someday!" After the fiery exchange, Hong Niang left without saying good-bye.

That night Zheng Heng thought out a plan. The following morning, he went to call on Mrs. Cui. Always partial to him, she explained what had happened and tried to comfort him with gentle words. Zheng Heng, however, began to tell a story he had made up the night before. He claimed to have seen Zhang Gong in the capital and to know what had happened to him. While touring the capital on horseback to celebrate his success in the imperial examination, Zhang was hit by a ball made of colored silk ribbons. It was thrown by the daughter of Minister Wei to select her future mate. Over a dozen men rushed out from Wei's house and escorted Zhang inside. When Zhang mentioned he already had a wife at home, Minister Wei insisted that his daughter would be the principal wife, with Yingying reduced to the status of a concubine. Mrs. Cui took Zheng Heng at his word and began to swear at Zhang Gong. Finally she said to Zheng Heng, "Well, since Zhang Gong has married someone else, you can select an auspicious date and become my son-in-law." Zheng

Heng was elated at his success.

However, the abbot told Mrs. Cui she had made a rash decision. He had just received news that Zhang Gong, reappointed administrator of Hezhong Prefecture, would soon come to assume office. As Mrs. Cui refused to meet Zhang Gong, Fa Ben said he would go to the inn to meet him.

In the meantime, Zheng Heng chose his wedding day and readied some wine and betrothal gifts. Unfortunately for him, Zhang Gong arrived in Hezhong on that very day. Without lingering in his office, he headed straight for the monastery. When he knelt to salute Mrs. Cui, she turned away with annoyance. "Stop it! Since you are the son-in-law of another family, I no longer deserve your salute!" Bewildered, Zhang Gong asked the old lady to explain the cause of her displeasure. "You faithless man! But for the siege of the monastery, you would never have been received into the family of the late chief minister! What do you mean by marrying into Minister Wei's family and casting my daughter aside? Speak!"

"Where did you hear this story?" asked Zhang Gong.

"Zheng Heng has told us everything! He said you were hit by a colored silk ball thrown by Minister Wei's daughter!"

Just then Yingying walked in supported by Hong Niang. When they also began to blame him for going back on his word, Zhang Gong had a hard time defending himself. Fortunately, Fa Ben spoke up in his favor. "I am sure Mr. Zhang is incapable of such an act," he said to Mrs. Cui. "How could he have ignored your admonition? And how could he have forgotten the young lady? With General Du Que as a witness to the marriage, he is unlikely to change his mind like that. Please consider this!" Yingying thought the abbot's words reasonable. They would learn the truth, she said, upon the arrival of the White-Horse General.

By coincidence, Du Que had just been appointed military governor of Hezhong. Carrying some wine and gifts, he came to the monastery to congratulate Zhang Gong on his return in glory and to celebrate his wedding.

Zheng Heng, ignorant of the arrival at the monastery of the White-Horse General, came at the appointed time dressed as a bridegroom. Entering the gate, he caught sight of Du Que and Zhang Gong chatting at the table with Mrs. Cui in the Buddha's hall. He stepped back fearfully, but Du Que bade him stop. "Zheng Heng, what business has brought you here?" Zheng Heng, groaning inwardly, replied that he had come to congratulate the Number One Scholar on his return. "Really? So you come to offer your congratulations? But tell me, why did you try to seduce and abduct his wife? What do you have to say about that? By sending a memorial to the imperial court, I can easily obtain an order to have you beheaded!" Zheng Heng was scared out of his wits. As both Mrs. Cui and Fa Ben interceded, and Zheng Heng promised to revoke his engagement to Yingying and never come to harass Yingying again, Du Que agreed to let him go.

It was a festive day in the monastery. With Mrs. Cui presiding over the ceremony, General Du Que acting as witness, and Fa Ben attending to the detailed arrangements, Yingying and Zhang Gong were formally married at last. That evening the newly weds made a wish that all lovers under heaven could share their good fortune and be finally united in wedlock.

SORROW IN THE HAN PALACE

*Ma Zhiyuan**

When Emperor Yuandi of the Han Dynasty ascended the throne, he had every reason to be complacent. The Han Empire, founded by his grandfather, Liu Bang, was free of internal strife and incursion from the outside, enjoying abundant harvests year after year thanks to a favorable climate. Emperor Yuandi therefore showed no interest in holding audiences and attending to state affairs, but preferred to spend his time in the company of his many concubines and palace women in the rear palace. However, many palace women had been sent away after the death of the previous emperor. Those remaining, though still numerous, did not strike Emperor Yuandi as particularly attractive, and this made him quite unhappy.

In the imperial court was an official named Mao Yanshou, a crafty sycophant. He had established himself in the good graces of the emperor by inducing him to indulge in sensual pleasures. One day he said to Emperor Yuandi, "Your Majesty, when a petty landlord has enjoyed a good harvest, he celebrates his good fortune by taking one more concubine. As the Son of Heaven, you rule the entire land under heaven within the bounds of the four seas. Why not send some people on a

---

* The dates of both his birth and death are unknown, though it is certain he died before 1324. He spent his early years in the north, but was later made an official in the southern province of Zhejiang. One of the four great Yuan dramatists, Ma Zhiyuan is known to have written sixteen plays, seven of which have survived. *Sorrow in the Han Palace* is considered a representative work.

135

trip around the empire in search of young maidens? Any beautiful maiden between fifteen and twenty, whether from the family of a commoner, an official, or a prince, can be selected and brought to the palace to keep you company. Why can't we do this?"

"What a marvelous idea!" Emperor Yuandi cried with joy. "I will make you my special emissary and issue an edict to send you on the mission. When you complete the task, you must bring me the portraits of the chosen maidens so I can summon them one by one according to my liking. You will be handsomely rewarded on your return." Mao Yanshou sincerely thanked the emperor for entrusting him with such a delectable task.

Mao Yanshou had a passion for wealth. He summerized his philosophy of life in the following verse:

Big blocks of gold is what I seek;
Not even imperial decrees can stop me.
So long as I have wealth to enjoy in life,
Why should I care about curses flung before my grave?

His appointment to the beauty-hunting mission gave him an excelent chance to enhance his wealth. The next morning he set out without delay.

The imperial edict created a furor all across the empire. Many families, from commoners to lords and princes, were reluctant to send their daughters to the palace. This enabled Mao to extort huge sums of money. Of those families whose daughters were selected, some paid him bribes to have their names crossed out, while others offered him expensive gifts and asked him to accentuate their girl's beauty in the portrait so they would have a better chance to gain the emperor's favor. In this way, Mao Yanshou made a large fortune on his beauty-hunting trip.

After touring the better part of the empire, Mao Yanshou

had collected ninety-nine beauties, and intended to find one more before calling off the search. He arrived in Zigui County, where he failed to find anyone to his satisfaction, so he went to the villages on the outskirts of the city. Among the villagers summoned there was a man named Wang Zhangzhe who came with his daughter. That maiden of eighteen was a paragon of beauty. Her given name was Qiang, and her styled name Zhaojun. At the very sight of her Mao Yanshou added her name to the list.

Mao sent one of his followers to visit Wang Zhangzhe to extort a hundred taels of gold. Wang was told that if he paid the sum, Mao would put Zhaojun on top of the list of selected beauties. Once the emperor received the list, Zhaojun would no doubt win imperial favor, and the Wang family would be instantly elevated to the rank of nobility. Wang Zhangzhe, however, was a simple peasant. A hundred taels of gold was completely beyond his means. To Mao's great annoyance, several visits from his follower failed to exact the desired amount from Wang. "What a blockheaded old man!" he muttered to himself angrily. "No one has dared to treat me like this before!" He took up the brush and crossed Zhaojun's name from the list.

Walking back and forth in his room, Mao Yanshou was panting with rage when an idea occurred to him. "Why should I cross out her name? That's exactly what they want! How can I let them off so easily? Well, a true gentleman is not without venom!" What Mao decided to do was take Zhaojun into the palace but kept her forever from the emperor, so that she would spend the rest of her life in loneliness and isolation.

The following day Wang Zhangzhe was notified that his daughter had been selected and should sit for a portrait to be presented to the emperor. Reluctantly, Wang took his daughter to the guesthouse where Mao Yanshou was staying. After Zhaojun was seated, Mao Yanshou set down to work. He was dexterous with the painting brush, but at the end he added a finishing touch by presenting her with a cross-eye.

With a hundred beauties selected from all over the empire, and a fortune amassed along the way, Mao Yanshou returned to the capital with great satisfaction to report to the emperor. Emperor Yuandi did not choose to examine the beauties one by one. Instead, he had them taken to the rear palace, and their portraits left in his room. Whenever he felt the urge, he picked out one of them to keep him company for the night by flipping through the portraits. Because of the cross-eye in her portrait, Zhaojun never struck the emperor as attractive, so she remained unknown to him and was never granted a chance to meet him. Though some palace women knew the truth, they did not find it in their best interest to inform the emperor of the existence of a woman of unrivaled beauty. Thus Zhaojun lived in the rear palace for the next ten years, in total oblivion.

One evening Emperor Yuandi, instead of leafing through the portraits, chose to take a walk around the rear palace accompanied by a eunuch carrying a pair of lanterns. He stopped before a deserted house, attracted by the sound of a lute. The music reminded him of the mournful murmurs of a solitary spring, conveying a deep sense of sorrow and grievance. His interest aroused, he wanted to see the player. "Be gentle and mild," he admonished the eunuch. "Do not scare her."

Startled by the eunuch's shouts, Zhaojun came out and prostrated herself to receive the emperor. Emperor Yuandi looked down and, under the dim light of the lanterns, found to his delight that the woman was very pretty. "Who are you?" he asked good-naturedly. "Why was there a plaintive note in your lute? Don't blame me for never calling on you. Have I not come here today to make recompense? You are so pretty that you fully deserve such a favor. Look, my dear! The candle wicks keep breaking into flowers! That is a good omen for you!" As Emperor Yuandi was rattling away, Zhaojun knelt before him with her head lowered. To take a closer look, Emperor Yuandi bade the eunuch stir the lantern wick to make it brighter. This time, Zhaojun's visage and figure came clearly to the eye. "What a ravishing face! What an alluring figure!" the emperor exclaimed in wonder. "You even make the lantern shine more brightly!"

Zhaojun recovered from her surprise. In a low voice she said, "Your humble servant did not know Your Majesty was coming and asks forgiveness for failing to receive him properly." The emperor was pleased with her polite manners. "Where are you from?"

"I am from the Wang family in Zigui County. My given name is Qiang and my polite name Zhaojun. My father is named Wang Zhangzhe. Since the time of my grandfather, my family has made a living by tilling the land."

While listening to her reply, Emperor Yuandi went on to admire her beauty: her arched eyebrows, her dark, glossy long hair, her slender waist and her rosy cheeks. "I can hardly find a place in this palace deserving of your stay!" he said. "Heaven has sent you to my side. Otherwise how could you have come from a thatched house a thousand li away?"

He stopped abruptly, looking perplexed. The beauty-hunting trip was undertaken ten years before. Why had Mao Yanshou failed to mention the discovery of such an outstanding beauty? "With your exceptional charm and beauty," he asked, "why have you failed to attract my attention until now?"

"To answer Your Majesty's question: The imperial envoy, Mao Yanshou, extorted my father for money when I was selected to enter the palace, but my family was too poor to pay the huge sum. In his rage, Mao painted a cross-eye in my portrait so I would be neglected for ever by Your Majesty."

139

Wang Zhaojun fell on her knees to salute the emperor.

"What? I've never heard of such a thing!" Emperor Yuandi exclaimed in dismay. He ordered the eunuch to fetch Zhaojun's portrait at once.

The portrait was brought and shown to the emperor. At the sight of the cross-eye in the picture, Emperor Yuandi burst into a fury. "How could this have happened! Zhaojun has no cross-eye, but this Mao Yanshou must have an evil one! Pass on my order at once: Seize Mao Yanshou and behead him!"

Aware of the emperor's infatuation with her, Zhaojun took the chance to ask a favor for her parents. "Your Majesty, my parents are still living in poverty back in Zigui. Please bestow a little favor upon them!"

"Nothing could be easier than this! From now on they need no more carry vegetables in the morning, watch over melons at night, plant grains in spring or cultivate hemp in summer, for I will grant them exemption from tax and labor conscription. You will enjoy honor and wealth now that you are mine." The emperor, filled with elation, declared aloud, "Wang Zhaojun, starting from today you will be addressed by the title of Bright Consort!"

Zhaojun hastily knelt to thank him for the conferment. Well pleased with himself, Emperor Yuandi took her by the hand and led her into the bedchamber. He promised to come the following evening and told her jokingly not to play the lute again, for other palace women, learning of the incident, might follow her example.

The guards sent to seize Mao Yanshou returned empty-handed, as Mao had been informed of his impending arrest and absconded that very night to seek refuge in the northern state of the Huns.

The Huns were then a big headache for the Han Empire. Emperor Gaozu, founder of the Han Dynasty, had married one of his daughters to the Hun chieftain in return for peace along the northern border. This set a precedent. Subsequently, every Hun chieftain upon his ascension asked for a Han princess to be his wife. The present chieftain, Hu Hanye, had a hundred thousand crack troops under his command. Formerly, he had sent an envoy to the Han court with some gifts, asking for the hand of a princess, but Emperor Yuandi had declined on the pretext that all the princesses were still underage.

Mao Yanshou, arriving in the Hun state, asked to meet the chieftain. He was ushered into the palace, where he introduced himself to Hu Hanye. "I am Mao Yanshou, a minister of the Han court. I have come to report something to you." He took out a portrait. "When you sent an envoy to ask for an imperial princess, the beauty in this portrait, Wang Zhaojun, volunteered to go. However, the Han emperor did not want to part with her. I tried to talk some reason into him, advising him against placing a mere woman above interstate relationships. Instead of listening to my counsel, the Han emperor got angry and threatened to kill me. So I have come to present this portrait to you. You can go and ask the Han emperor for this very woman." He offered the portrait to the chieftain with both hands.

Hu Hanye had the portrait unrolled before him. The rare beauty of the woman depicted made him exclaim in astonishment. "I did not know such a beauty existed in this world!" He went into raptures over the portrait, convinced that nothing could make him happier than to have the woman for his wife. He immediately wrote a letter to the Han emperor demanding Wang Zhaojun be handed over, and dispatched an official with a huge entourage to carry the letter, which ended with a threat. If his request was rejected, the chieftain said, he would march north with his troops and topple the Han Empire.

After the envoy left, Hu Hanye summoned his troops, had them fully equipped with spears, swords, bows and arrows, and led them south on a hunting excursion. Thus a military invasion could be launched at short notice if that proved necessary for the procurement of Wang Zhaojun.

In the meantime Emperor Yuandi, ignorant of the intention of his northern neighbor, was having a great time in the rear palace, with Zhaojun always by his side. There seemed to be no need to trouble himself with state affairs, for the court officials would take care of everything on his behalf, and the Han Empire was apparently rock-firm.

One evening Emperor Yuandi went to the rear palace after supper and slipped into Zhaojun's room where he found her sitting at the dressing table busy with her toilet. Engrossed in watching her, he was quite annoyed when a eunuch announced that two officials had come to see him. With great reluctance, he had the two men ushered in. It was Wulu Congzong, director of the Imperial Secretariat, and Shi Xian, a palace attendant. "Bad news, Your Majesty!" they called out in a panicky voice. "An envoy has come from the Hun chieftain, Hu Hanye. Mao Yanshou offered the portrait of the Bright Consort to the chieftain, who now demands her for his wife. If we do not gratify his wish, he threatens to lead a hundred thousand troops southward to topple the Han Empire. What shall we do, Your Majesty?"

Emperor Yuandi felt as if a pail of cold water had been poured on his head as he shivered all over. The two ministers, looking grim and despondent, offered no solution but to appease the Hun chieftain by granting him what he wants. The emperor flew into a rage. "Troops are maintained for a thousand days so that they can be put to use at the right time. Why don't you court officials, who have enjoyed good salaries and high positions for so many years, come up with a better solution? Why should the Bright Consort be sacrificed because a bunch of cowards like you cannot cope with the barbarians?" He pointed his finger at the two ministers and rebuked them bitterly. "In times of peace you swagger around to show off your talents, but at a critical moment like this, you shrink back, fold your hands helplessly, and want my beloved consort to fight the enemy for you!"

Under this outburst the two ministers stared at each other, speechless. Wulu Congzong, as director of the Imperial Secretariat, was unable to shirk his responsibility for the situation, so he muttered in a trembling voice, "Your Majesty, that barbarian chieftain said you are ruining the Han Empire by neglecting state affairs and whiling away your time with Wang Zhaojun. If you do not marry him to Wang, he will launch a punitive expedition. Well, that reminds me of King Zhou of the Shang Dynasty, who ruined the nation because of his infatuation with Da Ji, his favorite concubine. Is that not a good warning against us?"

Emperor Yuandi's face almost flushed crimson with anger. "What rubbish is this? How can you compare me to that notorious tyrant? For one thing, I have not depleted national resources to build a pleasure house for my favorite! Why don't you compare yourself with Yi Yin, the capable minister who helped establish the Shang Dynasty? And why don't you emulate Zhang Liang, who achieved great merits in assisting Emperor Gaozu to found our Tang Dynasty? Are you dead to all sense of shame? You enjoy every convenience and luxury in your daily lives—all bestowed upon you by the imperial house! Yet when the northern barbarians come with their ignominious demand, you shrink back in fear, calling on a poor, frail woman to oppose the enemy in your stead! Do you feel no guilt at all for sending her alone to the cold, remote places beyond the northern frontier?"

Wulu Congzong, staggered by the emperor's fury, paused for a moment, then said, "Your Majesty, we don't have enough weapons and armor, nor do we have brave generals to command the troops. How are we able to withstand the attack of

144

the barbarians? What would be the consequences should we lose the battle? Therefore I hope Your Majesty will bear the pain and give away his beloved consort, so that war can be avoided, and the people saved from catastrophe."

Emperor Yuandi remained unwilling, and kept cursing his ministers for letting him down. The court officials, bathed in imperial favor, enjoyed every conceivable luxury under the sun. Each had a group of musicians and dancing girls to amuse him when at home, and each had resplendent clothes and precious adornments to wear when going out. When a border alarm was sounded, however, they all put their hands into their sleeves and keep their mouths shut, not even daring to cough. The emperor was vexed at the thought that Zhaojun, of all people, should have to shoulder the burden of saving the Han Empire. "Why do you bear her such an intense hatred?" he roared at the two ministers angrily. "Otherwise, why would you propose banishing her to the wilderness? Are all the ministers of the court no better than Mao Yanshou? In vain do I have three thousand officials and rule four hundred districts! Where on earth can I find a capable general? Who can share my burden and help me out of this calamity?"

Wulu Congzong fell silent again. "Your Majesty," remarked Shi Xian, "the Hun envoy is still waiting outside!"

"All right. Let him come in."

Hearing the summons, the Hun envoy pranced in with a stately air. Without kowtowing to the emperor, he bawled out in a boorish voice, "I am sent by the great Khan Hu Hanye to notify the Han emperor: Our northern state has always enjoyed a friendly relationship with our southern neighbor thanks to the link of intermarriage. Our chieftain has twice sent men to fetch a princess for his wife, but to no avail. A minister from your southern state, Mao Yanshou, has just presented our Khan with a portrait of a beauty, with whom he is very satisfied. He has sent me to ask Zhaojun to be his wife. Your Majesty is beseeched to grant our request. Otherwise, a million powerful troops from our nation will march south to challenge you. Your Majesty had better send Zhaojun to the north without delay if you want to avoid war."

While the emperor fumed at the menacing words of the Hun envoy, the court officials, who had come at the news, all turned pale with fright. None dared stand out to rebuke the Hun envoy. Emperor Yuandi had no choice but to order the envoy taken to the guesthouse to await a formal reply.

After the envoy left, Emperor Yuandi began to reproach his ministers. "Why did you remain speechless and allow that northern barbarian to act so insolently? Since the barbarian troops have approached the border, all of you, both civil and military officials, should work out a plan together to ward off the enemy and save Zhaojun from marrying that savage chieftain." The ministers, with idiotic looks on their faces, offered no reply. "Come on," urged the emperor, "speak up if you have any suggestions to make! I have no caldron here to boil anyone alive for giving the wrong answer, so what are you afraid of? You dare treat Zhaojun in this way because she is kind and frail. When the iron-handed Empress Lu ruled in the court, which minister dared disobey her! From now on I will have no more use for your services. Instead, I will replace you with a team of beautiful women and rely on them to pacify the empire!"

The court officials, though lacking in practical abilities, displayed unusual accomplishments in cultivating the virtue of patience, for they endured the emperor's abuse with great composure and equanimity. Emperor Yuandi raged and fretted in vain. In the meantime Zhaojun pondered over the situation at hand. The Hun chieftain was unlikely to withdraw his demand. By their silence the court officials had voted in favor of appeasing the Huns by giving them what they wanted. As for Emperor Yuandi, apparently he did not want to give her up, but there was simply nothing at his disposal to prevent the outbreak of war. She decided to sacrifice herself to save the situation. "Your Majesty," she said, "since I have received your unbounded favor, I should be given a chance to offer my service in return. I offer to go beyond the northern frontier and marry the Hun chieftain, so that war can be prevented and our people saved from carnage. The only thing I cannot bear is to be separated from you forever!" She stopped as her voice choked with tears.

"Neither can I bring myself to part with you!" Emperor Yuandi also began to weep.

When Zhaojun expressed her willingness to go, Wulu Congzong looked quite relieved. "Your Majesty," he said, "since Her Ladyship has volunteered to marry the Hun chieftain, you had better send her away without delay to save our nation from calamity!"

Though Emperor Yuandi knew he had no alternative, Wulu Congzong's words still exasperated him. "Maybe I should give you a bonus for acting as matchmaker for the Hun chieftain!" he said sarcastically. Wulu Congzong acted as if he had not heard the remark. "Take the Bright Consort to the guesthouse together with the Hun envoy," Emperor Yuandi ordered. "Tomorrow I will go to the Baling Bridge to see her off."

"Your Majesty must not go there," objected Wulu Congzong. "The barbarians will certainly laugh at us because of it."

Emperor Yuandi flared up in anger. "Why don't you let me do what I want, after I have agreed to your suggestion? I have to go and see her off myself! And I will always cherish you in my memory, my honored ministers, for separating me from my beloved!"

Zhaojun was grieved to find the emperor in such great distress. "Your Majesty," she said tearfully, "though I am willing to go for the sake of the nation, I cannot bear the thought of parting with you!"

"My beloved wife! How will you be able to swallow the unseasoned beef and mutton, or drink the smelly milk?" Emperor Yuandi walked away, covering his face with his hand. Wulu Congzong, Shi Xian, and the other ministers hastily escorted Zhaojun to the guesthouse.

The following day Wang Zhaojun left the guesthouse with the Hun envoy. They went out of the capital and came to the Baling Bridge. Filled with anguish, she had no choice but to accept what fate had in store for her.

Emperor Yuandi called a morning audience at which he announced that whoever came up with a plan to dispel the Huns and save the Bright Consort would be handsomely rewarded. But none of the court officials stood out to claim the reward. "The Hun envoy has already taken leave," a minister remarked. "How can Your Majesty revoke his edict now?" "What would that matter?" Emperor Yuandi retorted. "When a commoner embarks on a long journey he can, if he chooses, come home after going a short distance and put off the trip. Aren't you aware of this folk custom? Why can't my Bright Consort do the same?" However, as no one spoke in favor of this idea, Emperor Yuandi mounted his horse and set out for the Baling Bridge.

Zhaojun, sitting in the bridgehead pavilion, had tears in her eyes at the sight of the emperor galloping toward her. The band began to play a piece of farewell music. "Slow down the music," Emperor Yuandi ordered. "It doesn't matter if you play out of tune. Just make it slow so I can exchange some parting words with my Bright Consort!" The court musicians were eager to comply. The Hun envoy, however, was growing impatient. "It is getting late, Your Majesty. Please let Her Ladyship set out without delay!"

Ignoring the Hun envoy, Emperor Yuandi went up to Zhaojun and took her by both hands. "You are leaving right away. How can I bear this separation? Though you are still here, my heart has flown to the northern frontier to wait there for your arrival!"

"There is no telling when I will meet Your Majesty again after my departure today," said Zhaojun. "Though I belong to the Han palace, pretty soon I will marry into the northern barbarian state. Let me change out of my Han-style clothes." Thereupon she put on a dress brought by the Hun envoy.

Emperor Yuandi gazed sadly at the Han-style clothes Zhaojun had been wearing. Only a few days before, Zhaojun had danced for him in these very clothes, but now the cool autumn wind was blowing away the vestige of their fragrance. And he would return alone to the palace, to her room devoid of all joy. "Zhaojun!" he called out in great agony. "When will you return to your homeland?" Zhaojun could not answer. "Your Ladyship!" the Hun envoy urged. "Let's go! I have waited for over half a day!"

With a deep sigh, Emperor Yuandi bade his beloved farewell. After Zhaojun left, the court officials were evidently relieved, as if a heavy burden had been taken off their shoulders. Looking at the retinue of officials, Emperor Yuandi felt sick to his stomach. "Am I really ruler of the Han Empire? I feel more like a defeated warlord, forced to give his beloved to the victor!" "Your Majesty," Wulu Congzong said, "please don't take this to heart." "What?" Emperor Yuandi glared at the officials. "Just look at you! In peaceful times each regards himself as an indispensable member of the court, a pillar of the nation. At the mere prospect of spears and swords, all of you fall into fright and confusion, anxious to sacrifice my beloved wife to save your neck. Why can't anyone among you act like a man?"

Wulu Congzong chose not to answer the emperor's query, but kept advising him to calm down. "Your Majesty, please refrain from too much grief. Just let her go!"

Emperor Yuandi, aware that he had lost Zhaojun forever, kept casting glances in her direction.

The Hun chieftain was informed that Zhaojun was coming to marry him. Delighted, he headed south with his troops, coming to the Heilong River on the northern border of Han.

Zhaojun, well cared for by the Hun envoy, arrived at the Heilong River after many days of travel. Hu Hanye had a banquet prepared to receive her. When he offered her a cup of wine, Zhaojun did not decline. Cup in hand, she left the seat and walked toward the river. Not knowing what was on her mind, Hu Hanye followed close at her heels. "Your Royal Highness," said Zhaojun, "I will use this cup of wine to bid farewell to the Han court. After that I will follow you north." At this Hu Hanye felt quite relieved.

Zhaojun stepped forth and poured the wine into the river. Turning back, she found the Hun chieftain several steps away. "His Majesty the Han emperor," she prayed silently. "There is no hope for me in this life. Let me be reunited with you in my next life!" Then she threw herself into the river. Stunned, the Hun chieftain lunged forth but failed to catch her. In an instant, Zhaojun was swallowed up in the torrential waters.

The chieftain was filled with dismay and remorse. "What a pity!" he exclaimed. "So Zhaojun was actually unwilling to marry into our northern state. Now that she has killed herself, I end up with nothing but the hostility of the Han Empire." Then it occurred to him that Mao Yanshou was responsible for all this. In a rage he ordered Mao to be tied up and escorted back to the Han court. By this time Zhaojun's body had been found and retrieved from the water. Hu Hanye bade his soldiers bury her by the river.

When news of Zhaojun's death reached him, Emperor Yuandi was so grieved that he did not appear for audiences for many days. He lingered in the rear palace, where many sights stirred memories of his beloved Bright Consort.

Facing south, she poured out a cup of wine to bid her homeland farewell, then threw herself into the river.

One night he lit an incense burner and sat before it, hoping to invoke Zhaojun's spirit by the fragrant smoke. After a while, he grew drowsy and drifted into sleep. Suddenly he saw Zhaojun running into the palace. Panting heavily she said, "Your Majesty, I have run away from the northern barbarians!" Then he saw two Hun soldiers coming after her. Zhaojun moved quickly to duck them and was gone in a flash. Emperor Yuandi woke up with a start, finding to his regret neither Zhaojun nor Hun soldiers. The eunuch waiting on him by the side, sympathizing with the emperor, advised him to take care of himself and not allow distress to harm his health. Emperor Yuandi sighed deeply. "I can't help it! No one can keep from feeling distressed after suffering a bereavement like mine!"

Just then Wulu Congzong came with a message from the Hun chieftain. "Your Majesty, an envoy from the Huns has come and brought Mao Yanshou back. This tragic episode, he said, would not have happened but for Mao's evil attempt to sow discord among our two nations. Now that Zhaojun is dead, the Hun chieftain is willing to make peace with Han." Emperor Yuandi had no intention of maintaining hostilities with the northern state, so he readily agreed to making peace with the Huns. A grand banquet was given in honor of the Hun envoy. In the meantime Mao Yanshou was taken away by palace guards and executed, his head offered in sacrifice to the Bright Consort.

THE TIGER-HEAD BELT

Li Zhifu[*]

In times of war Shanshouma, a battalion commander garrisoned at Jiashan Pass, always bravely charged the enemy at the
head of the one thousand men under his command. During
peaceful intervals, while his battalion tilled the land and
cultivated crops in the fields around their campsite, he would
go on hunting trips with his well-trained eagles and dogs.

The frontier remained peaceful for a long time. One fine
day Shanshouma went out hunting with a few subordinate
officers while his wife, Chacha, and a servant named Liuer
were left at home. Unlike other women, Chacha showed no
interest in pretty clothes and spent little time at her dressing
table. Instead, she enjoyed riding horses, shooting arrows, and
wielding the spear or the sword, which lent her a peculiar
charm. After her husband left, she bade the cooks prepare
some wine and food, for Shanshouma was always very thirsty
and hungry when he returned from hunting. Just then two
guests arrived unexpectedly.

Shanshouma had an uncle named Yinzhuma who lived
with his wife at Bohai Village. Shanshouma lost both his
parents at an early age and was brought up by his uncle and
aunt who treated him like their own son and taught him to
use both the writing brush and the sword. Yinzhuma doted
on his nephew, and Shanshouma treated his uncle with filial

---

[*] Li Zhifu (c. 1271-c. 1320) was a playwright of Nuzhen nationality
in the early Yuan Dynasty. Of the twelve plays he is known to have
written, only *Tiger Head Belt* survives.

153

devotion. However, after Shanshouma was appointed battalion commander in charge of Jiashan Pass, a long distance from Bohai Village, they were separated from one another for five years. The old couple, missing their nephew, at last took the journey to Jiashan Pass. While busying herself to receive the old couple, Chacha sent Liuer away to bring back Shanshouma at once.

Liuer hastened to the hunting ground where he found Shanshouma about to shoot an arrow, with the eagle soaring overhead and the dogs running by his side. "My lord! My lord! Some relatives have come to visit!" Delighted, Shanshouma halted the horse and asked eagerly, "What relatives, Liuer?" Liuer was a trusted retainer who had served in the house for many years. Finding his master in an unusually good mood, he said jokingly, "My lord, they said they are relatives, but I don't know who they are!" Shanshouma began to guess, rolling out many names, but Liuer kept shaking his head in denial. Finally Shanshouma became vexed, muttering to himself, "Could it be my uncle and aunt from Bohai?" Liuer clapped his hands. "Right! Now I remember! It is your uncle and aunt!" Shanshouma at once called off the hunting and galloped back home.

Yinzhuma and his wife sat waiting in the hall for about the time it takes to eat a meal and began to grow impatient. "Why hasn't he come back yet?" they asked Chacha, who sent another household servant to fetch her husband, and then went out to the gate to wait for him.

Shanshouma galloped to a halt before the house, dismounted, and called out, "Where are my uncle and aunt?" He walked into the hall with giant strides and fell on his knees to salute his uncle. Pleased with the respectful air of his nephew, Yinzhuma helped him to his feet. "My dear child! How we have missed you in the past few years! That's why we have come for a visit without being invited!" As Shanshouma recalled how he had been brought up and taught by his uncle and aunt, he was greatly moved that the old couple had come such a long distance to see him. After an exchange of greetings, he bade the servants slaughter a pig and a sheep and the table was laid out for a grand welcoming feast.

While they were chatting away at the table, enjoying their food and wine, a guard came in to report that an imperial envoy had come with the emperor's edict. Shanshouma hastened out to meet the envoy, who read out the edict. The emperor, well pleased with Shanshouma's military exploits in guarding the Jiashan Pass, was promoting him to the rank of admiral and endowing him with a tiger-head gold belt, entitling him to make decisions independently and execute criminals without prior consent from the court. In his edict the emperor also charged Shanshouma with selecting someone to succeed him as garrison commander of Jiashan Pass and receive the plain gold belt he hitherto had been wearing.

The gold belts represented different levels of rank and status by displaying various designs. The gold belt worn by an admiral was decorated with a crouching tiger and embedded with pearls, whereas the one worn by a battalion commander was unadorned. A company commander, on the other hand, wore only a silver belt.

Yinzhuma felt tempted when he learned of his nephew's promotion to admiral and the mandate to choose a successor. "I served the nation wholeheartedly in my youth," he thought to himself, "but I failed to abtain an official rank. Now here is a rare opportunity bestowed by heaven. Why don't I have my wife ask Chacha to persuade my nephew to recommend me for the position of battalion commander? I will have a gold belt to wear and enjoy myself in my later years." When he dragged his wife aside and told her his idea, she expressed her doubts. Aware of his weakness for wine, she feared that he could not be trusted with the responsibility because of his heavy drinking. Beating his chest with his fist, Yinzhuma pledged, "If I am made a battalion commander, I will never touch a single drop of wine!" Finding him so determined, his wife agreed to take up the matter with Chacha.

Chacha, hearing her aunt out, knew at once it was her uncle's idea. As Shanshouma was in a good mood, she mentioned it to him. Shanshouma frowned, looking very grave. "Whose idea is this?" Chacha replied that her aunt had suggested it. Shanshouma hesitated. With his ability, Yinzhuma would make a good commander, but his drinking might bring about a catastrophe. When Chacha said Yinzhuma had pledged to abstain from alcohol if he were made commander, Shanshouma was delighted. Inviting his uncle to come over, he said, "Uncle, you have served the nation in your youth, and fully deserve the position of battalion commander. This gold belt is yours now!" Trying hard not to appear too eager, Yinzhuma received the gold belt. His wife was not a little pleased at the idea that she was now an officer's wife. "Uncle," Shanshouma admonished, "your life won't be the same after you put on this gold belt. In the past you were an ordinary citizen. Now you are an officer responsible for national security. From now on you must not be too fond of wine!" Yinzhuma nodded his head repeatedly. "You can trust me! After I put on this gold belt, I will never touch a drop of wine!" "Uncle," Shanshouma went on, "a son has a chance to display his filial devotion when the family is poor, and an officer has a chance to prove his loyalty to the emperor when the nation is in danger. In return for the favor of His Majesty, you must take every precaution to safeguard the Pass against the enemy!" Again Yinzhuma said aye repeatedly.

Having put everything in order, Shanshouma left with Chacha for Daxing to take office as admiral, while Yinzhuma went back to Bohai Village to pack up.

On his return to Bohai Village, the neighbors came to

congratulate Yinzhuma on his appointment and invite him to several farewell banquets. The celebrations lasted for a dozen days, and the old couple enjoyed themselves immensely. As the date for taking office drew near, Yinzhuma packed up his belongings, said good-bye to relatives and neighbors and embarked on his journey, arriving on time at Jiashan Pass to take over his nephew's old command.

After taking office, Yinzhuma carried out his duties meticulously, patrolling the area in the day and checking the campsite at night. He never dared become slack in his work, and half a year passed without incident.

Now it was autumn. For half a year Yinzhuma dared only sip a little wine surreptitiously now and then, and his guards always pretended they had seen nothing. He began to feel an intense craving to drink wine to his heart's content. In addition, long-time peace along the border also caused him to be less vigilant. When the full bright moon rose on the night of the Midautumn Festival, he had the table laid out with food and wine. Listening to the zither and flutes, with the bright moon in the sky and a sumptuous feast on the table, the old couple had a jolly good time. The table became cluttered with empty dishes and wine cups when a guard entered in great panic. "Bad news, sir! Bad news! Jiashan Pass has been captured by the enemy!" The shock instantly brought Yinzhuma back to sobriety. He neither panicked nor paid any attention to his wife's whimpering, but calmly told the guard to bring his armor and weapons. Shortly after, he galloped off with his troops toward Jiashan Pass.

News of Yinzhuma's drinking bout and the loss of the Pass to the enemy reached the registrar at the admiral's headquarters. The registrar, though aware of Yinzhuma's trespasses with regard to wine, chose to take no action, for he was, after all, the admiral's uncle. But now the situation was very serious. The Pass had been lost because Yinzhuma had treated himself to a feast and failed to patrol the border as required. It would be impossible for the registrar to overlook this incident, and he sent a few guards to bring Yinzhuma back for interrogation.

The troops at Jiashan Pass, made up of brave and strong soldiers picked and trained by Shanshouma, engaged the enemy in a fierce battle at the Pass from night till dawn, finally sending the enemy to their heels and recapturing the people, cattle and horses they had lost. After pursuing the enemy for some distance, Yinzhuma led the troops back. In the jubilant air of victory, all the officers came to congratulate Yinzhuma, who had the table laid out again and treated them to another feast.

Yinzhuma was celebrating the victory with his officers when the guards sent by the admiral's registrar came to arrest him. "How dare you?" roared Yinzhuma angrily. "Don't you know I am the admiral's uncle?" The guards, ignoring his protest, insisted he should go with them. At this, Yinzhuma ordered his soldiers to seize the guards and beat them.

When the guards failed to return for quite a long time, the registrar realized something had gone amiss, so he sent another squad of guards to arrest Yinzhuma. These guards, however, were again overpowered and beaten by Yinzhuma's men.

The third group of guards from the admiral's headquarters brought a thick iron chain, with which they tied Yinzhuma up and dragged him away. Yinzhuma, growing worried, called out to his wife, "It looks very bad! The admiral's office wants to punish me. How can I bear such harsh treatment at my age? Please bring a pot of warm wine with you and come after me!" His wife hastily picked up a pot of wine and headed for the admiral's headquarters.

After listening to the registrar's report, Shanshouma immediately went to hold court in the main hall, flanked on both sides by soldiers carrying sharp swords and heavy sticks. Aware of the admiral's anger, the guards escorting Yinzhuma wanted to return as soon as possible, but Yinzhuma deliberately dragged along in slow steps. The guards, not daring to hit him, urged him to hurry up. "What do I have to fear?" Yinzhuma looked disdainful. "I am the admiral's uncle. What's all this fuss about?"

Shanshouma was getting very impatient when the guards finally arrived with Yinzhuma. Yinzhuma was brought into the hall and the iron chain removed. At the sight of the plain gold belt he was wearing, Shanshouma charged the guards to remove it. Yinzhuma, raging inwardly, stood there without saluting the admiral, who was very much annoyed. "I was appointed admiral by His Majesty to govern this region," he thought to himself. "Though you are my uncle in the family, you are a subordinate officer in the army who must follow orders without fail. You have committed a felony by losing Jiashan Pass to the enemy, but you act as if nothing has happened, without pleading guilty or even kneeling to salute me." He turned to the registrar. "Ask him if he intends to admit his guilt and fall on his knees. If he won't kneel, bring the sticks and break his legs!" When the registrar stepped up to question him, Yinzhuma assumed an arrogant air and flatly refused to kneel. "I am his uncle. How can I kneel to my nephew?" However, when informed that the alternative was a severe beating with the sticks, Yinzhuma fell on his knees while muttering to himself indignantly, "Don't beat me, I am on my knees! What effrontery for you to order your uncle around like this!"

Shanshouma told the registrar to take a written statement to Yinzhuma and have him put his fingerprint on it. With a nonchalant air, Yinzhuma pressed his finger onto the statement, not even looking at it. Then, Shanshouma bade the registrar read it aloud. A detailed description of Yinzhuma's offense, it ran like this: "The garrison commander of Jiashan Pass, Yinzhuma, while drinking wine on the night of the Midautumn Festival, was surprised by the enemy. The Pass was lost, and many people, cattle, sheep and horses were plundered by the enemy. When guards from the admiral's headquarters went to apprehend him, he twice disobeyed. The punishment for such a heavy offense is death." Only then did Yinzhuma finally realize the gravity of the situation, and began to weep in despair. "It's not that I cherish no kinship feelings," said Shanshouma. "However, in the present case, the law of the state and the army takes precedence. Since you were appointed by the imperial court to garrison the Pass, how dare you surrender it to the enemy without a fight? How could you get drunk all day to the neglect of your duties?" The guards were called in to take Yinzhuma away and behead him.

Yinzhuma realized to his utter grief that nothing could save his life. His wife, who had been waiting outside the gate, rushed up to the guards. "Please tarry a moment! I am the admiral's aunt. Let me go in and talk with him." She burst into the hall and threw herself before the admiral. When Shanshouma went up and helped her to her feet, she broke into tears. "Admiral! It's not proper for me to be here, but I must talk to you for the sake of your uncle. As a baby you lost both parents, and it was your uncle and I who brought you up. Though I did not carry you in my womb for ten months, I did nurse you for three years. I always let you have what fine food we had and left the coarse food for myself. Though your uncle has committed a serious mistake, please spare him the sword for my sake and give him a beating with the sticks instead. That would be enough to give him a warning." Shanshouma took pity on her but remained unmoved in his decision. "How can I make you understand the duties of an officer?" he said. "He was entrusted with the task of guarding the Pass against the enemy, but what did he do all day except drink wine and listen to music? What he did is unpardonable!" "Your uncle is advanced in years and getting a little muddle-headed," she pleaded again. "Please let him off this time." Shanshouma disagreed. "My uncle is only sixty. Jiang Ziya did not meet King Wen of Zhou until he was eighty, and yet he was able to achieve great merits afterward. Compared with Jiang, My uncle is a young man. Since he has broken the military law, he cannot be pardoned!"

The old lady left the hall in great disappointment and went straight to the inner room to ask Chacha for help.

After listening to her aunt's tearful complaint, Chacha went at once to the main hall to see her husband. At the sight of her Shanshouma realized what was on her mind. "Chacha!" he bellowed. "What are you doing here?" Startled by the harsh tone of his voice, Chacha nevertheless plucked up her courage to speak out. "I am not fit to come to this place in ordinary times, but today the matter is entirely different. You lost your parents in early childhood. Without your uncle and aunt, you would not have lived to this day, much less achieved any rank and position. How can you have your uncle executed? Can't you pardon him, if only for my sake?" Shanshouma flew into a fury. "How dare you, Chacha, meddle in the affairs of the army? Who told you to do this? Well, from now on no officer will be afraid of breaking the law, for he could always rely on his wife to save him from punishment. What absurdity! Chacha, how did you learn about it so quickly? Who sent you here? Get out at once, otherwise don't blame me for being harsh with you!" Cowering in dismay, Chacha went back to her room. "The admiral is uncompromising," she told her aunt. "I cannot bring him around this time."

The old lady rubbed her hands and stamped her feet in despair. "What can we do? What can we do?" she muttered repeatedly. Just then Yinzhuma hit upon an idea. Looking around, he caught the registrar's eyes and made a bow, begging him to gather the other officers and make them petition the admiral to pardon him.

With Yinzhuma pleading in such humility and despair, the registrar agreed to help. He went out, got hold of the other officers and led them back to the hall, where they knelt before the admiral. The registrar, an experienced man with a ready tongue, spoke for the group. The admiral, he said, showed his loyalty to the emperor by sentencing his uncle to death for drinking while on duty and losing the garrison. However, as he had lost both parents as a child and had been brought by his uncle and aunt, he would be violating the principle of filial piety by executing his uncle. A solution should be found by which the admiral could fulfill his duties both to the emperor and to his uncle.

Shanshouma was not convinced. "He is my uncle, and I am his nephew—this much I cannot deny. But he has committed a serious offense, so I must punish him according to military law despite the kinship between us." His voice rose when he addressed the officers. "Listen, all of you! Though he is a relative of mine, he must be punished by law. Let this be a good example for you. Whoever among you commits an offense will never get away with it!" With a sweep of his hand, he dismissed them.

The registrar went out to see Yinzhuma. "The admiral refused to listen to us! Well, it was your fault after all. Why didn't you set out and attack the enemy after you lost the Pass?" "What an injustice!" Yinzhuma cried indignantly. "Who told you I didn't attack the enemy?" Then he described how he had led the troops to fight the enemy from night till dawn, recapturing the pass and bringing back all the people, cattle, sheep and horses looted by the enemy. Hearing this, the registrar rushed back to the main hall to see Shanshouma.

After hearing the registrar out, Shanshouma conceded

Shanshouma ordered the guards to give his uncle
a hundred strokes of the stick.

that Yinzhuma did not deserve a death sentence since he had recaptured the pass. However, he would not escape unpunished either. The statement of his offense was rewritten and the penalty changed to a hundred strokes of the stick.

Yinzhuma sighed with relief to learn his life was saved, but still felt unhappy about the corporeal punishment. "Though my head won't be cut off, the heavy beating on my bottom will probably be the death of me! What can I do?" Suddenly it occurred to him that he could ask help from a former steward in his house, who was now a trusted follower of the admiral. He sent his wife to find the steward, who readily agreed to help. But Shanshouma not only rejected his request but gave him a beating with the stick.

Yinzhuma was dragged away by the guards. With the registrar supervising the process, the guards began to beat Yinzhuma with thick sticks. Having spent his life in easy circumstances, Yinzhuma could hardly bear the pain. The registrar took pity on the old man and told the guards to stop after thirty strokes. But Shanshouma, who sat watching from a distance, ordered the registrar to go on with the punishment. Thus the guards went on with the beating until the count of one hundred. Yinzhuma moaned in excruciating pain, muttering he wouldn't survive for more than a few days. His wife wept bitterly and tried to comfort her husband while cursing her nephew. After the beating was over, Shanshouma said, "Uncle, you have received the penalty today all because of your overindulgence in wine. You should remember this day if you don't want another beating!" He turned to his aunt. "Tomorrow I will come to your house with a sheep and some wine to comfort my uncle!"

Yinzhuma, carried back to his house, kept swearing at his nephew for his cruelty. He told his wife to close the gate to all visitors while he stayed home nursing his wounds.

The following day Shanshouma bade the registrar prepare

some gifts together with wine and a sheep, and went with Chacha to visit his uncle. They found the gate firmly closed with no one in sight. Aware that his uncle was still furious with him, Shanshouma told a servant to go up and knock on the gate. When the servant knocked and shouted for all his worth without getting any reply, Shanshouma sent the registrar to have a try. The registrar, while knocking on the gate, called out to the old man. "Open the gate and come out! There's something I must tell you!" The gate did not open, but the old man's voice was heard. "I am not opening the gate to anybody!" The registrar threatened that his case was not cleared yet, so he must get ready to stand trial again. The old man remained unmoved. "Maybe you want to give me another hundred strokes of the stick! Whatever you say, I won't open the gate." The registrar did not know what to do next.

This exchange between the registrar and his uncle made Shanshouma quite uneasy. Though he did not regret having acted in the best interests of the country, he was unwilling to have his uncle bear a deep grudge against him. What could he do to alleviate his uncle's anger over the insult of the beating? He must go in and reason with the old man. So he asked his wife, Chacha, to shout at the gate. At Chacha's voice his aunt wanted to open the gate, but Yinzhuma stopped her. "Tell her," he said, "to take me for dead. Why didn't she plead for me yesterday instead of coming today with sweet words?" Shanshouma had no choice but to go up and address his uncle in person. "Uncle, your nephew has come to see you! Open the gate now!" Hearing Shanshouma's voice, his aunt knew it would not be proper to deny him entry, so she ignored her husband's objection and opened the gate. Shanshouma walked in with his company.

As Yinzhuma did not bother to get up from his bed to salute the guests, Shanshouma and Chacha walked up to him and knelt. At this the registrar and all the servants followed suit. Shanshouma apologized profusely to his uncle. "It was your nephew's fault! I have come to apologize to you!" "A good nephew indeed!" said Yinzhuma. "You are not ashamed to meet me, after what you did to me yesterday?" His aunt also blamed Shanshouma for being too severe, saying the punishment had nearly cost the old man his life. Shanshouma listened patiently until they had vented their anger, then said, "Dear uncle and aunt, it isn't that your nephew treated you with severity on purpose. Do you suppose I wasn't aware of uncle's old age? Do you think I was happy to have him beaten? I was merely acting in accordance with military law. Actually, I had nothing to do with the beating."

"What?" Yinzhuma's eyes bulged in disbelief. "You gave your old uncle a beating, and now you deny having anything to do with it?" Shanshouma took out the tiger-head belt and showed it to the old man. "Uncle, I didn't want to have you beaten, but the punishment was meted out according to the military rules inscribed on this belt. Didn't I know you are my father's brother? But how could I disregard the law on account of family relations?" He bade the servants slaughter the sheep and warm the wine. Cup in hand, he and Chacha offered wine to the old couple asking for their forgiveness.

Yinzhuma found his nephew's argument hard to refute. He admitted to himself that the punishment he had suffered was not undeserved. It would be impossible for his nephew to assert authority as admiral if he should bend the law out of personal considerations. The old man's anger subsided. By this time the table had been laid out, so the old couple took the seats of honor and began to enjoy the feast with Shanshouma and Chacha. The registrar also came up to propose a toast congratulating them all on the happy reunion of the admiral's family.

THE MONEY KEEPER

*Zheng Tingyu**

Jia Ren, a native of Caozhou Prefecture, lost his parents as a child and had no relatives to rely on. He could hardly read or write and lacked any practical skills. With no house to live in and no land to cultivate, he took shelter in a broken-down kiln. He became known among the locals as Penniless Jia. Jia Ren was not resigned to living in poverty, but dreamed of making a fortune someday. In the meantime he made a living by doing odd jobs such as carrying goods, building walls, and making bricks. At night he crawled into the kiln to sleep.

One day he went to build a surrounding wall for a local landlord. Working from early morning till noon, he began to feel drowsy, so he slipped into a nearby temple to take a nap. He kept cursing fate for his poverty until he drifted into sleep. The Buddha in the temple, hearing his complaint, summoned his spirit for an interrogation. Jia Ren, whining about his dire circumstances, begged the Buddha to bestow some wealth on him. The Buddha, being infinitely compassionate, took pity on him and sent for the God of Wealth. But the god was reluctant to help, saying that Jia Ren showed no respect for heaven and earth and no filial devotion to his parents, but had intense cravings for wealth and gambling. An evil person like that was destined to freeze or starve to death. But the Buddha expressed a different opinion. Since heaven cared for

---

* Zheng Tingyu was a renowned playwright in the early Yuan Dynasty. The history of his life is unknown. He wrote some twenty-two plays, five of which have survived.

every living thing under it, whether good or evil, it would be no big deal to grant Jia Ren a little wealth. Upon the Buddha's insistence, the God of Wealth agreed to let Jia Ren enjoy wealth for twenty years. But Jia Ren was such a greedy man that the more he got the more he wanted, so he asked the god to allow him ten more years of good luck. But the god refused, declaring that at the end of twenty years the wealth would be returned to its rightful owner. Grunting, Jia Ren woke up.

He looked up and found the sun was setting. He had to hurry back to finish his job, otherwise there would be no meal for him that day. Scrambling to his feet, he went back to the landlord's house. The unusual dream was still clear in his mind as he rammed the earth. Suddenly he heard a clinking sound underneath. Digging deeper, he uncovered a huge stone casket. He looked around warily. It was already dusk, with no one in sight near the courtyard, which happened to border on a stretch of wasteland. Lifting the stone cover, he found it filled with gold and silver ingots. Jia Ren could hardly believe his good fortune. He picked up a few ingots, placed them carefully into a pail, then covered them up with hay and limestone. After that, he put the stone cover back on and covered the casket with earth. At the end of the day he carried the pail back to the kiln. In this fashion he transported the contents of the stone casket to his kiln in just a few days, without anyone's knowledge.

From then on Jia Ren had no more use for the water pail or the mason's float. He moved to nearby Caonan County, had a huge estate constructed, and then opened a pawnshop, a bawdy-house, a flour mill, an oil mill, and finally a wine-shop. In no time he became a famed rich man, with not only money in his pockets but property on both land and water. No one called him Penniless Jia anymore. Instead, he became known as Jia the Miser because of his unusual stinginess. Whenever he paid someone a string of coins, he felt as if one of his tendons were being pulled out. In spite of the wide-spread distaste with which he was regarded, he felt quite pleased with himself as long as he was rich. However, he had no offsprings to inherit the huge fortune he had accumulated. This matter weighed heavily on his mind until he finally decided to purchase a boy to be his adopted son and heir.

Jia Ren mentioned this idea to his household tutor, Chen Defu. A native of Caonan, Chen studied Confucian classics as a small child, but the early death of his parents forced him to give up his studies and make a living. First he worked as a private tutor in a local family, then he was hired by Jia Ren. As Jia was childless, Chen Defu actually had no pupils to teach, but was made to keep the books in Jia's pawnshop and wineshop. When Jia Ren expressed his intention to purchase a son, Chen, who was well acquainted with his master's stinginess, did not take him seriously. However, as he grew older Jia became more and more worried over the lack of an heir and kept urging Chen Defu to inform the waiters in the wineshop of his intention, and told them to keep their eyes open.

It was customary for Chen Defu to go to the wineshop every four or five days and work on the accounts there. One day, when Chen was scheduled to come, one of the waiters got up early in the morning and took out a pot of wine. After offering a cup to the God of Wealth and the God of the Land, he sat down to wait for Chen. He would offer Chen a cup, then place the pot on the counter to serve the day's customers. It was snowing heavily, with few travellers on the road. The waiter looked out of the gate but failed to see Chen. Instead, a couple with a small boy was trudging through the snow toward the shop.

These three people journeying in the inclement weather used to be a wealthy family of Caozhou. The man, Zhou Rongzu, had come into a large inheritance, but finding himself inept at moneymaking, he chose instead to devote himself to study. That year the imperial court held a civil service recruitment examination in the capital. The Zhou family, though not lacking in wealth, did not enjoy high social status, so Zhou Rongzu wanted to go to the capital to try his luck, hoping to pass the examination and obtain an official post, which would bring glory to his ancestors. His wife, Zhang Shi, was a young woman unacquainted with hardship. She insisted on going with her husband so to enjoy the sights of the capital, the dwelling place of the emperor. The couple talked it over and decided to go together. The silver and gold ingots were buried in the backyard, and the house and its furniture entrusted to the household servants. Then, the couple set out for the capital taking their small son, Changshou, with them. As luck would have it, Zhou failed in the examination, and the family returned home in low spirits.

After Zhou's departure his servants loafed on the job and did not take good care of the house. It rained heavily several times until half the backyard wall collapsed. The servants, afraid of being blamed by their master on his return, hired Jia Ren to mend the wall, but Jia ended up stealing the hidden treasure. When Zhou came home with his wife and son, he found the stone casket completely empty. The three of them stared at one another in dismay. Now that all the family's wealth was gone, it soon became hard to make ends meet. It then occurred to Zhou that in the city of Luoyang he had a relative who was fairly well off. So they went to Luoyang, but failed to find the relative before their money ran out and they were forced to return home on foot. That snowy morning they arrived at Caonan County. Shivering with cold and hunger in the heavy snow and fierce wind, they could hardly continue on.

As the boy began to weep from hunger and cold, Zhang Shi asked her husband to find a place where they could take shelter from the snow. Zhou Rongzu peered around and caught sight of the wineshop sign. When the three came to the gate, the waiter greeted them in a cheerful voice. "Hi, come in, scholar, and take a seat. Some wine and food will soon warm you up. Where are you from? Why do you have to travel in such bad weather?" Zhou Rongzu sighed heavily. "Oh, brother! I'm afraid I don't have the money for wine and food! I am just a poor scholar. My family and I left home in search of a relative, hoping to take refuge in his house, but we failed to find him. On our return we were caught in this heavy snow. Now we don't have enough clothes on our back, or much food in our stomach. We have come to your shop just to shelter ourselves from the snow. Please take pity on a poor scholar and let us stay for a while." The waiter, being a kind-hearted man, allowed them to remain in the shop.

The snow grew heavier, and the wind stronger. Inside the wineshop the three travellers still shuddered with cold. Zhou Rongzu pulled Changshou over and pressed his freezing hands to his bosom. The waiter was moved with compassion to find them in such distress. Taking a cup of wine from the altar of the local land god, he offered it to Zhou. After drinking the wine, Zhou felt a surge of warmth all over his body, as if a cotton-padded jacket had been placed on his back. Thereupon his wife and son also begged for wine. The waiter decided to go all the way with his charity and offered each of them a cup. When Changshou's handsome looks caught his eye, he remembered his master's intention to adopt a child, so he advised Zhou to sell his son to save the whole family from starvation. Zhou and his wife talked it over. Although they loved their son dearly, they were indeed unable to support him. So they told the waiter they were willing to sell Changshou. A very wealthy man of the neighborhood, the waiter said, had no child of his own and wanted to adopt a son and heir. Hearing this, Zhou Rongzu comforted himself by saying that at least his son was going to join a good family.

Just then Chen Defu arrived to do the books. The waiter greeted him and told him about Zhou Rongzu and his son. Chen looked Changshou up and down and told Zhou he was quite satisfied. "Mr. Jia, my employer, has lots of money but no offspring. Once adopted by Mr. Jia, your son will inherit all his property." He then took the family to Jia's house.

When Chen Defu entered the house, Jia Ren was munching a frog leg over some wine. At the sight of Chen, Jia Ren again urged him to find a child for him. "I have found a boy for you now!" replied Chen. "Where is he?" asked Jia Ren in surprise, finding Chen all alone. The couple with the boy, Chen said, were waiting outside the gate. "What sort of a man is he?" asked Jia Ren. "A poor scholar." Jia Ren was highly displeased to hear the word "poor." "If he is a scholar, call him a scholar," he said irritably. "Why did you have to use the word poor?" "You are being unreasonable, sir," Chen Defu retorted. "You don't suppose a rich scholar would be willing to sell his own child?" Jia Ren, who had no answer to this, told Chen to bring in the scholar.

Seeing Chen Defu, Zhou Rongzu begged him to try to negotiate a good price for the child. Chen agreed to do his best and led him into the house. After inquiring about Zhou's native place and family name, Jia Ren could find no more questions to ask, but he wanted to put on the airs of a wealthy man, so he turned to Chen Defu and said, "This penniless wretch has lice all over his body. I detest penniless people like him! Tell him to step back!" Zhou Rongzu, already weighed down by his ill fortune, dared not talk back. He walked out, muttering complaints to his wife.

After Zhou Rongzu left the room, Jia Ren said to Chen Defu, "Well, a contract needs to be drafted if I am to purchase his son. I will dictate it to you." Chen Defu spread a piece of paper on the desk and took up the writing brush, then Jia Ren began to dictate. "The signatory of this contract, Zhou, has no money for food or clothing and therefore cannot support himself. For this reason, he is willing to sell his natural son, Changshou, to be the adopted son of a wealthy man, Mr. Jia." "Everyone knows you are a wealthy man!" interrupted Chen. "It would be enough to call you Mr. Jia. Why do you want to write 'wealthy man' into the contract?" Jia Ren flew into a tantrum. "What? Am I a wealthy man or a poor wretch? How dare you insult me in this way?" Chen Defu hastily apologized to his boss, "Of course, my master, you are a wealthy man!" Jia Ren went on with his dictation. "On this day an agreement has been reached by both parties and the witness on the price to be paid. Once this contract is signed, no party shall go back on his word. Otherwise he will be fined one thousand strings of coins, to be paid to the other party. This written statement is proof of the agreement." As Jia Ren failed to specify the price of the child, Chen Defu knew the stingy rich man was playing a trick against the poor scholar, so he tried to argue in a mild tone. "You said the party who breaks his word will be fined one thousand strings, but it is not mentioned in the contract what price will be paid for the boy!" Jia Ren told him to shut up. "That's none of your business! How much can they possibly want? As you said, everyone knows I am a wealthy man! I have only to snap my fingers, and he will have enough money to last him a lifetime!" Chen Defu dared not contradict his enraged boss again. He wrote down all the words dictated by Jia Ren and went out to see Zhou Rongzu, who then copied the contract in his own hand.

Reading over the statement, Zhou Rongzu found the words "wealthy man" a little offensive. "Sir," he muttered after a long pause, "it doesn't seem necessary to write the words 'wealthy man' into the contract!" Chen Defu realized the poor scholar had not detected the rich miser's trick. "That doesn't matter much," he said. "If the master wants it that way, let it be. But there is a very crucial point in the contract. It says here the party who goes back on his word will be fined one thousand strings of coins." Zhou Rongzu suddenly caught on. "Yes! The fine will be one thousand strings for breaking the contract, but how much will I get for the child? It is nowhere mentioned!" Chen Defu then recounted what Jia Ren had told him. "I can't say how much you will get paid. He just said he is a very wealthy man. With a snap of his fingers he could save you from hunger and cold for a lifetime." As Zhou was not an experienced man of the world, he felt reassured and took up the brush to sign when he was stopped by his wife. "Wait a minute! Are we told how much we will be paid?"

Changshou, standing to the side, then learned from their conversation that his parents were about to sell him. He pulled at his father's leg and began to weep. "How can you sell me! I don't want to leave you!" The couple felt sorry for their son. However, Jia Ren was waiting in the hall for the contract. As there seemed to be no alternative, Zhou Rongzu copied the contract in a hurry and handed it to Chen Defu. All three members of the family, holding on to each other's hands, burst out crying.

Chen Defu went in and gave the contract to Jia Ren, who read it out aloud. "The signatory of this contract, Zhou Rongzu, has no money for food or clothing and cannot support himself. Therefore he is willing to sell his natural son, Changshou, who is seven years old, to be the adopted son of the wealthy man Mr. Jia." Jia Ren tweaked at his beard in satisfaction. "Well written! Very well written! Chen, bring in the boy and let me look at him." When Changshou was led into the hall, Jia Ren was pleased to find him quite handsome. "My son!" he said. "From now on you are my son. If people in the street should ask, tell them your family name is Jia." Changshou, in his sullen mood, was unwilling to acknowledge a strange old man as his father. "My family name is Zhou!"

he blurted out. "No, it is Jia!" Jia Ren bellowed, as his face flushed in anger. But Changshou was defiant. "My name is Zhou!" Unable to contain his rage, Jia Ren went up and slapped Changshou across the face. The boy cried out in pain. "Father! He is beating me!" Zhou Rongzu, though grieved to hear his son crying, dared not protest. He wanted to take the money and be done with it quickly. "Mr. Chen!" he called out. "Please send us away now!" Chen Defu also thought he'd better let the child's parents leave as soon as possible, so he told Zhou to wait while he went in to fetch him the money from Jia Ren.

Entering the hall, Chen Defu was about to speak when Jia Ren cut him short. "Has the scholar left? Well, I'll invite you to tea someday!" "What do you mean?" Chen Defu cried in dismay. "How could he be willing to leave? You haven't yet paid him for the child!" Jia Ren's eyes bulged with indignation. "Chen Defu, you are dead to all sense of reason! He has given his son to me because he has no money to raise the child himself. From now on the boy will eat three meals a day in my house. I am so generous that I won't ask him to pay for the food. How can he ask me for money?" Chen was at a loss to know how to cope with such sophistry. He tried to make Jia Ren give some money to Zhou, at least some traveling fare so they could get home. But Jia Ren would not make any concession. "Chen Defu! If he should refuse to sell his child now, he would be guilty of violating our contract. Give the boy back to him and let him pay me one thousand strings of coins for a fine!" Chen Defu was so indignant that he talked back to his boss. "Why should he pay you a thousand strings? It's you who should pay him some money!" Jia Ren found it unbearable that his tutor should speak in favor of the poor scholar. "Chen Defu!" he said harshly. "I don't think that scholar is so audacious as to ask money from me! You must be playing a trick against me!" "What you say is utterly groundless!" Chen Defu replied, not at all intimidated.

With great reluctance Jia Ren finally agreed to pay "one precious string of coins" as the price for the boy. When Chen Defu declared the sum too small, Jia Ren argued that it was quite enough. "You must not underestimate its value. Can't you see the word 'precious' engraved on every coin? Of course, it wouldn't cause you any heartache to see me losing money! For me, to part with a string of coins is like having one of my tendons pulled out. I can recover from the loss of a tendon sooner or later, but the loss of a string of money will give me everlasting pain! All right, here is the money. If he is a true scholar, maybe he will decline to accept it." Chen Defu took the string of coins and went out to give it to Zhou Rongzu. Seeing the money, Zhang Shi exclaimed in despair. "How can he pay one string for my son? The sum is barely enough to buy a child made of clay! Though I am a poor scholar, how can he look down on me like this! What's the worth of a string of money?" Zhang Shi said tearfully that she wanted her son taken back from the miser. In sympathy with the couple, Chen Defu told them to wait while he went in to reason with Jia Ren.

Entering the hall, he hurled the money back at Jia Ren. "They give the money back to you!" Jia Ren was very pleased. "What did I tell you, Chen Defu? I knew they wouldn't take it!" "It's not that they wouldn't accept money for the child," said Chen Defu. "They found one string too small. It would not be enough to buy a pottery child, let alone a human one." Jia Ren disagreed. "Does a pottery child have to eat three meals a day? Chen, haven't you heard the saying, 'No matter how much money you have, you should not buy a voracious child.' How ridiculous for them to want more money! Oh, I know, you must be instigating them!" Choked with indignation, Chen Defu stood there and refused to go until he got more money. At last Jia Ren produced another string of coins.

Jia the Miser shoved Zhou Rongzu into the snow, cursing loudly.

Chen Defu asked Jia Ren to advance him two strings of money against his salary, then he went out. Taking the four strings of coins, Zhou Rongzu thanked Chen for his kindness and began to curse Jia Ren. A miser like Jia Ren, he said, would someday grow carbuncles and contract febrile diseases, and his house would burn to the ground, leaving him a beggar. Hearing this, Jia Ren went out and shoved Zhou Rongzu, sending him sprawling. "You low-down knave! Get lost this minute! Don't show up again, or I will set my dogs on you!" Chen Defu persuaded Zhou Rongzu and his wife to leave the house before they got hurt.

Jia Ren was immensely pleased with the transaction. "Mr. Chen," he said, "thank you so much for your help. I would like to invite you to some wine, but unfortunately I am fully occupied now. Well, in the rear hall you will find a pancake left in the food box. You can take it for a light refreshment." Chen Defu, however, did not accept this gift. Utterly disgusted with Jia Ren's behavior, he subsequently left the house and opened a small drugstore of his own.

For the next twenty years Changshou was raised as Jia Ren's son. Memories of his early childhood gradually grew dim. As his foster father was immensely rich, he became known in the neighborhood as Master Rich. However, Master Rich was far from happy, for he had to wring every cent he needed from his father's tight fist. Then Jia Ren fell ill and became confined to bed. He could no longer attend to family business himself, much to the relief of Changshou.

One day Changshou told Jia Ren that he needed some money for a trip to the Temple of the God of Mount Taishan in Taian to redeem a vow. Jia Ren never liked his son's careless attitude toward money. But as he had no one else to rely on now that he was bedridden, he adopted a mild tone to admonish Changshou. "My son! Let me tell you how I fell ill. A couple of days ago I felt a great craving for roast duck, so I went in the shop intending to buy a leg. The duck was quite oily and smelled very inviting, but my heart ached at the thought of the precious money it would cost me. Well, I went over and clenched the duck with my hand, so that my thumb and fingers were all smeared with duck oil. Wouldn't that taste just as good as the duck itself? Why should I have to spend my precious money then? When I returned home to have my meal, I ate one bowl of rice after licking one finger, and in this way I ate four bowls of rice at one go, leaving the oily thumb for supper. But that confounded house dog licked my thumb clean when I nodded off on the bench! I was so grieved at the waste that I fell ill."

Listening to this story, Changshou didn't know whether to feel amused or disgusted. He advised his father not to take such a thing to heart, saying a wealthy man like him need not live in such hardship. Heaving a deep sigh, Jia Ren said, "You are probably right. Since I am dying, I might as well spend some money to enjoy myself. My son, go and buy one cent worth of tofu for me. I'll treat myself to a feast!" As he knew one cent could only buy half a cake of tofu, Changshou told Xing'er, the errand boy, to buy one string of tofu instead. Overhearing this, Jia Ren cried out in alarm, and Changshou had to call the boy back and tell him to spend no more than ten cents. Xing'er returned with only five cents worth of tofu, all that was left in the tofu shop. He mentioned that he left the other five cents at the shop and would settle the account next time he went there. "What's the name of the shop-keeper?" Jia Ren asked hastily. "Who is the neighbor to his left, and who is the neighbor to his right?" Puzzled, Chang-shou asked why he should want to known anything about the shopkeeper's neighbors. "If he should move away suddenly, how would I get my five cents back?" explained Jia Ren. Changshou then told his father he really worried too much.

While drinking the tofu soup, Jia Ren asked, "My son, if the worst should happen to me, how would you arrange my funeral?" Changshou replied without hesitation, "I would buy you a coffin made of cedar wood." Jia Ren was very displeased. "My son, never buy that kind of thing! Cedar wood is too expensive. Do you suppose a dead man can tell the difference between cedar wood and willow wood? There is a horse manger in our backyard. That will be good enough for the purpose." When Changshou asked in dismay how his body could be placed in the manger, which was very small, Jia Ren scolded him for being dull-witted. "Nothing can be easier than this! Though the manger is not long enough, you can make me shorter, can't you? Take an axe and chop me apart in the middle. Then I will fit nicely into the manger." Changshou's jaw dropped in disbelief, but Jia Ren had not yet finished. "My son, there is one more thing you must remember. Don't use our own axe to do the job. Borrow an axe from the neighbor." Seeing the blank look on Changshou's face, Jia Ren explained, "My bones are very hard, you know. If you use our own axe, the blade would probably be damaged, then you would have to spend a few cents to repair it. That would be too much of a waste." Changshou no longer wanted to stay by his father's bed listening to his ghastly calculations, and again asked for some money for the visit to the temple. Grumbling, Jia Ren finally yielded. "All right, I'll let you take three strings. No more than three!" Xing'er, who was standing aside, gave Changshou a wink, and the two left the room. "Why do you have to listen to the old man's blabbering?" said Xing'er. "You can go straight to the storeroom, take ten gold ingots, ten silver ingots and a thousand strings of coins, and spend them all on the trip!" Changshou thought it a great idea. So he went to the storeroom, took the money, and left for Taian accompanied by Xing'er.

They arrived at the temple in the evening and found the

place overcrowded, with people coming from everywhere to burn incense and redeem vows, for the next day happened to be the birthday of the God of Mount Taishan. There was hardly space to plant one's feet in the temple. Catching sight of a nice spot occupied by an old beggar couple who had come earlier, Xing'er went over and drove them away. Thus Changshou and Xing'er were able to spend the night in the temple. The following morning Changshou burned incense and prayed for the recovery of his father. The old beggars also burned incense and asked the God to bless their son with good health.

Changshou returned home to find his prayer unanswered, for Jia Ren was already dead. The old beggar couple, after leaving the temple, also went to Caonan County. When they passed before the wineshop, the old woman was suddenly seized by an intense heartache. Her husband helped her sit down on the ground and went in to ask the waiter for a cup of wine to warm her up. When he learned the old woman was suffering from heartache, the waiter told the old man that medicine for treating acute attacks of heartache was being handed out for free at the drugstore across the street; that would be more effective than a cup of wine.

The owner of the drugstore was none other than Chen Defu. When the old beggar came to the drugstore, Chen doled out some medicine for him. "Its effectiveness is guaranteed," he promised, "and you don't have to pay for it. If your wife gets well, just tell people Chen Defu has done a good deed." That name rang a bell for the old couple. Searching his memory, the old beggar suddenly realized Chen was the witness when he sold his son. When he introduced himself as Zhou Rongzu, Chen Defu gazed at the old couple for a long time until he finally recognized them. Since Jia Ren was dead, Chen Defu immediately went and introduced Changshou to his natural parents. When Changshou knelt to salute his

Changshou knelt upon being reunited with his parents.

parents, the old couple broke into tears, torn between joy and grief.

Remembering the kindness with which he had been treated by Chen Defu and the waiter in the wineshop, Zhou Rongzu bade his son reward them handsomely. He also told Changshou that, living in poverty for the past twenty years, he had often cursed rich people for their greed and cruelty. Now that he was rich himself, he would rather share his wealth with the poor and needy than arouse their hatred by being mean and callous. Though brought up by Jia Ren, Changshou did not share his foster father's attitude toward money. He therefore had no difficulty following his natural father's instruction, spending money to help the poor in the county. Many people thought it a good joke that Jia the Miser had turned out to be a slave, taking care of other people's money for the last twenty years of his life.

THE ZHAO ORPHAN

*Ji Junxiang**

During the Spring and Autumn Period, Duke Ling ruled
the state of Jin. Under this fatuous ruler, upright officials were
persecuted while treacherous sycophants gained power and
prestige at court. Duke Ling led a life of luxury and dissipation
and cared not at all about the welfare of the common people.
He had a high tower built in his palace which he sometimes
ascended to amuse himself by shooting passers-by outside the
palace walls with his slingshot. At court, the civil officials
were headed by Zhao Dun, while Tu Anjia was the leading
military man. Zhao Dun worked piously to make his nation
strong and prosperous. Whenever the duke did something at
the expense of the common people, such as building a high
tower from which to shoot people for fun, Zhao would openly
protest. The duke, therefore, did not like him. Tu Anjia, on
the other hand, often abetted the duke in his villainous
conduct. He regarded Zhao Dun as his arch enemy and tried
every way possible to get rid of him.

On one occasion, Tu Anjia hired a brave warrior named
Chu Ni to assassinate Zhao Dun. Chu Ni came to Zhao's
residence at night, dagger in hand. He leapt over the wall,
landed in the courtyard soundlessly, and hid himself behind
a big tree. After a while he saw Zhao Dun come out of the
studio to burn incense in the court while praying for the

---

* Ji Junxiang was a contemporary of Zheng Tingyu, but little else
is known about his life. He wrote six plays, of which only *The Zhao
Orphan* has survived.

everlasting prosperity of the state of Jin. "How can I act against the will of heaven by killing a man so devoted to his nation? But if I don't kill him, how can I escape from the persecution of Tu Anjia, who is extremely cruel and merciless?" Chu Ni thought hard but could find no way out, so he committed suicide by smashing his head against the tree trunk.

Tu Anjia did not give up after this aborted attempt. Soon after, an envoy from a neighboring state brought Duke Ling the gift of a very large and fierce dog called the divine hound. Duke Ling gave the dog to his favored minister, Tu Anjia, who found a special use for it. First he locked up the dog in an empty room for several days without feeding it. The dog leapt and howled in hunger. In the meantime he had a scarecrow made and dressed to the exact likeness of Zhao Dun: a purple robe fastened by a jade belt, a pair of black boots, and an ivory writing tablet in its hands. Sheep heart and lungs were also stuffed inside the chest of the scarecrow. The dog was then freed and led to the scarecrow. The famished dog leapt and barked at the smell of mutton. The instant the servant unfastened the chain, the dog threw itself on the scarecrow, bit into the purple robe, and grabbed the sheep heart and lungs out for a good feast. After that, Tu Anjia trained the dog in this manner many times, for a hundred days.

At an audience with the duke, Tu Anjia remarked that the divine hound, after being carefully trained, could now recognize disloyal and unfilial people. Delighted, Duke Ling told the court officials that in the time of the ancient sage kings there had been a divine animal capable of recognizing evil people. Now that he himself had such a dog, he would like to test its ability at once. So he ordered Tu Anjia to walk the dog around the court officials. When the famished dog was brought in, Zhao Dun was standing next to the duke, dressed in a purple robe and jade belt. At the sight of Zhao Dun, the dog leapt on him, eager to enjoy its usual feast. Zhao Dun dodged by moving around the pillars, with the dog close at his heels. This so enraged Ti Miming, head of the imperial guards on duty, that he lifted his hammer and knocked the dog to the ground. Grasping it by the legs, he tore the dog apart and hurled it out of the palace gate.

Zhao Dun, leaving the palace, ran toward his carriage only to find two of the four horses missing and one of its two wheels gone. Apparently Tu Anjia had thought of everything. Zhao Dun mounted the carriage and tried in vain to drive away. At this critical moment a hefty man appeared who, with one hand lifting one side of the carriage and the other goading the horses, was able to get the carriage moving.

Thus Zhao Dun was able to make his escape from the palace. But who was the man who rescued him? Actually, Zhao Dun had met him once previously. It had been a spring day and Zhao Dun was on a tour of the countryside to inspect the progress of farming, when he noticed a big man lying motionless with his mouth wide open under some mulberry trees. Surprised, Zhao Dun went up to ask why he was acting that way. The man introduced himself as Ling Zhe. He had just been driven out by his employer, who appreciated his strength but couldn't bear having him eat enough for several men. Though hungry, he didn't want to pick mulberries from the trees for fear he would be accused of stealing. So he chose to lie under the trees, his open mouth awaiting berries to fall right into it by chance. He would rather die of hunger than be accused of stealing. After hearing him out, Zhao Dun thought Ling Zhe a man of courage and character, so he bade the servants give him a good meal with wine. After eating his fill, Ling Zhe wiped his mouth and walked away without a word. Expecting nothing in return for his gesture of kindness, Zhao Dun did not take offence at this seeming ingratitude.

His judgment of the man's character proved sound, as Ling Zhe later repaid his kindness by rescuing him at the risk of his own life.

Enraged by Zhao Dun's escape, Tu Anjia told Duke Ling that the entire Zhao family was treacherous and must be eliminated. Duke Ling, a fatuous ruler if there ever was one, believed whatever Tu said. Tu was thus put in command of a squad of troops to surround and ransack Zhao Dun's residence. Over three hundred people of the Zhao clan were thus wiped out. The only one who escaped the massacre was Zhao Dun's son, Zhao Shuo. As Duke Ling's son-in-law, he lived in the residence with his wife, the princess. Determined to kill the Zhao clan to the last man, Tu Anjia finally decided to eliminate Zhao Shuo by fabricating an edict from the duke.

Though he was the duke's son-in-law and a high-ranking officer, Zhao Shuo sensed that his life was in imminent danger after the disaster visited upon his family. He told his wife, who was many months into pregnancy, of his worries. Should she give birth to a son, she must name him "the Zhao orphan" and bring him up properly until the day he would avenge the Zhao family. Deeply grieved, the princess gave her promise.

The young couple was interrupted by the arrival of an envoy dispatched by Tu Anjia. The envoy entered the main hall and ordered Zhao to kneel while the fake edict was read out. "The Zhao family has been wiped out for their treacherous, unfilial, dishonest and unlawful acts. Considering his relationship with the ruling clan, Zhao Shuo is exempt from spilling his blood on the execution ground. Instead, he is presented with a bow and arrow, a bottle of poisoned wine, and a dagger, from which he may choose one to end his life. The princess will henceforth remain in her residence, prohibited from any contact with her relatives and friends." The envoy, having read the edict, felt sorry for its recipient, but duty compelled him to urge Zhao Shuo to take his life without delay.

Just then the princess, who had hidden herself outside the hall, overhearing everything, burst into the hall in tears. The sight of his grief-stricken wife added to Zhao Shuo's rage over the enormity of the injustice. It was incredible that as the duke's son-in-law he could not even save his own life. In a burst of indignation he blurted out to the envoy, "My family served the sovereign heart and soul, and ended up being wiped out to the last man; but Tu Anjia, a most wicked man and the scourge of the nation, lives on in wealth and honor! That is what we get in return for our loyalty and devotion!" The princess, standing helplessly by her husband's side, could only weep and curse Tu, their persecutor. After she affirmed her promise to carry out his instruction, Zhao Dun took up the dagger brought by the envoy and cut his own throat. With a loud scream the princess passed out.

When the envoy returned, Tu Anjia made him tell every detail of what had taken place, and was alarmed when he learned of the princess's pregnancy. Didn't that mean the Zhao family still had an heir? He immediately sent some men to keep a close watch over the princess's residence.

Soon afterwards the princess gave birth to a boy, whom she named "the Zhao orphan." When the news reached Tu Anjia, he realized at once that Zhao Dun must have left her a will before his death. As Duke Ling might want to take a look at his grandson, Tu thought it inexpedient to murder the baby at once. He would have to wait for at least a month before taking action. However, someone might try to smuggle the baby out during this time. Tu thus ordered Han Jue, a junior general, to encircle the princess's house with his troops and thoroughly search everyone leaving. If anyone should be discovered trying to smuggle the baby out of the house, his entire family, including all relatives, would be beheaded. This order was carried out without delay. The house became so closely surrounded that not even a drop of water could leak out unnoticed.

The princess knew she must bring up her child so that one day he could avenge the annihilation of the Zhao family and rid the nation of that scourge, Tu Anjia. However, since the baby was not safe with her, she had to consign him to a family she could trust. But the house was heavily guarded by Han Jue's men. Moreover, where could she find someone with whom to entrust the orphan? After much deliberation, she decided on Cheng Ying, a private physician who had been a trusted advisor to her late husband. Cheng was so close to the family that he could almost be regarded as one of its members. He had not been included in the death roll during the massacre merely because his family name was Cheng instead of Zhao. The princess, having reached her decision, sent a servant to fetch Cheng, saying she needed herbal medicine to restore her health after childbirth. Cheng arrived at once and was received into the hall.

The princess, informed of Cheng's arrival, had him brought to a small studio where he found her in tears, her face covered in both hands. When he went up and began to inquire after her illness, she sighed deeply. "What cruelty the Zhao family has suffered!" Startled, Cheng hastily looked around the room, and was relieved to find no one in sight. The princess, after describing how the Zhao family had been persecuted by Tu Anjia, begged Cheng Ying to take the baby out of the house and entrust him to a dependable family, where he could be brought up and someday avenge the wrongs committed against his family. Cheng Ying, a man of high moral integrity and a strong sense of justice, held Zhao Shuo in high esteem and destested Tu Anjia for his misdeeds. But the task the princess put in his hands was so weighty as to make him think twice. "You may not be aware of this," he said, "but Tu Anjia knows about the birth of the Zhao orphan and has taken precautions. Your house is surrounded by troops, and notices are posted at the four city gates warning against any attempt to save the baby; punishment for the offender is elimination of his entire clan. How can I possibly smuggle the baby out under such circumstances?" The princess threw herself to the ground and begged him to save the child in the name of righteousness. "Cheng Ying! In times of emergency one thinks of his relatives, and in times of danger one places hope in old friends! By rescuing this baby you will save the Zhao family from extinction. Please take pity on the three hundred people of the Zhao family who all came to such a miserable end! The Zhao orphan is our only hope to avenge this gross injustice!"

Hastily, Cheng Ying went up and helped the princess to her feet. He told her his fear that should the secret leak out, whatever he did would be in vain. "Suppose I succeed in carrying off the baby. When Tu Anjia comes to seize it, you will probably reveal my name under torture. My entire family would then be eliminated, but the worst thing is that the baby would not survive after all." The princess realized Cheng Ying had doubts about her ability to keep this secret and decided to sacrifice herself to save the baby. "You don't have to worry on that account, Cheng Ying. I have the solution for it!" Her voice was choked with tears. After a pause, she went on. "Remember to tell the baby that his father was persecuted and killed by the archvillain Tu Anjia, and his mother died soon afterwards." She handed the sleeping baby to Cheng Ying. Then she hanged herself.

Despite his grief, Cheng Ying made no attempt to stop the princess. He opened his medicine chest, put the baby inside, placed some herbs on top, then closed it. With the chest on his back, he said a pray to heaven, then turned to whisper, "Little baby, on no account must you make any noise!"

Cheng Ying walked out of the gate and saw sentries and

patrols all over the place. His steps became a bit irregular as he was seized by fright. Han Jue, the junior general, spotted him at once and ordered a guard to bring him over. "Who are you?" he demanded. "Where are you coming from?" "I am Cheng Ying, a private physician," Cheng was able to reply in a calm voice. "I went to the princess's house to prescribe and stew some herbs for Her Highness."

"What was your prescription?"

"Nourishing soup for childbirth."

"What is in this chest you are carrying?"

"Nothing but raw herbs."

"What raw herbs?"

"Well, things like roots of balloon flower, licorice, and peppermint."

"Anything else?"

"None."

"In that case, you may leave," said Han Jue.

Greatly relieved, Cheng Ying walked on toward the gate. He was so eager to get out that he quickened his steps without realizing it. Han Jue, who had been watching him closely, called out behind him. "Come back, Cheng Ying! Tell me again what is in your chest!" Cheng Ying walked back to the general and insisted he was carrying nothing but raw herbs. He denied having anything else hidden in the chest. "All right, I'll let you go then." Han Jue said.

Cheng Ying was about to step out of the gate when Han Jue called out again. "Hey, Cheng Ying! There's something strange in your behavior! When I let you go, you scurried off like an arrow leaving the bow. When I called you back, you moved as if you were dragging your feet through mud. Something must be wrong here!" Panic-stricken, Cheng Ying was at a loss what to do. "Cheng Ying, do you think I don't know you?" Han Jue went on. "You were an honored guest of Zhao Dun. As a general serving Minister Tu, I will not let you get away with the Zhao orphan!" Cheng Ying was struck speechless with terror.

After sending away his soldiers, Han Jue beckoned Cheng Ying to him. Making sure that no one was around, he lifted the cover of the chest. "You only mentioned the roots of balloon flower, licorice, and peppermint, but I've found ginseng in here!" Cheng Ying dropped to his knees, trembling in fear. Taking no notice of him, Han Jue gazed at the baby lying all crumpled in the small chest, its forehead covered in sweat and its eyes gazing back at him. Han Jue could not help feeling sorry for it, and for the Zhao family. Though he was under the command of Tu Anjia, he had no sympathy for Tu's evil deeds, especially his ruthless persecution of the Zhao family. In his opinion, only by employing loyal ministers like Zhao Dun and dispelling evil men like Tu Anjia could the state of Jin maintain its newly attained stature among the rival nations. The duke, however, was ruining his state by acting to the contrary. When he received orders to surround the princess's residence, Han Jue had then decided to act according to his conscience.

While Han Jue was thus lost in thought, Cheng Ying kept begging for mercy on his knees. Having made up his mind, Han Jue told Cheng to stop blabbering. "Cheng Ying, I suppose you received much favor from the Zhao family." Cheng Ying believed Han was going to take the baby to Tu Anjia in return for a handsome reward. "Yes, I received much favor from the Zhao family," he replied. "I am only too glad to have a chance to pay them back!" Han Jue knew he had been misunderstood, but he had no time for a lengthy explanation. "Cheng Ying, I will give you the chance to repay the kindness you received. Take the orphan away! As for Tu Anjia, I'll cope with him." Though surprised, Cheng Ying did not delay by asking questions, but took up the chest and left without a word. After a few steps, he returned and knelt again

Sending the soldiers away, Han Jue went up to
search the casket himself.

before Han Jue. "What's this about?" asked Han in surprise. "Didn't I promise to let you go? Do you think I was making fun of you? Leave here at once!" Cheng Ying expressed his gratitude and stood up to go. But again he returned after taking a few steps to kneel before Han Jue. Irritated, Han began to rebuke him. "If you are a coward, why should you try to save the orphan in the first place? If you are afraid of danger, why should you try to prove yourself a true friend of the Zhao family?" Then Cheng Ying expressed his worries. He was afraid that Tu Anjia would soon learn of his escape and send troops in pursuit. Han Jue realized what Cheng was driving at. "Cheng Ying, you want to save the orphan because you were Zhao Dun's friend, but I am no friend of Tu Anjia and have no intention of acting on his behalf. Why should I compromise myself for his sake? As you are loyal to your friend, so am I true to my word. As you are willing to risk your life, so am I ready to cut my own throat. Now you must leave at once with the baby. Take him away to the remote mountains, where you can bring him up, teach him both the letters and the art of war, so that one day he will lead troops to eliminate the scourge of our nation. Cheng Ying, your secret is forever safe with me!" He then drew his sword and cut his own throat.

Deeply moved, Cheng Ying nevertheless did not take a second look at the general but left at once carrying his medicine chest. Approaching the city gate, he saw a crowd gathering around an official notice posted on the wall. After Cheng Ying left the princess's house, Han Jue was found dead by his soldiers who reported the news to Tu Anjia at once. From the deaths of both the princess and the junior general guarding her house, Tu deduced that the orphan must have been taken away. There was no time to lose. At his order, official notices were put out at the four city gates and all over the city, stipulating that all babies between one month and six months old must be taken to his residence. Whoever dared disobey would have his entire family eliminated. As for the babies thus collected, Tu planned to kill every one of them. Only then could he ensure the death of the Zhao orphan, who would otherwise grow up to become his worst enemy. "What a vicious man!" exclaimed Cheng Ying on reading the notice. Then he hastily put his hand over his mouth, for fear someone might hear him. After some consideration, he went out the city gate and headed for Peace Village.

One of the residents of Peace Village was Gongsun Chujiu, a retired minister who had served in the court together with Zhao Dun and Tu Anjia. An honest and upright man, he was a thorn in the side for Tu Anjia, but was widely respected among his peers. Advanced in years and dissatisfied with Tu's behavior, he resigned from his post and returned to live in his home village. Cheng Ying and Gongsun Chujiu, who became acquainted in Zhao Dun's house, regarded one another as trustworthy friends.

Cheng Ying had come to the village to entrust the baby to the old man, but he acted with great caution. Before calling on Gongsun Chujiu, he found a deserted shed in which he hid the medicine chest. Gongsun Chujiu went to the door to receive Cheng Ying. After an exchange of greetings, he began to inquire about the latest news at court. Cheng Ying mentioned a few things, then changed the topic to the Zhao family. Apparently Gongsun Chujiu still believed that, all the members of the family had been killed, and knew nothing about the newborn baby. "The Zhao family has an offspring!" Cheng Ying told him. Greatly excited, Gongsun Chujiu wanted to know more about the boy--whether he had been rescued, and where he was hiding. Convinced of his old friend's sincerity, Cheng Ying came out with the whole story. Afraid that the baby might come to harm, Gongsun Chujiu urged Cheng Ying to take him to the shed, where they found the chest and brought it back to the house. Gongsun Chujiu sent away the servants and, opening the chest, found the baby inside, sound asleep. As he stood gazing at the child, events of the past few years raced across his mind: the confusion at court, the general decline of the state, and his failure to redress the situation due to his old age and lack of power. Heaving a deep sigh, he told Cheng Ying to take good care of the orphan and bring him up properly, so that one day he could take revenge on Tu Anjia and rid the nation of this evil man.

Cheng Ying found it necessary to inform Gongsun Chujiu of the imminent danger the orphan was facing, describing the notices Tu Anjia had posted all over the city. "I have brought the orphan here to hide him in this village in order to repay the kindness I received from Mr. Zhao and also to save the lives of all those innocent babies of our nation. My son, who is about a month old, can pass for the Zhao orphan. I need you to go and tell Tu Anjia that I have the Zhao orphan with me. That villain will then have me and my son seized and executed, and think the matter closed. In this way you will be able to bring up the orphan and have him avenge his parents one day. Don't you think this a brilliant idea?"

Though deeply moved, Gongsun Chujiu did not seem to find the idea brilliant. "How old are you?" he asked abruptly. "I am forty-five," replied Cheng Ying. "Why?" "It will take twenty years for this baby to grow up and avenge his parents. You will be sixty-five by then. But I am seventy years old already. You don't suppose I can live to ninety? Since you are willing to sacrifice your own son, bring it here. Then you must go and accuse me of hiding the Zhao orphan. Tu will then come and have your son and I killed. After that, you can carry the orphan away and bring him up in a remote place. That is what I call a reliable plan!" Cheng Ying conceded that the plan was indeed superior to his and would better ensure the proper upbringing of the orphan; however, it would mean the death of the old minister. His mind made up, Gongsun Chujiu refused to listen to Cheng's objection. Struck by the old man's earnestness and determination, Cheng Ying finally agreed to go along with him.

Having reached a decision, they sank back to their seats for a rest. Only then did Cheng Ying notice how old and decrepit Gongsun Chujiu looked, and a sense of doubt emerged in his mind. "Old minister, there is something else I am worried about," he remarked. Gongsun Chujiu asked hastily what it was. "Well, after I have denounced you to Tu Anjia, he will place you under torture to make you own up your accomplices. At your age, how will you be able to endure the torture? If you should succumb to it and name me, my son and I will die a worthless death, the Zhao orphan will be seized and killed, and you will suffer great pain to no purpose." The old man's face became grave. "Listen to me," he said solemnly. "My promise is as good as gold. I will stick to it even if they should throw me onto a hill of daggers. You only have to concern yourself with how to protect the orphan and bring him up." Fully reassured, Cheng Ying left the village and walked briskly home with the medicine chest on his back.

With the Zhao orphan safe at his own house and his son taken to Gongsun Chujiu, Cheng Ying presented himself at Tu Anjia's residence. Tu immediately had him brought into the main hall and ordered him to introduce himself and reveal the whereabouts of the orphan. "I am Cheng Ying, a private physician. The orphan is hidden in Gongsun Chujiu's house at Peace Village." When asked how he learned this, Cheng replied that during a visit to Gongsun Chujiu, whom he had met once before, he had been surprised to find a baby lying in a brocade mosquito net in the bedroom. "I didn't think the baby could possibly belong to Gongsun Chujiu, an old man past seventy. So I asked him if it was the Zhao orphan, the baby our admiral was looking for? His countenance changed at once and he refused to answer me. That's how I came to discover the Zhao orphan." When Cheng Ying finished speaking, Tu Anjia stared at him savagely. "Shut up, you knave!" he roared. "How dare you play such a low trick in front of me? Why have you come to accuse that old man, with whom you have never had a quarrel? What exactly is your motive? Speak the truth and you live; tell a lie, and you are as good as dead!"

Cheng Ying was well prepared for this outburst. "It is true that I bear no personal grudge against Gongsun Chujiu. However, by your order, baby boys all across the nation will be taken to your house and possibly killed there. I want very much to save these babies, and in particular my own. At forty-five, I have just had my firstborn. If it should be taken away from me, I would be left without an heir, and the Cheng family would become extinct. I told myself that the admiral merely wants to take the Zhao orphan's life. If the orphan could be found, the other babies, including my own, would surely be spared. Therefore I have rushed here to report to you as soon as I found out the orphan was in that village." Tu Anjia found this explanation quite convincing. Summoning some troops, he set out at once for Peace Village with Cheng Ying leading the way.

After Cheng Ying's departure, Gongsun Chujiu disposed of business in the household and prepared for his arrest. He did not have to wait long. A few hours later the village was suddenly surrounded by troops. When he saw Cheng Ying leading Tu Anjia toward the house, Gongsun Chujiu acted as if he had not seen them at all. Furious at the old man's insolence, Tu Anjia ordered his guards to seize him and bring him over. "Are you aware of your guilt?" Tu demanded harshly. Gongsun Chujiu replied he had no idea what the admiral was talking about. Tu smiled coldly. "How dare you act against my order by hiding away the Zhao orphan?" When Gongsun Chujiu flatly denied the charge, several guards were ordered to beat him with sticks. Gongsun Chujiu claimed he was wrongly accused, and asked Tu to name the accuser. When Cheng Ying's name was mentioned, Gongsun began to swear loudly, calling Cheng a worthless traitor and condemning Tu for his merciless persecution of the Zhao family.

Tu Anjia ignored the old man's curses but charged him to tell the whereabouts of the orphan. When Gongsun Chujiu refused to say anything, Tu ordered Cheng Ying to torture him. Stupefied, Cheng tried to decline. "You know, admiral, I am just a physician with barely enough strength to bind a chicken. Even when I pick out the herbs for a prescription, I feel weak in my arms. I am really not strong enough to wield a stick!" Tu Anjia responded with a snicker. "So you don't want to beat him, Cheng Ying! I wonder if it's because you are afraid to make him say something to your disadvantage?" Reluctantly Cheng Ying picked up a small stick and went up to the old man, but Tu called him back. "Why do you choose a small stick? Are you unwilling to hurt him?" When Cheng Ying put down the small stick and picked up a big one, Tu again stopped him. "What makes you choose the biggest stick here? You aren't going to beat him to death in a few strokes, are you, so that he won't have a chance to say anything against you?" When Cheng Ying asked with irritation what on earth he was supposed to do, Tu told him to select a stick that was neither too thick nor too thin.

Cheng Ying walked up to Gongsun Chujiu, stick in hand. "Old fellow," Tu called out. "Now you will be questioned by your good friend, Cheng Ying!" After receiving only three strokes, Gongsun Chujiu, being an old man, found the pain almost unbearable and began to lose control of his tongue. "When the two of us worked out a plan to save the orphan--"

199

Tu Anjia ordered Cheng Ying to beat Gongsun Chujiu
with a stick neither too thick nor too thin.

Cheng Ying was terrified, his face pale, his legs weak and trembling. "So there were two of you!" Tu Anjia cried out triumphantly. "Who is the other one? If you confess, I will spare you!" Then he turned to look at Cheng Ying. "Could that be you, I wonder?" Badly frightened, Cheng Ying kicked at Gongsun Chujiu a couple of times. "Old fellow, don't implicate innocent people by talking gibberish!" Gongsun Chujiu regained his self-control in time. "Did I say two people? I must have been delirious because of the pain. Actually, I did it all by myself!" Tu Anjia hit the roof. He was about to order the torture to be continued when two soldiers came in with a baby which they had found in a cave near the village. "Old fellow," Tu Anjia sneered, "didn't you deny having hid the Zhao orphan? Now tell me what this is!" With one hand he seized the baby, lifted it up for a closer look, then he drew his sword with the other hand and slashed at the baby repeatedly, killing it on the spot. Swearing at Tu Anjia for his ruthlessness and brutality, Gongsun Chujiu suddenly killed himself by dashing his head against the stone steps.

Having disposed of the Zhao orphan along with Gongsun Chujiu, Tu Anjia was very pleased. It occurred to him that Cheng Ying should be rewarded. "From now on you are one of my most trusted men," he said. "Let me find you something to do in my house, where your son will be well cared for. You can teach him history and literature, and I will train him in martial arts. I am in my late forties and have no child of my own, so I will adopt your son. When I retire at an old age, your son can have my position at court. What do you think?" Cheng Ying thought it a good way to protect the orphan, so he readily agreed. "I am so grateful for your kindness, admiral."

The Zhao orphan came to be known by two names, Cheng Bo—as Cheng Ying's natural son, and Tu Cheng—as Tu

Anjia's adopted son. During the day Tu Anjia taught him the use of weapons, and at night he studied history and literature under Cheng Ying's tutelage. Both strived to teach him well, though with different purposes in mind. Under Tu Anjia's instruction, the Zhao orphan mastered the use of various weapons, and even surpassed Tu in horsemanship and archery. According to Tu's plan, his adopted son would someday command troops to attack and kill the duke, so that he would become the new ruler of the state of Jin. On the other hand, Cheng Ying tried to inculcate the boy with the principles of loyalty, justice and integrity so he would not hesitate to avenge his family once he learned of his true origin upon reaching manhood.

Twenty years later, Cheng Bo had grown into a handsome young man full of vigor. Nearly seventy, Tu Anjia was eager to execute his plan and usurp the dukedom. Cheng Ying, now sixty-five, also grew anxious lest he should die without telling the Zhao orphan about his family history. Time was definitely not on his side. However, the lad had always held his foster father in high esteem; how could he be made to believe the contrary? After many days of consideration, Cheng Ying worked out a plan.

Cheng Bo practiced archery and swordsmanship on the drill grounds each day until dusk. One day, after returning home after the day's practice, he did not find his father waiting for him in the hall. Surprised, he went down to the studio where he saw Cheng Ying in tears. Being a filial son, Cheng Bo anxiously inquired what was troubling his father. "Even if I told you, you would be of no help. Go and eat your supper now!" When Cheng Bo refused to leave, Cheng Ying said, "I will go to my room to take a nap. After supper you can come to study in the studio." With this he went out.

While he was stepping out the door, Cheng Ying deliberately let a scroll drop from his sleeve. Curious, Cheng Bo picked it up and unrolled it and saw a series of pictures. In the first one, a man in red was setting a fierce dog on a man in purple, but another man used a big hammer to crush the dog to death. Next he saw a hefty man driving a cart with only one wheel. Then there was a general cutting his throat with a dagger, and laid out in front of him were a bow string and a cup of wine. Further on, a physician carrying a medicine chest was on his knees while a young lady handed him a baby. Then she hanged herself with a belt. Next there was a general who killed himself with a sword. In the final picture, the man in red was torturing a very old man. Looking through these pictures, Cheng Bo could not make out what the story was about, but he felt such an instinctive aversion to the man in red that he muttered curses against him. Assured that the lad could tell good from evil, Cheng Ying, who had hid himself behind a screen, walked out. When Cheng Bo asked him about the pictures, he decided to tell the whole story. Thereupon Cheng Bo learned that the vicious man in red was Tu Anjia, while the man in purple was his grandfather, Zhao Dun. The man who killed the fierce dog was Ti Miming, head of the palace guards. The big man who rescued Zhao Dun by pushing the broken cart was called Ling Zhe. The man who stabbed himself to death with the dagger was his natural father, Zhao Shuo, and it was his mother, the princess, who hanged herself with a belt. Han Jue, a junior general, was the man who killed himself with a sword. The physician with the medicine chest was none other than Cheng Ying, and the old man under torture was Gongsun Chujiu. Only then did the young man realize that his name was neither Cheng Bo nor Tu Cheng, but the Zhao orphan, and that Tu Anjia was his greatest enemy. Gnashing his teeth in anger, he wanted to set out at once and take revenge on Tu Anjia, but Cheng Ying stopped him, saying Tu had not dominated the court for such a long time without enlisting a great many followers. By acting rashly they would only prompt Tu to take preemptive measures. The Zhao orphan accepted this advice and agreed to take no action until the next day when he would denounce Tu Anjia to the ruling duke, expose his misdeeds to all the court officials, then set out to capture him. Cheng Ying, in the meantime, would lead some men to aid in Tu's arrest.

At that time, Duke Ling of Jin had been long deceased. His successor, Duke Dao, was quite dissatisfied with Tu Anjia's domineering manner at court. After he learned from Cheng Bo's memorial how Tu had massacred Zhao Dun's family on a trumped-up charge, he finally made up his mind to eliminate the wicked old minister. A senior minister named Wei Jiang was dispatched to see Cheng Bo and pass on to him the duke's order to apprehend Tu Anjia. Cheng Bo waited in ambush by the road Tu always took on his return home. At the sight of Tu, Cheng Bo galloped forth to block his path. Taken by surprise, Tu Anjia cried, "Tu Cheng, why are you here?" "You old scoundrel," Cheng Bo roared in anger. "I am not Tu Cheng; I am the Zhao orphan! Twenty years ago you killed three hundred members of my family. Today I will at last take revenge!" Tu Anjia was scared out of his wits, knowing he was no match for the Zhao orphan. He tried to spur on his horse to get away, but Cheng Bo closed in on him, lifted him up and dropped him to the ground. Then the guards swarmed in and tied him up. By this time Cheng Ying had also arrived on the scene, and together they escorted Tu back to the palace.

Wei Jiang, who was expecting them at the duke's order, was greatly pleased at Tu's capture. In the course of his long reign in the state of Jin, Tu Anjia had earned the bitter hatred of its people, so Wei Jiang thought he deserved to die by slow torture. He was thus tied onto a wooden frame and cut to pieces on the execution ground.

Now that the Zhao orphan had avenged his family, Cheng

Ying began to feel sad at the thought of his own son. "You have taken revenge at last and can now revert to your family name of Zhao. But poor me! From now on I will be quite alone, with no one to rely on!" The Zhao orphan hastily tried to set the old man's mind at ease. "Father, no one could be so generous as you have been to me, sacrificing your own son to save my life! I will be forever indebted to you and will always treat you with filial respect and devotion."

Just then Wei Jiang arrived with an edict from the duke. The Zhao orphan was renamed Zhao Wu by the duke and allowed to inherit his late father's court position and manor. Han Jue received the posthumous title of senior general. A large piece of fertile land was bestowed on Cheng Ying, enabling him to live a comfortable life in his old age. A grave was to be constructed and a stone tablet erected in honor of Gongsun Chujiu. Other people who had died under Tu's persecution also had their cases redressed and received post-humous honors.

LI KUI BEARS THE ROD

*Kang Jingzhi**

Song Jiang, a petty official in the city of Yuncheng, had been imprisoned for killing his wife. After escaping from prison, he joined the rebels at Mount Liangshan in Shandong Province. Upon the death of their leader, Chao Gai, the rebels elected Song Jiang as their new chief. With its well-trained troops, Mount Liangshan gained resounding fame in Shandong and the adjacent regions.

The strength of Mount Liangshan, lay in the strict discipline of its soldiers. Song Jiang forbade his officers and men from taking anything from the common people. No one was allowed to leave the mountain without authorization lest he should harm the local inhabitants. In compensation, the troops enjoyed two three-day vacations each year, first during the Qingming festival in the third month, then at the double ninth festival in the ninth month.

At the Qingming festival one year, the three-day vacation was proclaimed as usual for officers and men alike on Mount Liangshan. Toward the end of the third day, Song Jiang went to seat himself in the main hall, accompanied by Wu Yong, his chief of staff, and Lu Zhishen, the camp superintendent. All officers were required to report to the tent on time; punishment would be meted out for the slightest delay.

An incident then took place on the third day that nearly resulted in a civil war on Mount Liangshan. At the foot of the

---

* Kang Jingzhi was a playwright in the early Yuan Dynasty. Practically nothing is known about his life.

mountain was a village called Apricot Cottage, which had a small wineshop run by an old widower, Wang Lin, and his daughter, whose maiden name was Mantangjiao. As she had to help her father with cooking, warming the wine and running the shop, she was still unbetrothed at eighteen. The father and daughter managed thus to eke out a living from the wineshop. Many officers from Mount Liangshan were patrons of the shop, and they always paid their own way, for which the old man was very grateful. One day Wang Lin had just put out the shop's signboard when two men walked in and introduced themselves as Song Jiang and Lu Zhishen. Wang Lin, who had never seen them before, felt flattered by their visit. He invited them to sit down and went away to prepare wine and food. To show his gratitude to the honored guests, he told his daughter to come out and fill the cups for them. Though she had never done this for any guests before, she had no choice but to do her father's bidding.

At eighteen she was at the height of her charms, her face shining like a spring flower. The two customers, stunned by her beauty, decided to take her away by force. The man who called himself Song Jiang tried to conceal his lust by telling the girl not to walk too close to him, as he was allergic to the smell of makeup. But he took the cup of wine she offered him with great eagerness and downed it at one go. Then he filled the cup and offered it to Wang Lin, who dared not decline. "Why, your clothes are so worn out!" he said to Wang Lin. "There are holes all over them." He took off a red silk bag strapped around his waist and told Wang Lin to mend his clothes with it. Again, the old man dared not decline. The other customer, alias Lu Zhishen, spoke up. "Listen, old man! Do you know what kind of wine you have just drunk? That was the betrothal wine, no less. Do you know what kind of gift you have just accepted? That was the betrothal gift. My elder brother, Song Jiang, wants to take your daughter as his wife. Let him take away your daughter for three days. On the fourth day we will bring her safely back to you." Without waiting for the old man's reply, the two bandits carried the girl away with them. Wang Lin could only watch on helplessly. Dropping to the ground, he beat his chest and railed loudly against heaven and earth.

Among the officers on Mount Liangshan was one named Li Kui, known by his nickname Black Whirlwind. Coarse in manner but honest at heart, he had a weakness for wine. Subject to strict disciple on the mountain, he did not have much chance to indulge in this pastime. On the third day of the Qingming festival, he decided to visit Wang Lin's wineshop and treat himself to some good wine. With giant strides he walked down the mountain, heading for Apricot Cottage. The distant hills were shrouded in mist. The mountain path was lined with poplars, and a stream rushed down the cliff, creating pearl-like bubbles along the way. Peach trees were swaying gently in the spring breeze, with petals falling into the water and carried down the stream. Though a hard-boiled rebel, Li Kui felt a simple delight at this splendid view. Dipping into the stream, he caught some of the petals in his palm and looked at them with a grin. "Mount Liangshan not only has great rebels but a great view as well!" he muttered to himself. "I dare anyone to deny this!" While enjoying the surrounding scenery, Li Kui walked briskly down the road and reached Apricot Cottage a short while later.

"Wang Lin!" Li Kui called out before he crossed the threshold of the wineshop. "Do you have any wine today? Warm some for me—I have ready money to pay you!" Despite the loss of his daughter, Wang Lin had to serve his clients. Taking the money, he went in and returned with a wide dish of cooked mutton and a big pot of warm wine. Li Kui drank directly from the pot, and helped himself to the mutton with his hands. In a moment both the mutton and the wine were gone. When he looked up to ask for more, he noticed for the first time something unusual in the old man's behavior. With a woebegone look on his face, Wang Lin kept mumbling to himself and did not attend to his customer with his usual alacrity. "Wang Lin!" Li Kui bawled out. "Didn't I pay you money for the wine? Why do you treat me with such indifference?" When Wang Lin replied he was worrying over something else, Li Kui urged him to blurt it out. Thus the old man recounted tearfully how his daughter had been abducted by two officers from Mount Liangshan the day before.

Li Kui did not believe Song Jiang and Lu Zhishen capable of such a vile deed. In a rage, he charged the old man to give evidence for this accusation. And when the old man produced the red silk waist bag, Li Kui thought it was evidence enough. "Wang Lin!" he said to the old man, beating his chest. "Don't worry about it. I will go straightaway to reason with them and bring your daughter back to you today. Prepare a jug of wine and slaughter an ox to welcome me!" Wang Lin expressed his utmost gratitude. "Elder brother! If you return my girl to me, I will not grudge my own life to repay you, much less a jug of wine and an ox!" Li Kui stepped out of the wineshop to leave, then went back again. "Old man! I will go to the tent now, bring Song Jiang and Lu Zhishen here, and then question them before you. You must not let me down by getting cold feet at the last minute!" "I can recognize the two villains," Wang Lin replied, stamping his foot. "I hate them so much I want to set my teeth into their flesh. Why should I be afraid to confront them?"

Seething with indignation, Li Kui rushed back to Mount Liangshan. Being an honest, upright man who wouldn't put up with foul deeds, he was furious that Song Jiang should have abducted a woman to be his wife. He climbed up the mountain in a short time and found Song Jiang and his assistants registering returned officers in the Hall of Loyalty and Righteousness. Li Kui rushed to the gate of the hall like a whirlwind and shouted at the top of his lungs, "Li Kui is back!" The guards hurried inside to inform Song Jiang, who ordered Li Kui to come in.

Entering the hall, Li Kui headed straight for Wu Yong, offering no salute to Song Jiang or Lu Zhishen. "Brother Wu, we have great news today. Why don't we sing the tune: 'With a brand-new hat and a gown with narrow sleeves, what a handsome bridegroom he makes!' Where is my brother, Song Jiang? Why doesn't he come over to exchange greetings with me? I have some money left in my pocket to offer to my new sister-in-law as a greeting gift!" Song Jiang was offended by such disrespectful remarks. "How dare you be so rude, black fellow! Why don't you salute me, and only speak to Mr. Wu? And what are you blabbering about?" Li Kui turned to Song Jiang. "What do I have to say, my sworn brother? I can only congratulate you." Bewildered, Song Jiang told him to explain what he meant. Li Kui replied by asking where Song was keeping his bride. Then he turned to Lu Zhishen, calling him a skinhead ruffian and condemning him for acting as middle-man in this foul match. Both Song Jiang and Lu Zhishen were irritated by such unjustified abuse. Song Jiang, as the leader of Mount Liangshan, was able to restrain his rage, knowing that some incident must have befallen Li Kui down the mountain to make him rattle on incoherently like this. He told Li Kui to take his time and speak out his grievances to Wu Yong.

When Wu Yong advised him to take a rest and regain his breath before speaking, Li Kui cried out with great impatience. "Our Brother Song Jiang has taken a bride by force!" he blurted out. "And that skinhead ruffian Lu Zhishen was his matchmaker!" Seething in anger, he tore off his shirt and took out a pair of axes. "There is no more justice on Mount Liangshan! So we have no more use for that yellow banner!

Fellow outlaws stop Li Kui from cutting down their banner.

Let me cut it down once and for all!" He dashed toward the commander's banner, which was made of yellow silk and embroidered with the words "Enforce Justice on Behalf of Heaven." The other officers swarmed up to stop him, grabbing him by his arms and legs and taking his axes. They all urged him to calm down and described what really had happened. Pinned down on the spot, unable to stir, Li Kui was compelled to give a disjointed account of what he had heard from Wang Lin at the wineshop in Apricot Cottage. After listening to this story, Song Jiang knew the truth of the matter at once. To get more information from Li Kui, he deliberately assumed a nonchalant air. "So that old man, Wang Lin, accused me of taking away his daughter. Well, I didn't do it. But if I did, do you think the old man would be happy or sad?" "How could the old man be happy with his daughter taken away from him?" he said angrily. "His heart was filled with hatred when he looked at Mount Liangshan!" He recounted how Wang Lin had wept and cursed, unable to sit squarely in the day or go to sleep at night. "Mount Liangshan produces unrighteous people and sour water" had been the old man's very words. Aware that Mount Liangshan's reputation was at steak, Song Jiang was determined to solve the problem without delay. "Mr. Wu," he said, "it must have been a couple of bandits who committed this atrocit in the name of Mount Liangshan. As for you, Li Kui, you should at least get some evidence to show us." When Li Kui produced the red silk bag, Song Jiang denied it had ever belonged to him. A written oath was signed on the spot by Li Kui and Song Jiang, each pledging with his life the truth of his words. Wu Yong, acting as witness, was made to keep the statement.

Convinced he had Song Jiang by the neck after the oath was signed, Li Kui embarked on a stream of invectives against his chief, calling him a hypocrite, a black-hearted ruffian who had abducted a poor old man's daughter to satisfy his own lust.

Though greatly annoyed, Song Jiang chose not to argue with him but suggested they set out for Apricot Cottage the next day. At this, Li Kui jumped onto a stone seat to address the officers. "I am taking Song Jiang and Lu Zhishen to face the old man at the wineshop. Once he recognizes them as the villains, don't think I will spare them! With one stroke of my axe I will chop that monk in two! With the same axe I will send Song Jiang after him to the underworld! No one can stop me!" The following day the three of them left the mountain, heading for Apricot Cottage.

On their way Li Kui kept close to his two companions for fear they would try to escape. When Song Jiang and Lu Zhishen walked fast, he cried out, "Slow down and wait for me! Are you so eager to meet your father-in-law that you have to run so fast? I can hardly keep up with you." Song Jiang said to Lu Zhishen in great annoyance, "Listen, brother! What a wicked tongue that black fellow has!" Then he turned to Li Kui. "Don't expect me to spare you, once Wang Lin tells the truth!" Nevertheless, he and Lu Zhishen slowed their pace. However, a moment later Li Kui began to find fault with them again. "Hey, skinhead! You don't have bound feet, do you? Then why are you dragging your legs like that? Are you afraid to face the victim of your matchmaking deal? And you, Brother Song, quicken your steps, will you? Are you feeling a bit ashamed of having abducted the old man's daughter?" The more he looked at Song Jiang and Lu Zhishen, the more convinced he was of their guilt. Song Jiang tried to assuage his hostility by reminding him of the brotherhood they had shared. "Do you remember the time you came to join us at Mount Liangshan, and the two of us became sworn brothers? You have treated me as your big brother since that day!" "I remember it very clearly, big brother!" Li Kui rejoined quickly. "It's no use reminding me of the old times after what you have just done! I will not let you off on any account because it's a

213

matter of right and wrong, not a private quarrel!" When they reached the wineshop, Li Kui cautioned Song Jiang and Lu Zhishen not to make any noise and startle the old man, while he went up to knock on the door himself.

After Li Kui's departure the day before, Wang Lin began to prepare for his daughter's return. He got up in the morning and laid out the table for Li Kui, without opening the shop or putting out the signboard. He was by turns hopeful and uncertain, and the thought of his daughter still brought tears to his eyes. Finally he grew sleepy and nodded off in the kitchen. He was awakened by a thunderous knocking on the door, with Li Kui's voice shouting, "Wang Lin! Open the door! I have brought back your daughter!" Wang Lin jumped to his feet and scrambled to open the door, his eyes scarcely half open. Taking Li Kui into his arms, he burst into tears. "My poor daughter!" Li Kui quickly pushed him away. "Open your eyes and see who I am! I shouted and shouted, but you did not answer the door. When I called out your daughter's name, you came out and mistook me for your daughter. What a joke! Well, stop lamenting and howling, old man. Come and identify the thieves who took away your daughter!" He beckoned Song Jiang and Lu Zhishen into the shop and warned them against intimidating the old man.

"Come over, old man," said Song Jiang after taking his seat. "I am Song Jiang, no less. Tell us if I am the bandit who carried your daughter away. You must tell the truth because both Li Kui and I have staked our heads on it." Li Kui, standing close by, urged the old man to go and take a look. Trembling, Wang Lin walked up to Song Jiang and peered at him. "He is not the one," he said. "What do you have to say now?" Song Jiang turned to Li Kui. Anxiously, Li Kui told Song Jiang to lower his voice for fear of scaring the old man, and insisted that Wang Lin take another look. Wang Lin looked again but reaffirmed that Song Jiang was not the man.

Frustrated, Li Kui told him to look at Lu Zhishen, the matchmaker. The old man walked around Lu Zhishen looking him up and down, and pronounced this was not the matchmaker. "What do you have to say, Li Kui?" Lu Zhishen called out triumphantly. Pacing in the room in distress, Li Kui kept urging Wang Lin to look more carefully. Under Li Kui's fierce stare, Wang Lin did not waver. According to him, one of the bandits was tall, and the other had sores on his head, but now he found Song Jiang a short, dark man and Lu Zhishen a monk. Song Jiang turned to Lu Zhishen. "Wang Lin has looked at us carefully and declared we are not the men he wants. Let's return to Mount Liangshan first and think about how to deal with Li Kui when he comes back." They bade the old man farewell and took their leave. Deeply vexed, Li Kui felt the urge to beat up the old man and burn his wineshop to the ground, but on second thought he realized the old man was not to blame. He had no choice but to accept his bad luck. With great despondency he left the wineshop and made his way back to Mount Liangshan.

When the three men were gone, Wang Lin began to worry about Li Kui, who would lose his head as a forfeit. But what could he do to save him? Just then the two bandits returned to the shop with Mantangjiao. "Where is my father-in-law?" yelled the fake Song Jiang. "Come out to meet us! Didn't I promise to bring your daughter home in three days? This is the third day, and here we are! I have never told a lie in my whole life, you know." At the sight of her father, the girl threw herself into his arms, and both broke into tears. The fake Lu Zhishen, standing close by, greeted the old man and congratulated him on his good luck. Afraid of offending the two ruffians, Wang Lin compelled himself to answer them politely. But the two bandits did not have much interest in talking with the old man. They took the girl into the inner room and helped themselves to the food and wine there. "My daughter has already been humiliated by these two bandits," Wang Lin thought to himself. "Why don't I let her keep them company here and rush overnight to Mount Liangshan to seek help? If I can get Li Kui to come and seize the bandits, I will not only avenge my daughter's insult but also save Li's life." His mind made up, he went into the inner room with still more food and wine and bade his daughter help the bandits drink their fill. Then he unbolted the door quietly and slipped out, heading for Mount Liangshan in the night.

On his return, Song Jiang summoned all the officers to the Hall of Loyalty and Righteousness and dispatched some soldiers to wait for Li Kui, who deserved to be beheaded according to the military oath he had signed. But Li Kui was not in a hurry to return. Dragging along the road, he cursed himself for his rashness in signing the oath. What could he do to save his neck now? He sat down before a ravine, listening to the wind rustling in the pine woods. Then an idea occurred to him. Why not show his contrition by carrying some sticks on his back and asking Song Jiang for punishment? No sooner thought than done. He hacked away at the chaste trees, picked out a few smooth twigs to carry on his back, and made his way back to the mountain.

On reaching the mountaintop, he entered the hall and met Song Jiang who watched him with interest. "So you are back, Li Kui! What are you carrying on your back?" Li Kui had no choice but to beg for pardon. "Big brother, I was wrong in treating you that way. Please punish me with these sticks!" "The forfeit for losing the bet is your head, not a mere beating," said Song Jiang, straight-faced, and bade the guards take Li Kui out and return with his head on a plate. Li Kui turned to beg Wu Yong who was standing close by to speak up for him, but Song Jiang refused to listen to anyone. Driven to despair, Li Kui sighed deeply. "Oh well, I give up. Instead of going to the execution ground, I might as well do it myself.

Li Kui kneels before Song Jiang to plead for mercy.

217

Big brother, please lend me your sword. I will use it to cut my throat." Unperturbed, Song Jiang took off the sword he was wearing and handed it to a guard, who passed it on to Li Kui. Gazing at the sword in his hands, Li Kui was overwhelmed with grief. He had found the sword on a hunting trip with Song Jiang and given it to him as a present. Little had he expected to use it to take his own life! He burst into tears at the thought of parting from his brothers with whom he had shared joys and woes for the past ten years.

At this juncture Wang Lin arrived, panting heavily. When he saw from a distance Li Kui standing in the hall about to cut his throat with a sword, he shouted in alarm, "Put away the sword!" Pleased with the interruption, Song Jiang bade Li Kui put down the sword while a guard led Wang Lin into the hall. After a pause to get back his breath, the old man told Song Jiang that the two bandits, back in his shop, had been made dead drunk by his daughter. He begged Song Jiang to send an officer to seize them. Song Jiang was glad to be given a reason to spare Li Kui. "Li Kui, I will let you go to the village now. If you catch the two bandits, you will atone for your crime; if you commit another offense by failing to catch them, no one will be able to save you then. Do you have the courage to go?" Jumping with joy, Li Kui beat his chest, saying the two bandits were a sure catch. Wu Yong, being a cautious man, suggested that Lu Zhishen go along, but Lu Zhishen pulled a long face. "Li Kui swore at me repeatedly, called me all kinds of names, and tried his best to make the old man at the wineshop identify me as the villain. Well, since he is so capable, let him go and catch the two bandits all by himself. I will have nothing to do with him." However, he agreed to go when Song Jiang asked him to do so in the name of righteousness. That night Li Kui, Lu Zhishen and Wang Lin left for the village.

It was already daybreak when they arrived at Apricot

Cottage. Eager to make amends for his mistake, Li Kui rushed into the shop first. The two bandits, just awakened after a night's sleep, were calling the old man to serve them. "Scoundrels!" roared Li Kui, his eyes red with rage, an axe in each hand. "Your father-in-law is here!" Stupefied, the fake Song Jiang asked who he was. "Listen carefully, you scum! I am none other than the Black Whirlwind from Mount Liangshan, and my companion is Lu Zhishen! You have sullied the reputation of Mount Liangshan by insulting an innocent woman in our name. Unlucky for you to fall into my hands! Now have a taste of this axe of mine!" The bandit was scared out of his senses. "They are real bandits from Mount Liangshan!" he called out to his mate. "We are no match for them. Let's get out of here!" But Li Kui and Lu Zhishen blocked their way and, in a short moment, struck them down and bound them up. Wang Lin, supporting his trembling daughter, went up to Li Kui and they knelt by way of gratitude. Li Kui helped Wang Lin to his feet. "Don't thank me, old man. If you really want to express your thanks, come and pay respects to my big brother Song Jiang tomorrow." Bidding the old man good-bye, he and Lu Zhishen escorted the two bandits back to Mount Liangshan.

As soon as Li Kui came to the foot of the mountain, sentries hastened back to the main hall to report to Song Jiang and Wu Yong, who had been waiting in the Hall of Loyalty and Righteousness. A moment later the four reached the gate. The bandits were brought into the hall and interrogated. The two men, named Song Gang and Lu Zhien, had committed all sorts of atrocities like murder, robbery and rape by pretending to be Song Jiang and Lu Zhishen and taking advantage of the local people's reverence for Mount Liangshan. Their crimes were pronounced unpardonable, so Song Jiang had them taken out and beheaded, and their heads displayed on flagpoles. A great feast was then prepared in honor of Li

Kui and Lu Zhishen, who had achieved great merit by catching the bandits. This is the end of the tale, which is summed up in the following quatrain:

Song Jiang upheld justice on behalf of heaven;
Heroes from all sides gathered on Mount Liangshan.
Li Kui drew his axes to protect the innocent;
Wang Lin was reunited with his daughter.

ZHANG YU BOILS THE SEA

*Li Haogu**

In Chaozhou there lived a young man named Zhang Yu who
had lost his parents at an early age. In spite of his erudition
he had failed to secure an official position and therefore chose
to relieve his melancholy by roaming from place to place.

One day while travelling along the coast of the East Sea
accompanied by his errand boy, he caught sight of an ancient
temple on a hill and headed for it. He found a little novice
monk standing at the gate and asked if the temple had a
name. The boy looked offended by the question. "How can a
temple do without a name? You must have heard the saying,
'An unnamed hill may be fascinating, but an unnamed temple
is a bore!' This is the famous Monastery of the Stone Buddha!"
Attracted by the serene atmosphere of the place, Zhang Yu
wanted to take a look around, so he asked the boy to send his
greetings to the abbot. Somewhat reluctantly the boy went in,
and came out presently with the abbot's invitation.

After greeting the abbot, named Fa Yun, Zhang Yu
expressed his desire to rent a room in the monastery where
he could study the classics in quiet. The abbot readily agreed
and bade the young monk clean up a room in the southeast
corner of the monastery. Zhang Yu offered two taels of silver,
which the abbot accepted with a smile. Then the abbot went
back to his own quarters to meditate, after instructing the boy

---

* Li Haogu: Nothing is known about the life of Li Haogu except
that he wrote three plays, of which *Zhang Yu Boils the Sea* is the only one
extant.

to provide the young scholar with some vegetarian food. As soon as the abbot turned his back, the little monk made a face at Zhang Yu, saying, "Scholar, you will find yourself in a very quiet room. There you can kick around, do somersaults, play the ghost, or play all kinds of mischief to your heart's content. No one will come to bother you." Ushered into the room, Zhang Yu put away his zither and sword and took out the books he had been carrying. He spent the entire afternoon studying the classics, never hearing so much as a footstep to break the silence. At nightfall he closed his book and bade the errand boy light some incense, then began to play his zither. The music poured out from his fingers, stirring the heart and refreshing the mind like a stream rushing down a high mountain.

It happened that Qiong Lian, third daughter of the dragon king of the East Sea, was close enough to hear the music that night. A sprightly young girl, Qiong Lian slipped out of the underwater palace with her maid, Mei Xiang. Half transparent under the bright moonlight, the boundless water of the sea appeared like a gigantic piece of emerald. After a stroll on the waves, they floated up into the sky to gaze down on the human world below. "The world of humans must look very different from ours under the ocean," remarked Mei Xiang. "Of course," her young mistress said. "The towers and pavilions on the land of man are no match for the buildings in my father's palace!" The bright maid took the chance to pay her young mistress a compliment. "As the sights of the human world are no match for the treasures of our palace, so can no human beauty compare with you!" Hearing this, Qiong Lian gazed at her own reflection in the water: her beautiful glossy hair tied into a bun, her slender waist brought out by the floating dress, her hands white as jade, and her tiny feet in a pair of embroidered shoes. Endowed with such charm and grace, where could she find a worthy man to entrust herself to? A sense of sadness welled up in her heart. Unaware of her changing mood, the maid rattled on, "Sister, I dare say nothing in the human world is as good as what we have!" "I agree," Qiong Lian said. "The prosperity of the human world is no more stable than bitter fleabane; the next thing you know, it has gone with the wind. The cocks' crow in the morning and the tolling of bells at night count off days, seasons, and years. You find yourself at the end of life's journey before you have time to awaken yourself!"

When Qiong Lian mentioned the bells at night, her maid's attention was caught by a distant sound. "What's that?" she asked. Qiong Lian listened attentively, but for a moment could not place it either. Somewhat like the wind bustling in the pine wood, a stream dashing into a deep valley, the rowing of a boat by a lotus-gathering girl in the lake, or the whistling of a fisherman, but it was none of these things. Finally she realized someone was playing the zither.

Mei Xiang looked down curiously into the monastery. Sure enough, the sound came from the zither being played by a fine-looking young man in a scholar's robe. Turning to tell what she saw to her young mistress, Mei Xiang found her absorbed in the music. The undulating sound reminded Qiong Lian of chrysanthemums quivering in the breeze, the fragrance of laurel blossoms wafting through the fresh air, or green bamboo twigs rustling in the autumn wind. Captivated, Qiong Lian could not help looking down for the source of the music. She saw the young scholar, handsome and graceful, sitting in the monastery with the zither in his hands. A sense of deep longing seized her heart. "Sister," remarked the maid, who noticed the young lady's intense reaction. "With your knowledge of music you know how to appreciate it. But even to my unschooled ears the sound from the zither is so sweet and touching!" Qiong Lian was so enchanted that, without realizing it, she had descended from the sky and was making her

223

Enchanted by the music, Qiong Lian made her way
into the monastery.

way into the monastery.

Zhang Yu was fully absorbed in playing the zither when one of the strings burst. "What made the string break?" he muttered to himself. "Someone must be overhearing the music. Let me go out and take a look." He went out of the room and came face to face with Qiong Lian. Each marveled at the other's charm. "Where are you from, young lady, and why do you come here late at night?" asked Zhang Yu. "I am from a very powerful family far away over blue waves in the azure sky," replied Qiong Lian, sounding very mysterious. "Our household servants are all dressed in scaly armor. My family name is Dragon." "That's an unusual family name," remarked Zhang Yu, "but I remember reading about it somewhere. What's your given name then? And please tell me why you are here!" Qiong Lian disclosed her maiden name and said she had traced the alluring music into the monastery. Zhang Yu was delighted to find a music lover in the beautiful maiden. He invited her to come into the room, offering to play another tune for her.

Qiong Lian accepted his invitation with alacrity. After they were both seated, she asked him to tell something about himself. "My family name is Zhang, and my given name Yu. I am a native of Chaozhou. I lost my parents at an early age and I have studied the classics assiduously, but have not yet attained fame and position. I am here to study." Zhang Yu paused, then added, "I don't have a wife yet." "What impudence!" cried Mei Xiang with a straight face. "Who cares whether you have a wife or not?" The errand boy was quick to respond. "My master doesn't have a wife, and neither do I." Oblivious to the squabble between the maid and the errand boy, Zhang Yu fixed his gazed on the young lady, whose beauty, in his opinion, was unsurpassed in the whole world. He decided to come straight to the point. "Can you overlook my poverty and be my wife?" he asked. For her part, Qiong

Lian, who had stayed in the dragon king's palace for years on end without seeing any man, let alone such a handsome and graceful scholar, was just as unwilling to let the opportunity slip away. "Scholar, I admire you for your unusual talents and graceful manners, and am very willing to tie the love-knot with you. Since my parents are still alive, I have to ask for their consent and blessing. Please come to my house for the Midautumn festival; with my parents' approval we shall be married on that very day."

Zhang Yu was overjoyed to have won the young maiden's hand, but he was so impatient that he wanted to get married on the spot. However, Qiong Lian would not agree to this. When Zhang Yu asked the whereabouts of her house so he could come to visit her on the appointed date, Qiong Lian replied that she lived amid the blue waves of the ocean. Uncertain if Qiong Lian would keep her word, Zhang Yu declared himself a man of honor and beseeched her not to let him down. Qiong Lian comforted him, saying, "On the Midautumn festival, the full moon will rise in the clear, cloudless sky over the sea. You and I will stand among a myriad of flowers and drink wine from jade cups served on gold plates. What a happy couple we will be!" When Zhang Yu asked her for a love token, she gave him a silk handkerchief. Seeing this, the errand boy suggested to Mei Xiang that she also owed him a token. "If you need a token," responded the sharp-tongued maid, "I will give you a tattered fan, so you can do a better job fanning the stove!"

"When you come to visit, ask for the Dragon family," said Qiong Lian. "No harm will come to you. When you present yourself at my house out in the blue waves, you won't have to trouble yourself with formalities as in those rich families of the mundane world. Promise to meet me on the Midautumn festival!" She bade him farewell and returned with her maid to the dragon king's palace.

After Qiong Lian's departure, the image of her beautiful features filled Zhang Yu with a restless longing. The Mid-autumn festival was still a long time away, but he was too agitated to sit and wait in the monastery. Telling the errand boy to pack up, he set out for the coast carrying the silk handkerchief. The errand boy sat in the room, blaming his master for his foolishness. How could a scholar like him believe the words of that strange girl? What if she turned out to be a monster? The errand boy decided to inform the abbot and ask his advice.

Taking the silk handkerchief with him, Zhang Yu walked all the way to the coast without finding any trace of Qiong Lian. Looking around, he could see nothing but high cliffs and undulating hills. By his reckoning, Qiong Lian could not be living beneath the sea, so he went searching for her among the hills. For a long time he trudged along the stone mountain path lined with pine trees and wild flowers until, overcome with thirst and fatigue and weighed down by sore disappointment, he slumped to the ground.

At this juncture a young woman emerged at the far end of the path. When she came close, Zhang Yu found her dressed in Taoist robes, so he got to his feet and bowed with clasped hands. "Please, Sister, could you tell me what place this is?" The Taoist nun looked him up and down but did not answer his question. Instead, she asked who he was and why he had come there. "I am Zhang Yu, a humble scholar. I have come here on a study tour and have taken lodging in the Monastery of the Stone Buddha. Last night I was playing the zither when a young lady accompanied by a maid came to listen. She said her family name was Dragon, and her given name Qiong Lian. We made an appointment to meet again along the coast on the Midautumn festival. I could not bring myself to wait that long, so I searched along the coast hoping to find her. Unfortunately I lost my way." Drifting into a reverie, he muttered to himself, "Oh, what a charming figure she has! There is no match for her in the whole world!"

Amused by his infatuation, the nun said with a smile, "You'd better be careful, Mr. Zhang. You don't seem to be acquainted with the people of the Dragon family. They have a dark blue complexion, a fierce temper, and a propensity to kill anyone who happens to displease them." "Are they really like that?" asked Zhang Yu, growing a little apprehensive. "Yes," said the nun. "By shaking its head and extending its claws, the dragon can topple mountains and create storms. It can grow so big that the world hardly has enough room for it, or so small that a mustard seed becomes its comfortable dwelling place. It is very powerful, so beware of its temper!" "The young lady told me she was from a family named Dragon," said Zhang Yu, puzzled. "But you seemed to be talking about the divine animal called dragon!" Only then did the nun explain to him that the young lady Qiong Lian was actually the third daughter of the dragon king of the East Sea.

The Taoist nun turned out to be an immortal woman sent by the East Flowery God to instruct Zhang Yu. "How can you hope to meet the dragon king's daughter?" she asked. "Our meeting is predestined," replied Zhang Yu confidently. "How do you know that?" "Otherwise, why should she have made the appointment to receive me in her home on the Mid-autumn festival, when we will celebrate our wedding? Moreover, she has given me this silk handkerchief as a love token." The nun took a look at the handkerchief and seemed convinced. "So Qiong Lian has taken a fancy to you, Mr. Zhang. However, how do you plan to persuade the ill-tempered dragon king to consent to this marriage?" Zhang Yu was at a loss to answer. After a moment's thought, the nun said, "Well, young scholar, I want to do you a favor. Here are three magic treasures. With these you can bring the dragon king to submission and make him agree to the marriage." She then produced a silver pot, a gold coin, and an iron ladle. Zhang Yu took the three charms and asked to be taught how to use them. "Use the ladle to fetch seawater for the pot, throw the gold coin into the pot, then build a fire with charcoal to boil the water. When one tenth of the water in the pot has boiled away, the level of the sea will be reduced by one tenth. When all the water in the pot has boiled away, the sea will have dried up to its bottom. Before that happens, the dragon king will surely find it very uncomfortable in his underwater palace and send for you to be his son-in-law!" Delighted to have such magic treasures at his disposal, Zhang Yu headed straight for the sea to try them out. After taking a few steps he turned back and begged the nun to show him a shortcut to the sea. The immortal woman pointed, saying the coast of the Shamen island was only a few dozen *li* away. Zhang Yu thanked her and set off at once.

After Zhang Yu left the monastery, the errand boy went to inform the abbot, then rushed down the road in pursuit of his master, finally catching up with him along a mountain path. With the errand boy carrying the three magic treasures, Zhang Yu continued his journey.

Upon reaching the seashore, Zhang Yu had the errand boy find three stones to prop up the pot. He then filled it with seawater from the ladle and dropped in the gold coin. Then they lit a fire under the pot and began fanning vigorously. A moment later the water in the pot began to boil, and so did the sea in front of them. "What a divine miracle!" exclaimed Zhang Yu. The errand boy also marveled at the magic powers of the three treasures. In the meantime the shrimp soldiers and crab officers guarding the underwater palace were plunged into commotion. As the palace became shrouded in steam, the dragon king's children and grandchildren were consumed with thirst, and fish and crabs darted and crawled in all directions. Even the dragon

In less time than it takes to cook a meal, the sea began to boil.

king himself was unable to maintain his majestic air but started to fidget on his throne. As Zhang Yu fanned the fire with all his might, the water in the pot boiled away rapidly. At his wit's end, the dragon king sent an envoy to the Monastery of the Stone Buddha, begging the abbot to mediate for him.

Fa Yun, the abbot, was sitting in his bed absorbed in meditation when the envoy from the dragon king arrived. After hearing him out, the abbot thought he'd better lend a hand to the dragon king, who could be considered a close neighbor since the monastery was located near the East Sea. The envoy left greatly satisfied, having secured the abbot's promise to persuade the young scholar to put out the fire. After seeing the envoy off, Fa Yun set out for Shamen Island at once.

When he arrived there, Zhang Yu was just directing the errand boy to add some dry twigs to the booming fire. Without much water left in the pot, Zhang Yu looked rather pleased with what he was doing. "Hey, young scholar!" the abbot called out. "Why do you come here to boil seawater?" Zhang Yu replied he was actually boiling the East Sea. "Why are you doing that?" Zhang Yu thought it unnecessary to keep the matter from the abbot, so he told him the whole story. Only then did the abbot learn that the young man was boiling the sea in order to get his bride. He tried to reason with Zhang Yu. "Listen to me, young man! A scholar who has studied the Confucian classics should be good-natured and ready to negotiate with others when there is a disagreement. How can you act so rashly, with no sense of distinction between right and wrong?" Zhang Yu, however, was determined to make the sea dry up. "Old monk, don't poke your nose into my business! If you want to beg for alms, go somewhere else!" Fa Yun stayed there and kept urging him to stop. Finally Zhang Yu said, "All right, abbot. If you can do me a favor by making the young lady marry me, I will return the favor by putting out the fire." "So you do not mind causing a catastrophe merely for the sake of a beautiful woman!" remarked the abbot. "You can say what you like," responded Zhang Yu indifferently. "For my part, I will keep the fire burning until the young lady comes out to marry me." As the dragon king's palace was almost on the verge of collapse, the abbot reached a quick decision. "Listen to me, young man," he called out. "The dragon king of the East Sea has asked me to propose marriage between you and his daughter Qiong Lian. You are invited to attend the wedding in the underwater palace. What is your reply to that?"

Zhang Yu, overjoyed at first, quickly felt a sense of apprehension, wondering if it could be a trap. After a pause he said, "Old monk, please stop pulling my leg! The East Sea is a stretch of boundless water; how can a mortal like myself find my way to the underwater palace? You must be playing a trick on a poor scholar!" Before Fa Yun could answer, the errand boy cut in. "Master, there is no problem at all. You can follow the old monk closely. If he doesn't drown, neither will you!" "Yes," agreed the abbot. "The power of the gods is beyond our imagination. Since you are an honored guest and future son-in-law of the dragon king, he will create a smooth path in the midst of the sea to facilitate your passage. What is there to be afraid of?" "Even if water can be turned into solid ground, how can I find my way around in the pitch darkness?" The abbot assured him that there would be lights even in the bottom of the sea. Zhang Yu, though a bit doubtful, decided to take the risk as he remembered the old saying, "He who wants to get the tiger's cub must venture into the tiger's den." "Since you have come here to mediate," he said to the abbot, "I will put away the magic weapons and go with you. But make sure the wedding will take place!" The errand boy had something else on his mind. "Abbot," he said, "as my master will take Qiong Lian for his wife, I might as well take the pretty maid, Mei Xiang. Otherwise I will try these magic weapons again!" Zhang Yu paid no attention to the boy's joking. His mind was filled with the image of Qiong Lian, her lovely visage, slim figure and gentle disposition. With the errand boy left on the bank to tend after the magic weapons, Zhang Yu and the abbot headed for the dragon king's palace.

As they reached the sea, the water parted to clear a path leading straight to the bottom of the deep. All the court officials stood outside the palace to welcome the bridegroom. The dragon king, to keep his promise, had a grand feast prepared for the marriage of his daughter Qiong Lian to the young scholar. As soon as he walked into the palace, Mei Xiang led him away to meet her young mistress. Qiong Lian was delighted to find him as handsome as ever. "I didn't expected us to meet so soon after that night!" she said with a sigh. "I was afraid the waves would keep us apart. To me, our reunion is a miracle!" At the very sight of the young lady, Zhang Yu seemed to undergo a metamorphosis; the lines on his face softened, his voice became gentle, and when he opened his mouth to speak, his words were sweet and comforting. Oblivious to their surroundings, they poured out their longings for each other. After a while it occurred to Zhang Yu that he had seen few people around. "Where are all the people living in this palace?" he asked. "Never mind them," Qiong Lian said. "In this palace we have turtles and alligators for guards, and shrimps, crabs and fish for household servants. No need to bother about them. Just look at these piles upon piles of pearls, gold and jade. Have you seen anything like that in the world of man?" Zhang Yu looked around and found the place glittering with jade and gold. "Such wealth is indeed incomparable!" he marveled.

Their tete-a-tete was interrupted by a turtle dispatched by the dragon king with an invitation for Zhang Yu. The young couple followed the turtle to the front hall of the palace. The dragon king, taking a close look at Zhang Yu, acknowledged to himself that his daughter had made a good choice. "Qiong Lian, why did you promise your hand to this young man when you met him for the first time that night? How did you make the decision?" Qiong Lian, no coy maiden of the human world, answered the question without embarrassment. She had detected a longing for love in Zhang Yu's music, a feeling she had shared. That was why they had fallen for one another at once. The dragon king, satisfied with this reply, turned to ask Zhang Yu how he had come by those magic weapons. When Zhang Yu told him an immortal woman had lent them to him, the dragon king realized he was no ordinary mortal and did not pursue the question. "You nearly boiled me to death, you know," he said with a sigh. "But I suppose my daughter is to blame for all this." "You are being unfair, father," protested Qiong Lian. "This wedding would not have taken place if he had not boiled the sea." "She's right," said Zhang Yu. "But for the magic power endowed by the immortal woman, I would never have been united with my love!" The dragon king realized he had better hold his tongue and let the young couple enjoy themselves, so he announced the opening of the banquet.

The festivities in the underwater palace were brought to a halt by the sudden arrival of the East Flower God. When the dragon king hastened out, followed by Zhang Yu, Qiong Lian, and the court officials, the god shouted in a loud voice, "Dragon king, pay attention!" The dragon king fell on his knees. "Zhang Yu is not your son-in-law, neither is

Qiong Lian your daughter," declared the god. "They are former residents of the land of immortals, banished to the mundane world for showing an improper interest in worldly pleasures. Now they are ordered to leave for the land of immortals!" Thus Zhang Yu and Qiong Lian bade farewell to the dragon king and followed the East Flower God to their native land high above the clouds.

CASE OF THE CHALK CIRCLE

*Li Qianfu**

In the city of Zhengzhou there lived an old woman, Mistress
Liu, whose husband, Zhang, came from a family of scholars.
Their children, a son named Zhang Lin, and a daughter
named Haitang, both learned to read and write at an early
age. Haitang, the brighter of the two, was pretty, clever, and
talented in dance and music. The family enjoyed a happy time
together until Zhang suddenly died of an illness and the
financial situation of the family deteriorated rapidly.

After the death of her husband, Mistress Liu had no
source of income whatsoever. Her son, Zhang Lin, could quote
a few lines from the classics but did not have any practical
skill. Haitang's deftness in singing and dancing proved more
useful. She became a courtesan who received guests at home.
With money and gifts from her patrons, Haitang was the
family's breadwinner.

Though he did nothing to support the family, Zhang Lin
held his sister in great contempt and kept abusing her for
sullying the family name. One day Haitang was so exasperated
that she answered back. "Brother, if you are a real man, you
should do something to support Mother." Struck speechless,
Zhang Lin was shamed into anger and raised his fist to beat
his sister, but Mistress Liu came between them to shield her
daughter. "Don't beat her, beat me instead!" she cried indignantly. "If you are ashamed of your sister, why don't you go

---

* Li Qianfu was a playwright of the Yuan Dynasty whose only
known work is *Case of the Chalk Circle*.

out and make some money to support the family? You would be doing all of us a big favor that way!" Zhang Lin realized he was in the wrong, so he did not say anything. "There is no reason why I can't improve my lot," he mused. "I don't think I will starve to death by leaving home!" Thus he bade his mother farewell and left for Kaifeng, the imperial capital, hoping to get a job from his uncle there.

Disturbed by the behavior of her son, Mistress Liu was seized by a severe pain in her stomach and took to bed. As Haitang waited on her mother, she shed silent tears at the thought of her miserable life. Among her patrons only Ma Junqing took her seriously. A good-natured scholar conversant with the Confucian classics, he was fairly well-off and enjoyed a good reputation in the neighborhood. As his wife was barren, he proposed more than once to take Haitang for a concubine. Haitang was willing enough to quit her trade, but Mistress Liu, dependent on her daughter's earnings from her various patrons, was reluctant to let her go. After her brother left, Haitang again begged her mother to consent to the marriage. Mistress Liu, aware that she could not keep her daughter forever, finally agreed.

Learning of Haitang's quarrel with her brother, Ma Junqing intended to visit her again with his marriage proposal, but on second thought he stopped, for fear that Zhang Lin would make a scene. After he found out that Zhang Lin had left Zhengzhou, Ma Junqing chose an auspicious date to call on Haitang, bringing money and gifts with him. Haitang met him at the gate and told him in a whisper about her mother's consent. Together they entered the room to see Mistress Liu.

Ma Junqing took out a hundred taels of silver, offering it to Mistress Liu. "Dear Madam, please accept my gift for taking away your daughter. After you hand her over to me, you can come to my house if you need anything, and I promise that you will never lack clothes, food or money. Today is a very lucky day; please give us your blessing!" According to the old saying, a marriage offer will be granted if it comes with handsome gifts. Looking at the silver and listening to Ma's solemn promise, Mistress Liu felt inclined to agree, but she had to make sure her daughter would have a good future. After a pause, she said, "Mr. Ma, I know my daughter cannot live on with me forever; for her, marriage is a very good option. The problem is, you already have a wife at home. When Haitang enters your house, she will probably be subject to abuse from your principal wife. If that kind of thing should happen, I would say Haitang might as well not get married at all. You must solve this problem before I will give my daughter away."

Under the circumstances Ma Junqing would say anything to get the old woman's permission. "I am not the kind of person to let you down," he said emphatically, beating his chest. "And neither is my wife. When Haitang enters my house, she will address my principal wife as elder sister, and I will treat them without any partiality. When she gives birth to a baby, be it a boy or a girl, all my property will be left to her!" Mistress Liu, convinced of Ma's sincerity, consented to the marriage. Each gained something from the arrangement: Mistress Liu received a handsome betrothal gift to ensure a good living for the rest of her life, Ma Junqing obtained a pretty concubine, and Haitang settled down to domestic life with a husband and a home. She was quite satisfied with her married life in Ma's house.

Ma Junqing's principal wife, Ma Shi, was an ugly woman with intense jealousy. She had no liking for Haitang, though she did not show it, as she was not well established in her husband's favor because of her barrenness. Haitang soon became pregnant and in due time gave birth to a son who was named Shoulang. In his joy, Ma Junqing showered his favors on Haitang, buying her fine clothing and jewelry, and all but treated her as the mistress of the house. Ma Shi, consumed with rage and jealousy, schemed day and night against her rival. In the meantime she showed unusual partiality for Shoulang and kept him always with her except when Haitang took him away to breastfeed him. Both Ma Junqing and Haitang were pleased that she should love the boy so much. Little did they suspect that it was part of Ma Shi's long-term scheme.

The family had been living in peace for five years when Haitang's mother died, and Ma Junqing took care of her funeral arrangements. Apart from that, Haitang never gave her husband any reason for worry during those five years. She also tried her best to stay on good terms with Ma Shi. However, Ma Shi was always involved in some clandestine relationship in spite of her looks, so she often found Haitang in her way, and grew impatient to get rid of her.

On Shoulang's fifth birthday, Ma Junqing and Ma Shi took him out to tour the temples, where they burned incense and prayed for good fortune. Haitang was left at home to tend the house and direct the servants in preparing a sumptuous meal.

Now relieved of her household duties, Haitang strolled to the gate and lazily gazed out. To her dismay she saw her brother, Zhang Lin. Luck had been against him since he left home five years before. In Kaifeng he failed to find his uncle, who had left for somewhere else. Stranded in a strange land with no kin to turn to, he led a very hard life, not knowing when or whether he would get his next meal. Then he became so sick that he almost died. When he finally recovered, he struggled back to Zhengzhou, only to find his mother dead and buried, and the house sold. Left with no alternative, he plucked up his courage and came to visit his only relative, Haitang.

It is well said by the ancients that poverty teaches humility. Seeing his sister, Zhang Lin went up to salute her first. As for Haitang, the unexpected encounter brought back memories of her past grievances. Without returning his salute, she stared at his sallow face and ragged clothes. "Oh, I almost failed to recognize you!" she said sarcastically. "So it's my dear elder brother! Judging by your shining appearance and fine clothes, you certainly did the right thing by leaving home! You have returned home in such splendor to build a grave for Mother and offer sacrifices to her, if I guess correctly?"

Zhang Lin knew his sister was making fun of him, but he swallowed his pride and admitted he had no money. He also apologized for having treated her unfairly. Haitang stopped ridiculing him, but she still had an offended look on her face and refused to talk to him. Zhang Lin then begged her to give him some money to pull him through.

Haitang was actually willing to help her brother, but as far as money was concerned, she had no say in the house. "Brother, why do you come to me for help? Didn't you make up your mind to support yourself?" When Zhang Lin urged her to lend him a hand for the sake of kinship, Haitang was brought to the verge of tears. "Brother, don't be fooled by the clothes and jewelry I am wearing—they are gifts from my husband. Apart from these I don't have a single coin to my name. How can I help you? You'd better go and think of something else!" She went back to the house, leaving him at the gate with a despairing look on his face.

Unacquainted with the situation in the Ma family, Zhang Lin was sorely disappointed by what he considered Haitang's total lack of sympathy. He turned to walk away, but on second thought he stopped, as he had really nowhere to go. He decided to wait for Ma Junqing's return, hoping that Ma would at least give him something.

In the meantime Ma Junqing was taking his wife and son to the temples, burning incense and praying for good luck for the boy. When they arrived at the Temple of the Goddess of Fertility, the abbot asked Ma for a donation to help renovate the temple. Ma told his wife and son to return home first while he stayed to discuss the matter with the abbot.

From a distance Ma Shi saw a man loitering in front of the house, his arms folded on his chest, his head sunk. After a closer look she recognized him, but she deliberately asked who he was and why he was standing there. When Zhang Lin described his difficulties, Ma Shi realized she could exploit the situation to her advantage. "Since your sister gave birth to a son, the property of the family has been under her charge. Without a son of my own, I have no say in this house. Wait here for just a minute. Let me go in to talk with your sister and try to make her spare a few coins for you." Zhang Lin was very grateful to her, and considered her a much kinder woman than his own sister.

Walking into the house, Ma Shi was met by Haitang and started blaming her for not helping her brother. Haitang replied bitterly, "How can I be unwilling to help my own brother? But I have nothing that is worth anything, except my clothes and jewelry, and these are gifts from my husband. How can I give them away?" However, Ma Shi told her to go ahead and give some to her brother, promising to explain the matter to Ma Junqing herself. At this Haitang took off an outer garment and a piece of jewelry and made for the door, but Ma Shi went up and snatched them into her own hands. "Trust me!" she said. "Let me give them to him!" Though puzzled by Ma Shi's unusual warmth, Haitang did not suspect anything.

Ma Shi handed the dress and jewelry to Zhang Lin and said in an indignant voice, "That sister of yours is so heartless! She has heaps of fine clothing and jewelry, but she would not give you anything. For my part, I cannot bring myself to turn my back on a poor relative. Here is something for you from

241

my own dowry. It's not worth much, but please accept it! My husband is not home so we can't invite you to lunch. You'd better leave now." Zhang Lin thanked her gratefully, then went away.

The abbot took Ma Junqing around the temple and showed him where its wall had collapsed. Ma donated some money, then took his leave. Greeted by his two wives on his return, he noticed Haitang was not wearing her outer garment, and a piece of jewelry was missing from her hair. When Haitang went away to fetch tea, he asked Ma Shi about it. This was exactly what Ma Shi wanted. "I came back to find Haitang with a man," she said. "She took off a piece of clothing and some jewelry from her hair and gave them to him. I stopped her when she tried to find something else to wear and told her to meet you like that. You have doted on her just because she has given you a son, but all the while she has been getting on with a lover behind your back. I am not making this up, you know!"

In spite of his partiality for Haitang, her disreputable past remained a sore point for Ma Junqing. Ma Shi's words plunged him into such fury that he grabbed Haitang and gave her a sound beating. Haitang tried to tell him what had really happened, but with Ma Shi contradicting her every word, Ma Junqing would not believe her. Ma Shi urged him to beat Haitang to death as a punishment for her disgraceful conduct. The house was thrown into great commotion.

Burning with rage, Ma Junqing fell ill suddenly and took to bed. When he told Ma Shi to cook ginger soup for him, she sent Haitang to do the job while she remained sitting beside his bed. After a short while Haitang brought the soup. Ma Shi took a sip and told Haitang to bring some salt and soy sauce. As soon as Haitang left the room, Ma Shi turned her back to her husband, took out a small packet from her sleeve, poured its content into the soup, and threw away the paper wrap. She had just enough time to finish doing this when Haitang returned with the salt and soy sauce. Ma Shi told her to pass the soup to Ma Junqing, who took the bowl and drank up the soup. Haitang then put away the bowl and helped him lie down in bed. No sooner had Ma Junqing closed his eyes than he was stabbed by an intense pain in his chest and became soaked with sweat. He uttered a shrill scream, then breathed his last.

Ma Shi made a few tearless howls to show her due sorrow. Haitang, stupefied and badly scared, wept bitterly over her husband's body.

The murder had been carefully planned. Though she was no beauty, Ma Shi liked to wear gaudy clothes and heavy makeup in order to attract the attention of other men. At last she succeeded in securing a lover named Zhao, who worked as a clerk in the local yamen. Though Zhao was more attracted to her means than her looks, she regarded him as her true love and wanted to marry him. Therefore, at the first opportunity, she did not hesitate to murder her husband with the poison Zhao had given her.

Claiming that Haitang had poisoned her husband to death, Ma Shi told her to choose between a public and private settlement. At a loss, Haitang asked what she meant. "If you want it settled in public," replied Ma Shi, "I will sue you at the yamen, and you will be punished for the crime of poisoning your husband. If you want it settled in private, simply get out of here and leave the child and all the property in this house to me. This is the only way you can save your life." "You are so black-hearted!" Haitang cried with indignation. "The child is mine; how can I let you take him from me? I did not poison my husband; why should I be afraid of punishment? I will fight it out with you at the yamen."

Haitang's reaction surprised Ma Shi, who had become used to her docility. Instead of going to the yamen straightaway, she had some arrangements to make. Apart from informing Zhao of the case, she bribed everyone who might be summoned for testimony. Only then did she take Haitang to the yamen and cry "injustice!" at the gate.

Su Shun, the governor of Zhengzhou, happened to be an official well-known for his stupidity and greed. He had no idea how to try a case properly, and would always leave it to his subordinates as long as he was properly bribed. For this reason the people of Zhengzhou referred to him as "Muddle-Headed Su" and composed a couplet to describe him:

His Excellency knows nothing about the law;
Whoever offers more silver will win the case.

When Ma Shi and Haitang arrived at the yamen, Su Shun had just taken his seat in the main hall ready to hold court. As soon as Ma Shi introduced herself as the widow of the late Lord Ma, the governor fell on his knees to salute her, much to the astonishment of the two women. The runners, who knew the governor well, realized at once that he had mistaken Ma Junqing for a superior. They helped him to his feet while explaining that the so-called Lord Ma was merely a wealthy landlord. Su Shun dusted his robe and went back to his seat. As Ma Shi began rattling away, he could not make head or tail of the case and hastily sent for his clerk, who turned out to be Zhao, Ma Shi's lover.

Entering the hall, Zhao sat down, rolled up his sleeves, and brought the wooden slab down on the table with a loud bang. He ordered Haitang to confess how she had murdered her husband and attempted to rob Ma Shi of her child and property. Naturally, Haitang denied all these charges. At this, he went on to ask how she had come to marry Ma Junqing and what she had done for a living before her marriage, In this way he tried to prove her a licentious woman with an ignominious past. While Haitang claimed that except for her brother Zhang Lin, she had never met another man since her wedding day, Ma Shi insisted she had a secret lover. Zhao quickly decided that Haitang had indeed poisoned her husband, and urged her to explain why she tried to rob Ma Shi of her son. Filled with indignation, Haitang retorted, "It is I who gave birth to the child. What has made him hers? To learn the truth, sir, you only have to ask Mrs Shi, the midwife, and Mrs Zhang, the woman who shaved the child's fetal hair, and some other neighbors." "Your words sound reasonable," Zhao remarked, knowing that Ma Shi had bought off all these people. He sent runners to bring them to court at once.

When Mrs Liu and Mrs Zhang arrived, they both testified in favor of Ma Shi's claim to the child. The neighbors, who had all received money from Ma Shi, provided additional proof, describing how they had offered congratulatory gifts at the birth of Ma Shi's son, and how Ma Junqing had invited them to a feast when the child was one month old. Having secured all these testimonials, Zhao ruled that the child had been borne by Ma Shi and should therefore belong to her.

Haitang was struck speechless with grief, but she was unwilling to give up. She requested to have the child himself point out his mother. What she did not expect was Ma Shi had prepared for this moment many years before. Feigning a strong affection for the child, she had actually taken him away from Haitang since the day he was born and reduced Haitang to the status of wet nurse. Therefore, when Haitang asked Zhao to let the child speak, Ma Shi was not in the least perturbed. Taking the child by the hand, she bade him call Haitang "wet nurse," which he did without hesitation. Haitang burst into tears. Ma Shi then told the child to acknowledge her as his mother. "Mother!" the boy called out. Zhao brought down the wooden slab with a loud bang. "Zhang Haitang, what do you have to say now? The boy, like all our witnesses, has proved that Ma Shi is his natural mother. There is no doubt that you are trying to rob an innocent woman of her son! I wouldn't be surprised if you are also trying to rob her of her rightful property. Now confess to everything, including the murder of your husband!" He bade the runners give her a sound thrashing. The runners, who had also received money from Ma Shi, were eager to comply. Several times Haitang fainted under the brutal beating, then recovered. Finally she could bear it no longer and made her mark on the confession, against her will. She was put on a heavy rack and thrown into prison, to be transported to Kaifeng prefecture for a final sentence.

Zhao left the hall and sent for Dong Chao and Xue Ba, the runners who were to escort Haitang to Kaifeng. He gave each of them five taels of silver and bade them finish her off in a quiet place on the way to Kaifeng the following day. Dong and Xue, who were prepared to do anything for money, agreed to the deal.

The next morning Haitang embarked on her journey to Kaifeng amid heavy snow and a strong wind. With a heavy yoke around her neck and aching all over from the flogging, Haitang plodded on with great difficulty. When they came to a village outside Zhengzhou, a wineshop on the roadside caught the runners' attention and they asked Haitang to buy them a few cups. Haitang said she had no money with her. When Dong Chao raised his club to beat her, Xue Ba stopped him and urged Haitang to quicken her steps. Haitang tried to walk faster, but the ground was slippery because of the frozen snow, and she tripped and fell. "You bitch!" Xue Ba cursed loudly. "I told you to move faster, but you disobey me on purpose! Why should you slip on the ice when everyone else walks on it perfectly well?" He was about to beat her when he slipped. In his rage he lifted his club and beat Haitang until she cried out in pain.

The three of them were soon coming up a hill when they

saw a man dressed in uniform walking briskly in the snow. With her sharp eyes Haitang recognized the man and called out his name. It was her brother, Zhang Lin. After the encounter at Ma's house, he left for Kaifeng where he sold the dress and jewelry and used the money to secure a position in the yamen. Acting with the utmost prudence and servility, he was able to get successive promotions until he became head runner of Kaifeng Prefecture. He was hurrying in the snow on his way to meet Lord Bao, the prefect of Kaifeng, who had been away on an official mission. He was astonished to run into his sister and find her in such dire circumstances. At first he ignored her call for help, for he still remembered vividly how she had ridiculed him and refused to give him any money. When Haitang begged him again, he replied that he would be willing to help if only she had given him a piece of clothing or jewelry the last time they met. Hearing this, Haitang told him in a choking voice that the dress and jewelry was the beginning of her misfortune. Zhang Lin asked in surprise what she meant. After hearing her out, he felt terribly upset, knowing himself to be the cause of all her trouble. He decided to try his best to help her, so he invited Dong Chao and Xue Ba to a wineshop where he treated them to wine and food and asked them to escort his sister safely to Kaifeng Prefecture to await trial by Lord Bao. The two runners, eating and drinking their fill, promised to do as he said.

In the meantime Zhao was getting anxious lest Dong Chao and Xue Ba fail to dispatch Haitang, so he took Ma Shi with him and left the city to go after them. The heavy snow compelled them to enter the wineshop for shelter. At the sight of them Haitang cried, "Brother, here are the couple of adulterers! Let's seize them!" Pushing away the wine cup, Zhang Lin leapt to his feet and rushed toward Zhao, only to find his way blocked by the two runners. Zhao took the chance to slip away. Haitang grabbed Ma Shi by the hand, but

Ma Shi gave her a shove that sent her falling to the ground, then took to her heels. In his rage Zhang Lin seized Xue Bao and began to beat him, while Dong Chao took this chance to strike Haitang. The four of them, grappling with each other, then made their way to Kaifeng Prefecture.

By this time Lord Bao had returned to his yamen. While reading the case files, he came across Zhang Haitang's case. She was charged as adultery, the murder of her husband, and the attempt to rob the principal wife of her son and household property. At first Lord Bao felt a strong aversion to the accused woman, but as he read on he grew increasingly doubtful. Who was Haitang's lover? Why did she want to rob the principal wife of her son? The file was ambiguous in many crucial points, and the conclusions seemed not well supported. He thought for a moment and decided to send some men to Zhengzhou to fetch the plaintiff and witnesses for a retrial of the case. It was at this juncture that Dong Chao and Xue Ba arrived, escorting Haitang, with Zhang Lin close at their heels. Lord Bao had them brought into the hall. He began by questioning Haitang, asking in what family she had been born, how she had met Ma Junqing, to whom she had given the clothing and jewelry, how her husband had died, why she had tried to seize Ma Shi's son, and how the neighbors had testified against her. Eager to prove her innocence, Haitang answered every question in minute detail.

Lord Bao, who already knew what the case was about, asked Haitang why she had signed her confession. "The governor of Zhengzhou did not want to find the truth," replied Haitang. "Ma Shi bought off people high and low, and the governor simply ordered me to be beaten soundly. I fainted and recovered several times until I could not bear the torture anymore. So I admitted to all those charges." Lord Bao called Zhang Lin to him and whispered a few words of instruction. After Zhang Lin left, Lord Bao went on to ask

As Ma Shi pulled with all her might, Haitang let go of
the boy for fear of hurting him.

Haitang why she had tried to rob Ma Shi of her son. Haitang replied that she was really the boy's mother.

At this Lord Bao beckoned a runner over and sent him away with a few words. The runner returned in a short while with a pail of whitewash and proceeded to draw a white circle on the ground. Lord Bao turned to speak to the two women, "I will have the child, Shoulang, placed in this circle. Zhang Haitang and Ma Shi, you may stand close by the circle facing each other and pull at the child by his arm. Whoever succeeds in pulling him out of the circle shall be considered his natural mother." Delighted, Ma Shi snatched at Shoulang's left arm, while Haitang took him by the right hand with some reluctance. As soon as Lord Bao gave the signal, Ma Shi started pulling at Shoulang with all her might. Unwilling to inflict pain on her son, Haitang let go of his hand.

"Zhang Haitang," remarked Lord Bao, "this boy does not seem to be your son. Otherwise why didn't you pull forcefully? Because of this you should be birched!" After the runners came up and gave her two strokes of the birch, Lord Bao ordered the two women to do it again, admonishing Haitang to try hard this time. Again it was Ma Shi who pulled the child out of the circle. When Lord Bao reproved Haitang for not trying hard enough, she said tearfully, "For ten months I carried this child in my womb, and for three years I gave him milk every day. What hardship have I not gone through to bring him up! If both of us pull hard at him, he will easily be hurt. I just can't do that to my son!" In the meantime Ma Shi was rejoicing at her success. Lord Bao's method of deciding who the child belonged to suited her well. If Haitang got hold of the child, she would be the one to inherit most of the property left by Ma Junqing. By taking the child away from Haitang, Ma Shi would become the sole owner of the Ma house. Thus she spared no strength pulling the child and could not care less whether or not he was hurt.

Lord Bao, having drawn his conclusions about the case, brought the wooden slab down on the table with a loud bang. "Ma Shi, what a wicked, impudent woman you are! Shoulang is surely not your child!" He proceeded to give an analysis of the case and ruled that Shoulang belonged to Haitang.

As she had learned some tricks about lawsuits from her lover, Ma Shi tried to defend herself, but Lord Bao did not give her the chance. Dong Chao and Xue Bao, the two runners from Zhengzhou, were interrogated and made to confess to everything. Then Zhao was brought in by Zhang Lin. He tried to deny his guilt at first, but when Lord Bao confronted him with the two runners' confessions and threatened to have him beaten with heavy clubs, he broke down and admitted to the murder of Ma Junqing. At this Ma Shi had no choice but to confess. Lord Bao meted out punishment for the wicked couple according to the law and cleared the case for Haitang. As Lord Bao reached a just verdict by means of a chalk circle drawn on the ground, this story became known as the Case of the Chalk Circle.

JOURNEY OF QIANNÜ'S SPIRIT

*Zheng Guangzu**

In the city of Hengzhou there lived a happy couple, an official named Zhang Gongbi and his wife, Li Shi. When Li Shi became pregnant, Zhang was delighted and on one occasion mentioned it to his colleagues. One of them, Wang Gong, remarked that his wife was also expecting a baby. As Zhang and Wang were good friends, they agreed that if their wives gave birth to a boy and a girl respectively, the two children would unite in marriage on reaching adulthood in accordance with the common practice of "betrothal by pointing to the womb."

In due time the babies were born. Zhang Gongbi became the father of a daughter, named Qiannü, while Wang Gong had a son, Wenju. The engagement was confirmed, and the two families grew closer than ever.

As the old saying goes, human fortunes are as changeable as the weather. First Zhang Gongbi died of illness, leaving Li Shi a widow and Qiannü an orphaned girl. Shortly after, Wang Gong and his wife died of illness one after the other. Left alone in Hengzhou, Wang Wenju returned to his home village and lost contact with the Zhang family.

As the years rolled on, Qiannü grew into a beautiful maiden of seventeen who was fairly skilled at needlework. Her mother, Li Shi, recalled the betrothal arranged by her late

---

* Zheng Guangzu lived during the late Yuan Dynasty and is considered one of the four great Yuan playwrights. He wrote eighteen plays, of which eight have survived.

husband and tried to discover some news about Wenju. She learned to her delight that Wenju was a diligent young man well-versed in the classics, and still unmarried. She had a letter delivered to him, and Wenju wrote her back soon afterwards. Thus contact between them was resumed.

One day Li Shi got a letter from Wang Wenju saying he was going to the capital, Chang'an, to take the imperial examination. He intended to stop at Hengzhou to visit them and marry Qiannü. Li Shi, pondering over the matter, made a decision.

One day a servant came in to announce the arrival of a young scholar by the name of Wang Wenju. "Show him in!" Li Shi said. "I've been thinking about him, and here he is!" Entering the drawing room, Wenju went to his knees to salute Li Shi, his prospective mother-in-law. "Mother, please accept your child's respects!" Li Shi helped him to his feet and had him sit down. "Mother, I have come to pay you a visit, then I will get on my way to the capital to take the examination." At this Li Shi turned to a servant. "Tell Meixiang to ask her young mistress to come here and meet her brother."

Coming to the back door, the servant called out, "Attention! The young mistress is invited to come to the drawing room!" Qiannü left her boudoir for the drawing room, accompanied by her maid, Meixiang. "My child, come over to meet to your brother," said Li Shi. When Qiannü bowed to Wenju, Li Shi said to him, "This is Qiannü!" Then she sent her daughter away. Puzzled, Qiannü asked her maid, "Where does this brother of mine come from?" A smart girl, Meixiang had already learned everything from the other servants. "You don't know him, sister? It is Wang Wenju, the man you were engaged to before you were born!" Qiannü, who was aware of her childhood engagement, was filled with perplexity. She did not understand why her mother let her call her fiance "elder brother" unless she wanted to set a barrier between them, and in a gloomy mood she returned to her boudoir.

Wang Wenju was also feeling upset, not knowing why the old lady had changed her mind about the marriage. Unable to bring himself to ask a blunt question, he stood up to bid her farewell, saying he had to make his way to the capital. However, Li Shi asked him to stay with the family and study in the studio. After some reluctance, Wang Wenju agreed.

Qiannü was in a state of agitation after her meeting with Wenju. She was delighted to find him a handsome young man with graceful manners, but worried that her mother might break her promise and cancel the prearranged marriage. Weighed down by anxiety, she lost her appetite and spent many a sleepless night in bed until she grew rather thin and pale. She no longer did any needlework and seldom sat down at the dressing table to make up. Instead, she would sit by the window for hours, or lie brooding on the couch. She had no idea why her mother should want to obstruct the match and leave Wenju and her longing in anguish for one another. Naturally she could not turn to her mother for solace, so her maid, Meixiang, became her confidant as well as her messenger.

One night she tossed and turned in bed for a long time before drifting into a half-sleep, only to be awakened by the wind rustling against the window. The day was dawning. At the sight of the fallen leaves swirling in the courtyard in the autumn wind, Qiannü was overcome with sorrow and depression as she realized that she was just like a fallen leaf at the mercy of the wind, not knowing where she belonged.

When the maid entered the room in the morning she found Qiannü leaning languidly against the bed heaving deep sighs. "Sister, you must take care of yourself and stop worrying like this!" said Meixiang. Qiannü sighed again. "When will all this come to an end, I wonder? While I am sitting here in distress, he is suffering in the studio. If only I could go and comfort him at the studio, which is but a few steps away! Since you brought his poem the other day, Meixiang, I have read it over and over and found it filled with woe and grievances. Why should a young scholar of high aspirations be subjected to such treatment?" Qiannü then rattled on praising Wenju in an agitated voice. In her opinion, Wenju, who was comparable to the great masters in literary talent, would surely gain fame and glory at the imperial capital. Unlike the swallows, content to twitter their life away under the eaves, Wenju could be compared to a great whale with the vast sea as its playground. When Qiannü paused, somewhat cheered, Meixiang took the chance to break the news she had come to deliver. "Mr. Wang is leaving today for the capital. Your mother will see him off at the Willow Twig Pavilion."

The day before, Wang Wenju had informed the old lady of his intention to leave. He had stayed long enough in the house, with no idea whether his engagement with Qiannü still held. Moreover, the examination was drawing near. Li Shi did not try to stop him, nor did she intimate anything about his marriage. "We will see you off at the Willow Twig Pavilion," she said simply.

Shortly after Li Shi and Wenju arrived at the pavilion, Qiannü also came with her maid. "My child," Li Shi said to her, "today we are sending your brother on his way. Pour a cup of wine and offer it to him." Holding the cup in both hands, Qiannü said in a tremulous voice, "Brother, please drink it up." Wenju took the cup and downed it in one gulp. As if emboldened by liquor, he decided to speak his mind. "Mother," he said to Li Shi, "I would like to ask you something before I leave. Formerly, the marriage between Qiannü and me was arranged by our two families before either of us was born. When my parents passed away, the matter was put aside. This time I have come with the intention of celebrating my wedding, but to my surprise you make me address Qiannü as younger sister. Could you please explain to me what this is all about?"

The old lady was no longer able to evade the topic. "Never in the past three generations has a young man without rank been received into my family," she declared. "What you must do now is go to the capital and take the imperial examination. If you distinguish yourself and subsequently become an official, you can come back to us and marry Qiannü." Wenju was eager to make his name in the capital, so he agreed readily to this, but Qiannü had her own doubts. In the imperial capital, she thought, there must be many young maidens from respectable families waiting to become engaged or married. With his talents Wenju will no doubt pass the examination with flying colors, thereby making himself an eligible young man for all those families in search of a son-in-law. If he should succumb to one of them, all her hopes and longings would be in vain. She became so worried over these dire prospects that tears streamed down her cheeks. Wenju went up to comfort her. "If I get to be an official, you will also receive a title as an official's wife!" However, Qiannü was more concerned about whether she would become his wife at all. "Keep me in your heart while you are away!" she said. The old lady, displeased that the young couple ignored her in their intimate talk, urged Meixiang to take Qiannü back home.

Qiannü was so grieved at the parting that her handkerchief became soaked with tears. Reluctantly she mounted the carriage with Meixiang to return home. In the glow of the setting sun the autumn wind swept across the road, scattering withered leaves in all directions. It grew a little chilly as a light rain began falling. Sitting in the carriage, Qiannü kept looking back until Wenju was out of sight, lost in the mist among distant hills. She felt as if her spirit had drifted away with him.

It was with a heavy heart that Wang Wenju left the

pavilion. After a day's travel he came to a river; the following day he boarded a boat to continue his journey. The willows and reeds trembling in the wind along the river banks filled him with sadness. At moonrise the boatman steered the boat ashore for the night. As he sat facing the cool waters Wenju recalled his parting with Qiannü. He picked up his zither, placed it on his lap and began to play. The music flowing from the strings seemed to be weeping and complaining.

Late into the night the surface of the river remained calm and chilly. All of a sudden Wenju heard to his surprise someone on the bank calling out his name in a familiar voice. "Is that Qiannü?" he asked. "Why are you here late at night?" It was indeed Qiannü who answered him. "Wenju, I left home to come after you without my mother's knowledge. Let's go to the capital together!" When the astonished Wenju asked why she had chanced such a daring act, Qiannü said she was unwilling to be left behind to pine away in anguish. Wenju then expressed his fear that her mother might come after her. "What of that?" responded Qiannü defiantly. "I have done what I think is right, so my conscience is clear!"

Wenju tried to dissuade her by quoting an ancient adage, "A woman who marries without parental consent cannot be made the principal wife." Qiannü remained unmoved. The only thing that worried her, she said, was that he might forget her after his success in the imperial examination and marry into a prominent family in the capital. Wenju grew a little suspicious on hearing this, wondering if she wanted to marry him merely for the sake of his prospective position and wealth. "If I should fail in the examination," he asked, "would you still marry me?" "Even if you fail, even if we have to endure great hardships, eating coarse meals and wearing crude clothes, I will stay by your side forever." Touched by her sincerity, Wenju agreed to take her with him. He helped her into the boat and told the boatman to set sail to avoid any

Wenju was playing the zither in the boat when a young woman
called his name from the river bank.

pursuers her mother might have sent after them.

Back at her home, Qiannü had become bedridden after seeing Wenju off at the pavilion. Hankering after her beloved, she pined away day after day. Eating little and sleeping less, she became emaciated and did not respond to any medication. Most of the time she was delirious and her maid, Meixiang, had to attend to her all day long. Waking up one day, she was told that it was already late spring in the fourth month. Through the window she could see the ground covered with red petals from withered flowers. She sighed as she recalled that Wenju had been away for quite some time without sending her a single letter.

Just then Li Shi came to inquire after her daughter's illness. Though she recognized her mother's voice, Qiannü deliberately asked Meixiang who it was. "I cannot see her," she said when Meixiang told her it was her mother. "Whichever way I look, I see Wenju!" When Li Shi asked if she was getting any better, Qiannü felt a surge of grief and sank into delirium. As she came to, she heard her mother talking about finding another doctor. "To have Wang Wenju back would be better than all the doctors in the world!" Qiannü blurted out. Even when Li Shi agreed to send for Wenju, Qiannü remained grumpy. "If it comes to that, why did you drive him away in the first place?" She turned her back to her mother and drifted into another dream. She felt as if she were floating into the air, and a moment later found herself beside Wang Wenju, who was wearing an official's robe.

Shortly after his arrival in the capital, Wang Wenju took the imperial examination, spending less than half a day to compose a long commentary on national affairs. The emperor was so pleased with the article that he made Wenju the Number One Scholar of the year. Overjoyed, Wenju wrote a letter and hired a servant named Zhang Qian to carry it to Zhang Gongbi's house in Hengzhou.

Arriving in Hengzhou, Zhang Qian located the house and shouted aloud at the gate. "A family letter! A family letter with good news!" Qiannü, lying in bed, bade Meixiang go and find out what it was about. Zhang Qian was ushered into the drawing room, where he handed the letter to Meixiang. As soon as she glanced at it, Meixiang exclaimed, "A family letter!" Qiannü broke into a broad smile. As if her illness was gone, she left her sickbed and walked unsupported into the drawing room. At the sight of Qiannü, Zhang Qian marveled at her striking resemblance to his master's wife back in the capital.

Qiannü picked up the letter eagerly and started to read. Meixiang was about to ask a question when Qiannü let out a scream. "What injustice!" Then she passed out. Meixiang hurried over to prop up the young lady, and Li Shi also arrived on the scene. Qiannü was carried back to her bed, where she finally came to after being pounded on the back and stroked on the chest.

The letter from Wenju stated the following: "Dear Mother: I arrived at the capital and came out first in the imperial examination. I am still waiting to get my appointment, after which I will return with my wife to visit you." It was the news that Wenju had taken another wife that plunged Qiannü into despair. Why should he want to bring her to Hengzhou? Overwhelmed with grief, Qiannü began blaming her mother for having obstructed her marriage and Wenju for his faithlessness. Zhang Qian, the servant, was touched by her pathetic outburst. "My master is really to blame! Why should he have sent me here? What I took for a family letter containing good news turns out to be a letter of divorce. No wonder the young lady passed out with rage!"

Wang Wenju in the meantime was made an official in the imperial capital, where he enjoyed a happy family life with Qiannü. At the end of three years the emperor was kind enough to reappoint him to assistant prefect of Hengzhou, his hometown. When he broke the news to her, Qiannü was delighted. "We can at last return home in glory!" she exclaimed. "This is my fondest dream come true!" Wenju had the luggage packed, and the couple set out in their carriage that very day.

During the journey they feasted their eyes on the spring sights, which seemed to mirror their joy, and arrived in Hengzhou in high spirits. The carriage pulled up before the gate of Qiannü's home. "Come after me," said Wenju. He entered the gate and was shown into the drawing room. When Li Shi, informed by the servants, came to meet him, Wenju fell on his knees to salute her. "Mother, please forgive my impudence!" The old lady asked in surprise, "What are you talking about?" "I should not have taken Qiannü with me to the capital without your permission." "What?" Li Shi cried in astonishment. "My daughter has been ill in bed all these years! How could she have gone to the capital with you? Where is your wife?" "Mother, here I am!" responded Qiannü, who had followed Wenju into the room. "Please accept the respects of your unfilial daughter!" "I must be looking at an evil spirit!" the old lady was badly alarmed. "This is an evil spirit!"

Qiannü could not understand why her mother should call her an evil spirit. She was so distressed that she burst out crying. His suspicion aroused, Wang Wenju drew his sword and pointed it at her. "Listen, spirit! Who are you? Where do you come from? You'd better tell the truth, or I will thrash you apart!" Qiannü was trembling all over with fear. It took her quite a while to calm down and try to explain the situation. "My mother must be playing a trick! She thinks my elopement with you is a family disgrace, so she wants to cast me out by calling me an evil spirit. How can you take her at her word? Don't you remember the happy times we have shared in the three years of our marriage? Give me a chance

261

Qiannü suddenly leapt forward and merged
with the sickly maiden in the bed.

to reason with my mother." Her initial shock over, Li Shi also grew cautious. "Put away your sword, Wenju. Since she denies being an evil spirit, we can take her to the boudoir and see if she can recognize the maid, Meixiang." Wenju thought it a good idea and put down his sword.

Qiannü headed straight for the boudoir and walked in. At the sight of her dressing table and toilet case, she began to feel dizzy in the head, as if in a trance. She was even more confused when, looking up, she saw a young lady in her own image lying in bed, surrounded by a few maids. Before Qiannü could open her mouth to say anything, the sickly young lady turned abruptly toward her. As if drawn by an invisible force, Qiannü lunged to the bed and, the moment she reached there, vanished out of sight. "Where is Wenju?" the young lady sat up in bed, as if just awakened, her illness gone and her spirits fully restored. "Where is my wife?" asked Wenju upon entering the room. As soon as she saw him, the young lady began repudiating him for finding another wife. "What is this about?" Wenju asked in great perplexity. "Didn't you stay with me in the capital for three years? And how come there were two Qiannüs merged into one?"

By this time Qiannü had recovered enough from her spirit journey to give him an explanation. "After we were separated at the Willow Twig Pavilion, I kept thinking about you and my spirit seemed to accompany you all along the journey. While I lay ill in bed at home, another part of me was spending time with you in the capital. Now that you have come home at last, I feel fully awake for the first time in years." The old lady, struck speechless for a long time, finally spoke up. "Let bygones be bygones! It happens to be an auspicious day today, so let's make it your formal wedding day!"

GRAIN SALE IN CHENZHOU

Author Unknown

For three years Chenzhou Prefecture had not seen a single drop of rain. The fields became scorched, and all the crops shriveled. The local people resorted to eating tree bark and grass, and in the more secluded places, cannibalism was reported. The local authorities kept sending petitions to the imperial court, imploring it to dispatch an official to relieve the famine victims.

Famine relief was the responsibility of the Ministry of Revenue, then headed by a renowned scholar named Fan Zhongyan. As petitions kept piling up on his desk, he reported the matter to the emperor, who ordered him to summon the relevant officials to a meeting and chose two capable and upright men for the mission. Once chosen, the two imperial envoys would set out for Chenzhou at once and sell grain from the local granaries to the people at the low price of five tales of silver for one dan of fine rice.

Thus charged by the emperor, Fan Zhongyan immediately invited the court ministers, Han Qi, Lü Yijian and Liu Yanei to his office to discuss the problem. "The relief operation in Chenzhou is both important and urgent," remarked Han Qi, the plain-spoken Vice Chief Minister. "The men chosen for the job must be honest, capable and uncorruptible!" "I agree with you," said Chief Minister Lü Yijian, who was careful not to offend anyone. Liu Yanei, however, was a brutal man given to riding roughshod over others. He once remarked that for him beating a man to death would be no big deal, as effortless as pulling a tile from the roof. When it was his turn to speak he declared that his son, Liu Dezhong, and his son-in-law, Yang Jinwu, were the best candidates for the job. Liu Dezhong was a notorious bully in the capital. Relying on his father's position, he threw his weight around and made a pest of himself wherever he went. And his brother-in-law, Yang Jinwu, acted as his right-hand man. Though aware of the infamy of the two men, Fan Zhongyan did not reject the recommendation outright for fear of an open confrontation with Liu Yanei. Instead, he suggested that the two men be brought in for scrutiny.

When Liu Dezhong and Yang Jinwu arrived, their fierce looks and crude manners caused the old ministers present to shake their heads in dismay. Fan Zhongyan said to Liu Yanei, "Judging by their manner and appearance, I'm afraid they seem unfit for this mission." Liu, however, insisted that his children were fully qualified. Han Qi spoke up in favor of Fan, saying the two young men were definitely not suitable. But Lü Yijian remained noncommittal and asked Fan to make the final decision. "Mr. Fan," said Liu Yanei hastily, "I am willing to make a written statement of guarantee for my two children. The court can hold me responsible for whatever misdeeds they might commit while in Chenzhou." Fan Zhongyan was compelled to give his consent. He told the two young men that they must stick to the price set by the emperor: five taels per dan. Liu Dezhong and Yang Jinwu paid scant attention to this admonition, but took their leave immediately, saying the mission was too urgent for further delay.

Liu Yanei accompanied them to the gate and said in a low voice, "In terms of rank and status I have no complaints, but we can do with a little more money in our family. When the two of you get to Chenzhou, double the price to ten taels per dan. You can also mix some sand and chaff into the grain, or make clever use of the balance and measuring vessels to get more money. Just go ahead and do it—I am here to back you up if there should be any trouble." Liu Dezhong remarked that he needed no instruction on how to cash in on the mission, but he was worried that the people of Chenzhou might grow discontent and rise up to create disturbances. Liu Yanei told him to wait while he returned to the hall to speak with Fan Zhongyan.

"Mr. Fan," asked Liu Yanei, "if there should be a riot in Chenzhou, how would it be handled?" Actually the emperor, anticipating the problem, had prepared a gold hammer. By using that hammer, the envoys could beat any rioter to death with impunity. Fan had deliberately withheld the hammer for fear that Liu Yanei's two children would abuse the people of Chenzhou with it. Now that Liu Yanei mentioned it, Fan reluctantly brought out the hammer and gave it to him, warning that it must be used with the utmost restraint. Overjoyed to have the hammer at their disposal, Liu Dezhong and Yang Jinwu set out for Chenzhou in high spirits.

Thus the meeting of the senior ministers came to an end. As Fan Zhongyan left to report to the emperor, Han Qi said to Lü Yijian with a sigh, "Those two will be up to no good once they are in Chenzhou. Someday I will have to bring them to account when complaints arrive from there." "You have always acted in the best interests of the nation and the people," said Lü Yijian flatly.

On their arrival in Chenzhou, Liu Dezhong and Yang Jinwu sent for the two clerks at the official granary for a briefing. "The two of us are now in charge here. The price of rice is set by His Majesty at ten taels of silver per dan; this cannot be changed. However, no one likes to do a job without gain. Why don't you use an oversized weight for the balance and a smaller-than-normal grain measure? In that way the two of us will be able to make a good profit, and the two of you will also benefit from it. How does that sound to you?" The two clerks, who were used to cheating in grain sales, agreed with alacrity. "We know what you mean, sir. You have promised us a small fortune, and in return we will help you gain a big one." They went away to fetch the treacherous balance and grain measure to be used for sales the following day.

When it was announced that the emperor had ordered rice to be sold to the famine victims of Chenzhou at a bargain price, people all over the region, though poverty-stricken, managed to scrap up some money in order to buy some food to tide them over the famine. The day the official granary was opened, the first customers were three peasants who came to purchase rice with twenty taels of silver. The two clerks took the silver when Liu Yanei said, "Examine it carefully! Don't let yourselves be cheated with fake silver!" The two clerks actually needed no such warning. They stared at the piece of silver for a long time before placing it on the balance, declaring it to be sixteen taels. The three peasants argued that the piece, instead of four tales short, was in fact half a tael in excess. When Li Dezhong heard this he began to swear, calling them troublemakers and threatening to use the gold hammer on them. The three peasants, though fuming with indignation, were forced to produce six more taels. The two clerks then measured two dan of rice with the undersized measure. Taking the bag of rice in his hands, one of the peasants realized immediately it was short in weight. When he took a handful of rice and let it stream down against the wind, a lot of chaff and sand were found. He sighed. "This is supposed to be two dan, but weighs only one sixty. With the chaff and sand removed, a little more than one dan will be all that is left. Why should people like us suffer one misfortune after another!" Carrying the rice, the three peasants left in low spirits.

Soon afterwards two men, Old Zhang and his son, came

to buy rice. Aware of his father's fiery temper, Little Zhang warned him not to make any offensive remark while buying rice. Old Zhang, however, would not listen. "The imperial court shows its concern for the people by this grain sale," he said. "But a bunch of corrupt officials are plotting together to seek private gains by exploiting us. How can we allow them to do this? If they keep on with their foul deeds I will accuse them to their superiors, and I won't be afraid to take the case to the imperial capital!" "Father!" pleaded Little Zhang. "How can you be so naive? What can you possibly do against those powerful officials? Why don't you simply accept our bad fortune?" But Old Zhang remained irate and went on cursing the officials and their clerks, comparing them to rats feeding on the official granary.

When one of the clerks caught sight of the father and son, both in ragged clothes and with sallow complexions, he yelled at them. "Hey you, old man, are you also coming to buy rice? First show me if you have any silver!" Old Zhang was not in the least pleased by this yelling. "Isn't this silver good enough?" he said, taking out a piece of silver. The clerk took it, weighed it in his hand, and put it on the balance. "Well, old man, that's eight taels from you!" "I have brought a full twelve taels!" exclaimed Old Zhang angrily. "How come it has shrunk to eight once you take it in your hands?"

Little Zhang, though usually timid, was also unwilling to put up with such an injustice. He stepped forth and demanded, "Look, this piece of silver is exactly twelve taels. Why should it weigh only eight on your balance? This is not being fair!" At this, the second clerk began to abuse Little Zhang. "Shut up, you knave! Look at the balance—it points to eight taels only. You don't suppose I have bitten a chunk off your silver?" When Old Zhang said he would weigh the silver himself, the two clerks would not let him. Finally Old Zhang, still fuming, conceded to count the silver as eight taels. But

Shamed into anger, Liu Dezhong raised
the hammer to hit Old Zhang.

the two clerks went on to give short measure, which caused the two Zhangs to protest again. "Who are these two officials sitting high above?" asked Old Zhang, pointing to Liu De-zhong and Yang Jinwu. "Why don't they do something to ensure fairness?" "You don't know them?" said the clerks. "They are sent by the emperor to take charge of the grain sale!" When Old Zhang remarked such officials were worth-less compared with Lord Bao of Kaifeng Prefecture, the first clerk warned him to mind his tongue. "Stop talking nonsense, old man! You are asking for trouble!"

Instead of holding his tongue, Old Zhang became more vehement in his curses, saying the officials were virtually robbing beggars of their last bowl of soup. Unable to make him stop, the first clerk went over to report to Liu Dezhong, who went into a rage and had Old Zhang brought to him. "Damned bandit!" he yelled at the old man. "How dare you insult me just because you don't have enough silver?" Pushed around, abused and threatened, Old Zhang nevertheless showed no sigh of fear. Instead, he looked at the two officials steadily in the face. "Corrupt officials like the two of you only bring misfortune to the people and our nation!" he called out angrily. Liu Dezhong, infuriated, lifted the gold hammer and hit the old man on the head. Old Zhang dropped to the ground unconscious, and Little Zhang began calling out his name tearfully. After a while the old man came to. Despite the searing pain in the head, Old Zhang mustered his last drop of strength to reprove Liu Dezhong. "I come here to buy rice. What right do you have to hit me?" "You know how much your life is worth?" Liu said with a sneer. "No more than a piece of lampwick, I tell you! I am sick of poor people like you and happy to bid you good riddance!" Old Zhang rebuked Liu for defying the law of the empire and told his son to bring the case to Lord Bao, who would surely uphold justice and mete out punishments against such wicked officials. Once he got to the underworld, he said, he would accuse the two officials to the gods there. Then he sighed deeply and breathed his last.

Little Zhang burst into a storm of tears over his father's body. Then, recalling his father's last words, he wiped off his tears and vowed to seek justice by going to the capital and lodging a complaint with Lord Bao. Hearing this, Liu Dezhong said to the clerks, "Let him go and complain to his heart's content. With my father in the court, what do I have to be afraid of? The Minister of Revenue, Mr. Fan, is a good friend of my father's. I have killed a poor old man—so what? It would make no difference even if I should kill ten!" Then he turned to Yang Jinwu. "I don't think anyone will dare to make trouble again. Why don't we skip off to Goutuiwan for a cup of wine with Wang Fenlian?"

Before long, news of the gross misdeeds committed by Liu and Yang in Chenzhou reached the capital. Fan Zhongyan reported the matter truthfully to the emperor, who had hitherto shown a strong partiality for Liu Yanei. Afraid of arousing further discontent in the court and among the common people, the emperor reluctantly agreed to do something about it. Fan Zhongyan was ordered to summon another meeting at which an upright official would be chosen to set out for Chenzhou, there to investigate the case and take over the relief operation. The official would be given a sword and a gold placard empowering him to carry out death sentences without the prior consent of the imperial court.

Fan Zhongyan took his seat in the Secretariat and sent for the relevant ministers. Han Qi and Lü Yijian soon arrived and were told about the imperial edict, but they had to wait for Liu Yanei before they could make a decision. Liu, in the meantime, was delayed on his way because of Little Zhang. Arriving in the capital, Little Zhang could barely find his way around and had no idea where to look for Lord Bao. Just then he caught sight of a high official with gray whiskers. This must be Lord Bao, he told himself, so he rushed up to block the path of the carriage and shouted "injustice!" Liu Yanei had him brought over and learned to his dismay that the yokel wanted to sue his own son and son-in-law. Pretending to be Lord Bao, he told Little Zhang to wait outside and hurried into the Secretariat Hall.

As Liu Yanei entered the hall with quick steps, Fan Zhongyan greeted him by saying, "What a couple of fine officials you recommended to us, Yanei!" Though startled, Liu tried to appear calm. "These two children of mine are really fine officials, I assure you!" When Fan Zhongyan, not mincing words, went on to describe the many atrocities committed by the two envoys in Chenzhou, Liu Yanei tried his best to find excuses for his children.

While the ministers were engaged in heated talk in the hall, Little Zhang began to get restless waiting outside, so he went over to a gatekeeper. "Lord Bao told me to wait for him here. He has been inside for a long time now. When will he come out?" The gatekeeper gave him a quizzical look and told him that the man who had gone inside was Liu Yanei, not Lord Bao. Dumbfounded, Little Zhang muttered to himself, "I almost threw myself into the tiger's den!" At this moment the gatekeeper caught sight of Lord Bao approaching the gate. "Here comes Lord Bao!" he told Little Zhang.

. Lord Bao was then edict attendant of the Dragon Diagram Hall and concurrently prefect of Kaifeng. During his official career of more than thirty years he had tried numerous cases, always endeavoring to uphold justice even at the risk of offending people of rank and power. On his return from an inspection tour at the emperor's order, he now was coming to meet the other ministers to report the results of his tour, when his entourage was halted by Little Zhang, who was on his knees uttering loud cries of "injustice." After hearing him out,

Lord Bao told him to wait outside, then entered the hall.

Stepping into the hall, Lord Bao exchanged greetings with the other ministers present. Fan Zhongyan, Han Qi and Lü Yijian all made solicitous inquiries after his journey and commended him for his loyalty and devotion, saying it was his uprightness and impartiality that made the corrupt officials of all ranks cower in fear. To their surprise, Lord Bao said it was not a good idea for him to go on incurring the wrath of the rich and powerful through his forthrightness, and he was considering retirement. "How can you leave us like this?" cried Fan Zhongyan anxiously. "The court is in great need of upright officials like you!" Liu Yanei, on the other hand, would be too glad to get rid of Lord Bao, whom he feared more than anyone else. "It is natural for you to think so," he said to Lord Bao. "At an old age, one can indeed retire from his post and stay home to enjoy family pleasures." However, Lord Bao had no intention whatsoever to resign from his post. He had mentioned his plan to retire in order to find out whether Liu Yanei had a guilty conscience, and Liu's response betrayed him. Without saying anything, Lord Bao took his leave and walked out of the hall.

As soon as he passed the gate, Little Zhang fell on his knees and cried, "Your Excellency, take pity on me!" Lord Bao bade him not to linger in the capital but rather return to Chenzhou at once, promising he would go there soon. Thus assured, Little Zhang headed back to his hometown. Lord Bao then walked back into the hall. "Why are you back in a minute?" asked Fan Zhongyan in surprise. "I've just been told that Chenzhou has suffered a severe famine," replied Lord Bao, "and some corrupt officials are exploiting the situation and harming the local people. Could you tell me which officials were sent there?"

Fan Zhongyan replied that the relief officials were Liu Dezhong and Yang Jinwu, who were, respectively, Liu Yanei's

273

son and son-in-law. Informed of their profiteering practices, the emperor had charged the ministers to send someone to Chenzhou to investigate and deal with the case. "I don't think anyone else is up to the task. Why don't you volunteer for it?" "I can't do it," Lord Bao responded. "If you can't, who else can?" remarked Lü Yijian. By this time Fan Zhongyan was fully aware of what Lord Bao had in mind, so he turned to Liu Yanei sitting uneasily by his side. "Yanei, Prefect Bao is unwilling to shoulder the task. Why don't you try to persuade him? If we can't make him go, you'll have to take the trouble of going to Chenzhou yourself."

Liu Yanei did not know what to say. "Old Bao just said he wanted to retire," he thought to himself, "and now he looks very unwilling to go to Chenzhou. I might as well say something to urge him as Fan suggested. When he declines again to accept the job, I can take it up myself, and no harm will ever come to my children." Thus he said to Lord Bao, "Why don't you take this trip to Chenzhou, old prefect?" "Since you say so," Lord Bao responded at once, "I will take the trip for your sake. Zhang Qian!" he called out to his servant. "Saddle the horse! We will set off without delay!" Filled with dismay and remorse, Liu Yanei muttered to himself, "What will happen to my children when this old fellow arrive in Chenzhou?" Ignoring Liu's sour expression, Lord Bao said to him, "Thanks so much for recommending me for the task!" "I didn't recommend you!" cried Liu Yanei in exasperation. "I never did!" But the other ministers all agreed to have Lord Bao chosen for the mission. Fan Zhongyan took out the gold placard and imperial sword given by the emperor and handed them to Lord Bao. Out of his wits, Liu Yanei stifled his rage and assumed an obsequious air to plead with Lord Bao. "When you arrive in Chenzhou, please take good care of my two children for my sake!" Lord Bao raised the sword and placard. "I will take good care of them with this!" Bursting into fury, Liu Yanei shouted, "You wouldn't dare kill my children! I am superior to you in both rank and wealth!" Lord Bao paid no attention to his threat and left immediately for Chenzhou with Zhang Qian.

Judging from Lord Bao's attitude, Liu Yanei knew his children were in imminent danger, so he asked the other ministers to help him. Mumbling a few noncommittal words, Han Qi slipped out of the hall, with Lü Yijian close at his heels. Fan Zhongyan, importuned by Liu Yanei, came up with an idea. "Take it easy, Yanei. Let's ask for an audience with the emperor, and I will obtain for you an imperial edict stating 'The living shall be pardoned, but the dead shall not.' I will also ask His Majesty to send you to carry this edict to Chenzhou. Everything will be all right then." Liu Yanei could not think of a better solution, so he followed Fan to the imperial court to see the emperor.

Lord Bao left for Chenzhou on horseback, with Zhang Qian following on foot carrying the imperial sword and gold placard. One day Lord Bao called Zhang Qian over and asked him what comments he had heard from the officials and common people along the way. "I would have told you, Your Excellency," replied Zhang Qian obsequiously. "When they are told that Prefect Bao is on his way to Chenzhou to take charge of the grain sale, they all cup their hands in respect and say, 'At last an official has come to uphold justice for the common folks!'" Lord Bao, however, did not take Zhang Qian at his words, knowing that he was definitely not popular with the corrupt officials and local bullies.

On approaching Chenzhou, Lord Bao dismounted and changed into plainclothes so as to gather some firsthand information from the local people. He ordered Zhang Qian to ride the horse and enter the city before him. Delighted, Zhang Qian leapt onto the horse. He was about to ride away when Lord Bao stopped him. "Bear this in mind, Zhang Qian! In the city you must not bully the common people. If you find me being humiliated, don't try to intervene. Now you can leave!" Zhang Qian answered aye and galloped off.

Lord Bao gazed after Zhang Qian until he vanished out of sight, then resumed the trip on foot. Ahead of him there was a woman riding a donkey. Somehow alarmed, the donkey suddenly took a leap, sending the woman sprawling to the ground. Lord Bao walked up and reined in the donkey, while the woman scrambled to her feet. Judging by her excessive make-up, she was apparently a woman of a disreputable profession. Taking Lord Bao for an old villager, she thanked him and asked him to help her onto the donkey.

The woman turned out to be Wang Fenlian, a prostitute in Goutuiwan Village. It was on her that Liu Dezhong and Yang Jinwu had spent much of their ill-gotten money from the grain sale. Leaving the granary to the care of the two clerks, they spent all their time in Wang's house and even kept the gold hammer there. Alarmed by the news of Lord Bao's coming visit to Chenzhou, they had a banquet prepared in the official reception hall and sent someone to fetch Wang Fenlian, intending to have her wait on Lord Bao. After delivering the message the man left, so Wang had to make her way to the reception hall on a donkey. When she unexpectedly ran into Lord Bao, she took him for a peasant and asked him to lead the donkey for her, to which Lord Bao agreed without difficulty. As they moved along he began to ask her questions. Wang Fenlian, boasting of her wealth, promised to tip the old man handsomely. When she mentioned the gold hammer, Lord Bao cried excitedly that the very sight of the hammer was said to dispel ill fortune. To further show off her importance, Wang said she would take him home to look at the hammer if he escorted her to the reception hall for a banquet. Lord Bao was eager to comply.

Shortly after, they arrived at the hall. Both Liu Dezhong

and Yang Jinwu came out to greet her with broad smiles, and Wang complained that the messenger had not waited for her, so she had fallen from the donkey. As the old peasant had escorted her all the way there, she suggested that he be given some wine and food. When one of the granary clerks brought the food over, the old man remarked, to the surprise of all, "Tell the official over there that I don't want this meat and wine. Feed them to the donkey instead." The clerk went in to repeat the old man's remark to Liu Dezhong, who flew into a tantrum and ordered the old man tied up and suspended from the old scholartree in the courtyard.

Liu Dezhong and Yang Jinwu waited and waited, but Lord Bao failed to show up. They were growing anxious when Zhang Qian arrived holding the gold placard in his hand and carrying the imperial sword on his back.

Intent on enjoying a treat, Zhang Qian walked straight into the hall without noticing Lord Bao hanging from the tree outside. "Excellent!" he cried out as soon as he stepped in. "Both of you are here. Lord Bao is on his way to arrest you, and he has sent me to come first. We know perfectly well what the two of you have been up to here!" Liu and Yang begged Zhang Qian to show some mercy. As Lord Bao hadn't arrived yet, Zhang Qian took this chance to brag. "Listen, the two of you! When court is held, Lord Bao is merely the sitting lord, while I am the standing lord. You can trust me with your problem." Taking the cup of wine offered by Liu and Yang, he was about to gulp it when he caught sight of Lord Bao hanging from the tree in the courtyard. His face turned ghastly pale, and his hands trembled with fright. But he recovered in an instant and threw the wine cup to the ground. "What a couple of knaves you are!" he roared, pointing at Liu and Yang with his fingers. "How dare you raise the official price of rice from five to ten taels? How dare you kill Old Zhang just because he tried to argue with you?" Pointing at

Lord Bao ordered Yang Jinwu beheaded with the imperial sword.

the scholartree, he demanded to know why they had tied and beat up an innocent person, then he pointed at himself and demanded how they dared try to bribe him with wine. "Lord Bao has already entered the city in plain clothes. Why don't you hurry to the east gate to receive him?" Scared out of their senses, Liu Dezhong and Yang Jinwu scurried out and rushed to the east gate.

After they left, Zhang Qian hurried over to untie Lord Bao from the tree. "A standing lord indeed!" Lord Bao said, giving him an angry stare. Zhang Qian dared not say a single word in reply. "How can I go back home when both of them are gone?" complained Wang Fenlian. "Old man, come over and help me get on the donkey!" Lord Bao stopped Zhang Qian from scolding her. He led the donkey over and helped the woman mount it. Before she left, Wang told Lord Bao that he could come to her house to take a look at the gold hammer at the next opportunity. When everyone else had gone, Lord Bao remarked to Zhang Qian, "Their crimes have been proven. I am determined to rid the empire of these two greedy, heartless men, even at the risk of my own life!"

The next morning Lord Bao held court in the yamen. As Zhang Qian brought in Liu Dezhong and Yang Jinwu, some runners were dispatched to seize Wang Fenlian. Entering the hall, Liu Dezhong and Yang Jinwu were flabbergasted when they recognized Lord Bao and dropped on their knees in fear. But they flatly denied their malpractices in the grain sale, such as raising the price of rice and giving short measure. A moment later Wang Fenlian arrived with the gold hammer, which she admitted had been given to her by Yang Jinwu. It did not take long for Lord Bao to reach his verdict. The imperial sword was handed to the executioner, who took Yang out and beheaded him. Little Zhang was summoned into the hall, where he was given the gold hammer to strike Liu Dezhong to death to avenge Old Zhang. After that, Lord Bao

279

had Little Zhang locked up in prison, knowing that Liu Yanei would think up something to rescue his children.

Sure enough, Liu Yanei soon arrived with the imperial edict stating "The living shall be pardoned, but the dead shall not," which he had managed to obtain from the emperor the day he followed Fan Zhongyan to the imperial court. "That old peasant is dead," he told himself, "and my children are still alive. With this edict, they can get away with whatever they did." He hastened to Chenzhou and read out the edict to Lord Bao, who pledged solemnly to carry it out without fail. Turning to Zhang Qian, Lord Bao asked, "Who are the dead and who are the living?" "Liu Dezhong and Yang Jinwu are dead, and Little Zhang is alive," was the reply. Lord Bao ordered Little Zhang set free on the spot, for the emperor had declared him not guilty. Thereupon Liu Yanei burst into bitter tears. Grieved at his children's death, he berated Lord Bao for his cruelty and blamed himself for bringing the edict that served to absolve his enemy instead of saving his own children. However, Lord Bao declared that according to Liu Yanei's written pledge, he should be held responsible for his children's guilt. Thus the runners were ordered to arrest Liu Yanei and take him back to the imperial capital to stand trial.

图书在版编目(CIP)数据

墙头马上:英文/陈美林改编.—北京:外文出版社,1997
(中国古代戏剧故事选)
ISBN 7 - 119 - 00342 - 9

Ⅰ.墙… Ⅱ.陈… Ⅲ.戏剧文学 - 故事 - 中国 - 英文
Ⅳ.I247.8

中国版本图书馆 CIP 数据核字(95)第 10168 号

墙头马上 —— 中国古代戏剧故事选

陈美林　改编

责任编辑　贾先锋　杨春燕

装帧设计　朱振安

＊

ⓒ外文出版社

外文出版社出版

(中国北京百万庄大街 24 号)

邮政编码 100037

北京外文印刷厂印刷

中国国际图书贸易总公司发行

(中国北京车公庄西路 35 号)

北京邮政信箱第 399 号　邮政编码 100044

1997 年(36 开)第 1 版

1997 年第 1 版第一次印刷

(英)

ISBN 7 - 119 - 00342 - 9 /I·291(外)

02980(平)

10 - E - 3113P